P9-BZR-157

#3

THE
UNDERTAKER

THE UNDERTAKER

The Legend of El Cajónero

Lauran Paine

Thorndike Press • Thorndike, Maine

Library of Congress Cataloging in Publication Data:

Clarke, Richard, 1916–
    The undertaker : the legend of El Cajónero / Richard
Clarke.
        p. cm.
    ISBN 1-56054-401-5 (alk. paper : lg. print)
    1. Large type books. I. Title.
[PS3566.A34U5   1992]   92-7112
813'.54—dc20   CIP

All characters and events portrayed in this work are
fictitious.

Thorndike Press Large Print edition published in 1992
by arrangement with Walker Publishing Company, Inc.

Cover design by Sean Pringle.

The tree indicium is a trademark of Thorndike Press.

This book is printed on acid-free, high opacity paper. ∞

CONTENTS

1. The Peralta Country 7
2. A Little Out of Hand 20
3. The Gift of Springtime 33
4. Butler's Decision 49
5. *Desplobado* 62
6. Caught! 75
7. A Dead Man 90
8. A Strange Night 105
9. A Day to Remember 119
10. Shanks' Mare 135
11. A Bad Night 148
12. Surprises! 163
13. Under an Overcast Sky 176
14. The Passing of Time 192
15. Water! 203
16. The Ride Back 221
17. The Return 235
18. Resolving Problems 250
19. A Loose End 263
20. A Long Afternoon 279
21. Into the Night 294
22. A Change of Luck 309

23. Showdown! 323
24. A Patron Saint 336
25. El Cajónero 349

CHAPTER ONE

THE PERALTA COUNTRY

Peralta was south of Albuquerque on the trade route from Chihuahua State in Mexico northward to the gringo towns of New Mexico and Colorado. It was also the traditional lying-over place for *arrieros* with their long pack trains, and for wagoneers (almost invariably *norteamericanos*) who traded and freighted as far northeast as Missouri.

The mostly desert country had loose soil and miles of candid hostility. Its trees had hooks, its bushes had thorns, its creatures had venom, its sun was pitiless, and its water was often unpalatable. What little water there was lay hidden in rocky places or deep in patches of nearly impenetrable thornpin, usually far from roadways.

To the natives with their meager squash, maize, and gourd patches, their thick-walled, plain but functional jacals of solid mud, the desert was a form of purgatory. To the Mexican *arrieros* with tiny bells on their trousers, huge sombrero hats, strings of small but incredibly tough Mexican mules, it was a continuation of the native soil, despite Mexico having lost it in a savage war. The common language was Spanish: the people were Mexican, had been for generations; their towns were Spanish-Mexican.

The conquerors were a minority. True, they had army posts, their law prevailed, they owned the best land and most of the sources of water, and controlled law and order. But they remained a minority.

Their control was tenuous. For one thing New Mexico was a territory, not a state. Territories were administered by the army, not civilians. Even in towns where gringos dominated the politics, the commerce, the authority to tax and to pass sentences, the army was usually too distant or too sluggish to respond quickly. So law enforcement was in the hands of the gringos, outnumbered or not; and while gringo law was not entirely different from the old-time Spanish and Mexican law, it was not free of discrimination.

Periodically, the native Mexicans had been targeted by every hostile element. The Apaches had massacred them, destroyed their ranches, emptied entire villages, and filled graveyards, but the authorities in Mexico City had refused to permit native Mexicans to own guns. They could make and use bows and arrows, or spears whose tips were hardened in flames — weapons that were pathetically inadequate in comparison to the rifles, carbines, pistols traded to the Indians — but owning guns was punishable by death.

When the gringos came it got a little better, but not very much. Although guns were available, for self-defense, ammunition was both scarce and very expensive for people who still made and used candles because they could not afford the coal oil or the lamps that burned it.

The relationship between conquerors and conquered was better than it had been for the natives under either Spanish or Mexican sovereignty, but only after a number of years had passed. And there were always gringos who scorned people whose existence required endless hikes into the desert with tiny burros for such a basic requirement as faggots for cooking fires, and whose deferential humility had been ingrained for centuries.

But in time the relationship improved, as in Peralta, where, despite each race having its own part of town, friendships were not uncommon between gringos — some of them anyway — and Mexicans.

The constable of Peralta was a rawboned, weathered man named Frank Butler. All manner of rumors existed about Butler; in fact, after seven years as the local law, everyone either knew of, or had seen, how capable he was with his bony fists, with his Colt, and with one of the big-bored scatterguns. He kept the scatterguns in a rack on the wall of the adobe *juzgado*, Peralta's jailhouse, which had walls three feet thick and had at one time been the residence of a local Mexican commandante.

Whether it was true or not that Marshal Butler had been an outlaw in Texas, a guerrilla with the Confederacy, or a notorious horse and cattle thief in Montana, one thing was certain: he maintained order in the Peralta countryside. Even when on several occasions he had brought lawbreakers into town from fifty miles out and was accused of exceeding his authority — which, as town marshal, did not extend beyond the town limits of Peralta — people said very little . . . if they said anything at all.

They recognized Frank Butler's authority and, after generations of abuse, appreciated his evenhanded enforcement. They also appreciated his insistence that stockmen, packers, freighters, and hurrying riders passing through obey Frank Butler's law or end up either injured or locked into one of the little gloomy, unpleasant cells of his jailhouse.

People said there was neither an outlaw he could not face down nor a crime he would not solve. Marshal Butler enjoyed his reputation, but he *did* have a problem that in seven years he'd been unable to resolve, or even fully understand; that was how to cope with local superstitions.

The latest manifestation occurred in the early spring, the only time the South Desert bloomed and blossomed. During this time, it had air as clear as glass, and fragrances from shy tiny flowers by day as well as by night.

It all started when a drunken *arriero* came up from Mexico, along with eleven other mule-train men. He tried to make love to a woman in Mex-town whose husband had been gone a month on a wild-horse hunt.

The woman struck the *arriero*. He struck her back, causing one eye to discolor and swell closed. An old man who came to her aid and attacked the Mexican with a stick was badly beaten by eleven *arrieros*.

The noise of this encounter was loud enough to empty the Mex-town cantina. The eleven *arrieros* were attacked by nearly twice as many Peralta Mexicans. One of the *arrieros* fired his pistol, wounding a native. It was this gunshot that brought Marshal Butler in a lope with

11

a sawed-off shotgun in his hands.

The packer who had shot the native made the mistake of firing at Butler. He missed, and Frank Butler blew him to mincemeat from a distance of sixty feet.

The other *arrieros* fled. Marshal Butler collared only two and locked them up overnight. In the morning, the other Mexicans and their pack train were gone. He freed his two prisoners with a solemn warning that if he ever saw them in Peralta again he would shoot them on sight.

Two days later, in an exact reenactment of legend, a man attired in black appeared astride a big black horse, which he walked through Mex-town to the mud house of the woman with the discolored eye. He tossed gold coins through a glassless window and rode away.

Frank heard about this only when he went up to Jess Hobart's saloon, Gringo-town's most favored watering hole. Jess, a burly, fleshy man who combed his hair straight down on both sides with a part in the middle, leaned atop his counter and held out a hand palm up.

There were two gold coins in his hand. He smiled at Marshal Butler's blank expression. "Got 'em from a Mex this morning for a bottle of popskull he wanted with him when he went looking for firewood."

Frank Butler looked at the coins without touching them. "Did he say where he got them?"

The heavy-jowled saloonman straightened back as he answered. "Yeah. *El Cajónero.*"

Butler leaned on the bartop. "Last night?"

"Yep. El Cajónero came in the night and tossed money to the woman who got hit in the eye." Hobart was pocketing the coins when he finished his statement. "You know what happens next?"

Butler knew what was *supposed* to happen, but he was skeptical. "He'll never find that *arriero.*"

The heavy man was regarding Marshal Butler steadily when he said, "Want to bet?"

Butler ignored the offer. "A beer, Jess. What did the man you got the coins from say?"

"That was all. El Cajónero came in the night, tossed the money through a window, and disappeared. That was all."

"Did he see him?"

"No. This morning the woman showed the coins around Mex-town. She told everyone down there what had happened. . . . Marshal?"

"What."

Jess Hobart stood a moment regarding the lawman's expression, then changed his mind about pursuing this topic. Instead, he went after the beer.

Marshal Butler would not have objected so much to the mythical horseman called El Cajónero by Mexicans, but his appearance invariably resulted in wild speculation — not only in Mex-town.

He did not exist. There was no such thing as a *fantasma,* in this case one whose legend went back over a century. The old people who swore they'd seen him in their youth were imagining things; they were illiterate, superstitious people. It was pure figment except for one thing: the gold coins.

El Cajónero was a very durable legend. Old people, and those who were not that old but who had the story from their parents and grandparents, invariably described him the same way. Nothing had changed in over a century: He was dressed in black, rode a big black horse, wore a gun with silver inlay in the wooden stock, always distributed gold coins to the injured, always tossed them through a window, and never came to Mex-town until after midnight.

He was a *vengador,* an avenger. He sometimes was called The Undertaker because after he caught up with people to kill them, their bodies rarely were found.

That part was not difficult to understand. The South Desert was huge, barren, and mostly empty. It had a thousand brushy arroyos where a corpse could dehydrate to mummihood and never be found. Occasionally dead men had been found, identified, and linked to some act against Mex-town's inhabitants, but only one thing convinced the people of Mex-town El Cajónero had killed them: a bullet hole in the center of the forehead. Always a bullet hole in the middle of the forehead, exactly as the legend had indicated.

Marshal Butler made his rounds of Peralta and returned to the jailhouse. Since he'd been the local law, El Cajónero had appeared five or six times. After the first couple of times, Butler could predict exactly what the consequences would be: exuberance and reaffirmation in Mex-town, even a little of the same in Gringo-town, and always the same arguments, which, in Gringo-town, were heavily tinged with scorn. After a while the talk would die, but those damned gold coins remained.

He got a cup of coffee from the little iron stove and returned to his desk with it. The legend of El Cajónero in itself was harmless. In fact, it probably did some good among people whose lot for centuries had been oppression. Except for two things, Frank Butler could have shrugged off The Undertaker. The first was the gold coins, which he could not satisfactorily explain, even to himself. The second was that El Cajónero killed people. At

15

least, *someone* did; and El Cajónero got the credit in Mex-town and the blame in Gringo-town.

He was sitting with his boots propped atop the desk when an old cowman named Hunter Calkins walked in beating off dust. They had known each other for years; in fact, they'd played Saturday-night poker at Hobart's saloon for nearly as long as Butler had been marshal.

Calkins was one of those longtime desert dwellers whose age was impossible to guess, except to say he was old. His skin was bronzed from lifelong exposure, his face lined and creased, his hide leathery. He had small, pale, shrewd eyes, and teeth worn down evenly all around.

He ran cattle and horses west in the area of the southward Navajo Reservation, and as far north as the Laguna Reservation. He could speak Navajo like a native, which was no small feat: Navajo was difficult to learn.

Hunter Calkins had been on the South Desert most of his life. There were the usual stories of his past, but as far as Frank Butler was concerned, in a country where the nearest people could come to having heroes was a legend of someone riding a black horse avenging wrongs, Hunter Calkins was a worthwhile individual. The marshal offered the old man coffee as the sinewy cowman sank into a chair. Calkins, who had just come from the cafe, declined, shoved out his saddle-warped legs, thumbed back his hat, and watched the lawman sip coffee for a moment before speaking.

It was indicative of the seriousness of what he had to say that Calkins dispensed entirely with the customary, traditionally mandatory comments about the prospects for rain, the condition of the range, and a little harmless gossip, and got straight to the point. He brought something from a pocket and placed it carefully on the marshal's desk.

The object was a magnificent crucifix of solid gold inset with jewels, clearly very old. It was as large as a man's hand, and heavy. Frank Butler gazed at it with an increasing sense of foreboding as the old stockman began to speak.

"Couple of my riders was silting out a water hole south of Laguna and north of Alamo, somewhere close to the middle of my range. They found it where they thought they'd found a grave; fresh earth, dragged over as though to conceal it, but not very well done. Maybe in the dark."

Calkins paused to round out a cheek with a cud of molasses-cured Kentucky twist. "There was one of those iron-bound bullion boxes. Heavy as hell by itself, but heavier because it was full of this kind of stuff."

As Frank Butler finally leaned to pick up the crucifix, Calkins said, "My guess is that the box had been buried out there maybe a week back. Maybe two weeks . . . Frank, that's isolated country. In a year we maybe see one or two riders passing through. Whoever buried that stuff most likely knew their cache would be safe, and it would have been except that every spring I send men out to open up the water holes."

Butler gently put the crucifix back on the edge of the desk and looked solemnly at the stockman. "Where is the box now?"

"Buried where we found it, covered and dragged over so's there'd be no sign my men had dug it up."

Butler smiled his approval.

Calkins did not smile back. "Figured you'd want to know, an' I didn't want 'em to come back and find their cache gone. We're pretty isolated out yonder. I've fought off my share of border jumpers, In'ians, and whatnot for more years than you been alive. I learnt long ago not to go out of my way to fire 'em up. They've ambushed a lot of men."

They sat a moment regarding the beautiful old church artifact. Then Calkins spoke again, very dryly. "It's the same routine they've used since I been down here."

Marshal Butler inclined his head without speaking.

"It's a wonder to me, Frank, there's anything of value left in Mexico."

The marshal raised his eyes to the old stockman's craggy face. He roughly knew the area where the cache had been found. There was no reason for anyone to cross that country, except for Hunter Calkins and his riders, mostly vaqueros and an occasional Indian who worked for him.

Calkins sat back studying the scuffed toes of his boots. "I haven't heard of anything happening down there. Have you?"

Frank shook his head.

"Well, maybe what we stumbled onto was part of the plan to get things organized before they pronounce, eh?"

Butler thought it might be. "They'd know in Mex-town. I'll ask around. You want to keep the crucifix?"

"No. Put it in your safe. If they come back, I can look 'em straight in the eye and say I don't have anything from their cache."

Chapter Two

A LITTLE OUT OF HAND

Frank Butler sat admiring the crucifix long after Hunter Calkins had departed. Eventually he wrapped it in cloth and locked it inside his massive, squatty iron safe.

Then he went down to Mex-town. A soft, fragrant breeze raised tiny devils of dust under a flawless turquoise sky.

Mex-town, much older than Gringo-town, had grown up around a large plaza. In the middle of the plaza was a large circular wall of adobe bricks about knee high to keep small children, drunks, and animals from falling into the well where women congregated to draw water, do laundry, and gossip.

Whereas the streets of Gringo-town were straight, those of Mex-town meandered around stick corrals for goats and sheep, the occasional cow, and of course, horses. It made its widest deviation around a three-room adobe residence in front of a network of faggot corrals where Jésus Obando, Peralta's only *arriero,* kept his mules and horses. The dusty roadway had been etched out and around those corrals generations earlier.

The father and grandfather of Jésus Obando had also been *arrieros.* At one time, before the arrival of the big wagons with their over-size rear wheels for traction in sandy soil, mule-pack trains had been the only method employed to move goods north into gringo country and southward toward Old Mexico.

At the north end of Mex-town stood an old, fortresslike church. It had a typically splendid long Spanish name that commemorated saints and the greatness of God. There used to be a bronze bell cast long ago in Mexico, but it had since been removed and recast into weapons; now the bell tower housed a wooden cross that slanted woefully sideways, despite innumerable vows by the devout that someday they would climb up there and straighten it.

Residences surrounded the plaza. They ranged from humble one-room adobe jacals to three- and four-room adobe houses. Mex-town had its own small stores, its cantina where women were not allowed, all of which faced the plaza.

It also had dogs. Marshal Butler's experience had taught him to be wary of Mex-town's

21

dogs. When he crossed the plaza under dozens of watchful eyes, the dogs appeared. He ignored them, even the bold ones that snapped at him from a distance.

As he was passing down a narrow, crooked street an old man emerged from shade to laugh at him and wag a finger. He said in Spanish that dogs never forgot, that it had been passed along in their mother's milk how the first *norteamericanos* had treated them.

The marshal smiled without replying and was almost past when the old man said, this time in English, "Somewhere there is a man made dead for striking Señora Elizondo in the eye."

Butler stopped, looked steadily at the old man, and said, "El Cajónero, *viejo?*"

"Certainly," the old man replied in Spanish, and the marshal walked away in the direction of the three-room adobe of Jésus Obando.

The *arriero* was gone, his handsome and robust wife told Frank Butler. Had been gone for two weeks with his mules. She did not expect him back for another week, perhaps less. She smiled and shrugged. "*Quien es?* Who knows? After nine years of being married to him, I know that he will return only when I see the mules coming."

Frank stood on the small porch under its ramada of fronds. He and the woman's husband had been friends for years. As he stood there, the woman's dark eyes studied him. Eventually she said, "Trouble, Marshal?"

He smiled. "There's always trouble, señora."

"About my husband?"

"No. Did he go south?"

"Yes. With goods from Grover's store to be delivered in Angostura and Rincón."

Frank twisted to gaze elsewhere and saw several heads quickly pulled back from behind walls and fences. He faced her again, wearing a crooked smile. "Nothing changes, does it?"

She smiled understanding. "Nothing. As long as we stand in plain sight. Can I help you?"

He doubted it. "I wanted to know if Jésus has picked up anything down south about a revolution."

The woman's dark eyes widened. *"Pronunciados?"*

"Yes."

"He hasn't said anything to me. I don't think so. We hear about things like that in Mex-town."

Marshal Butler nodded. It had been a source of amazement to him how the *huaracha* telegraph worked. Before he or anyone else in Gringo-town heard of trouble in Mexico, the residents of Mex-town knew about it in detail.

"I'd like to see Jésus when he gets back," Butler said. He touched the brim of his hat and turned back the way he had come.

The handsome woman leaned in her doorway watching him pass from sight, then stepped back and closed the door. As she did this, all the watchful eyes disappeared. It was said of Gringo-town that there were no secrets. In Mex-town, there was not even a chance for secrets.

Marshal Butler stopped by the cantina for a tepid *cerveza,* and the smoke-filled, windowless room fell silent. Mexican beer tasted less of yeast than did gringo beer.

The barman was a toad of a man with unruly, lank black hair that overhung his forehead. He was short and thick, and darker than an Indian. He smiled widely as he set up the tin cup of beer and leaned across his counter to speak in English.

"Somebody stole a horse?"

Frank grinned. "No."

"Some goats, then, some sheep?"

Men chuckled around the room, and Frank laughed with them. "No. I like the *cerveza.*"

"Better than gringo beer?"

"Yes."

The barman scuttled for a large dark bottle to top up Frank's cup. From among the loafers an old man quietly said, "You heard about

El Cajónero. You want to catch him?"

Frank turned, cup in hand. The old man was fair except for black hair and black eyes. A *gachupín,* no doubt. "I don't want to capture him, old-timer. Tell me, how does one capture a ghost?" he asked in Spanish, and the chuckles returned.

Frank downed the beer, put the cup aside, smiled at the old man, and walked out of the saloon.

When he returned to the jailhouse John Grover, the paunchy individual who owned the Peralta Emporium, or general store, was waiting. Grover was a man of medium height who seemed smaller because of his heft. He was nearly bald and had the look of someone who rarely stood for long in sunshine.

He was shrewd, successful, wore a big gold watch chain across his front, and usually had a cigar in his mouth, which he never lighted. He chewed cigars. He'd formerly chewed molasses-cured, but his wife loathed chewing tobacco. She tolerated cigars because in this part of the country cigars were a sign of affluence. He had a cigar in his mouth as he sat down on a wall bench opposite Frank Butler's old desk and said, "Is there trouble brewing down over the line?"

Butler stared. "Why did you ask that?"

Grover's stogie slid almost mechanically to

the other side of his face before he replied. "A freighter who hauls to me from up north saw a band of *bandoleros* a week or so back."

"Where?"

"Going east a few miles north of town. Frank, it usually happens like that before marauders come charging up out of Messico. It's been quiet for a long time, four or five years."

The marshal leaned on his desk. "How many *bandoleros?*"

Grover did not know. "He said a band of them. I expect that might be fifteen or twenty. . . . Have you heard of trouble starting down there again?"

Butler shook his head. He hadn't actually heard of any trouble, but he had a strong feeling that before long he would. As Grover had said, it had been a few years. Uprisings by armed bands who pronounced against Mexico's central government were frequent, and for many reasons they most commonly came in springtime.

"Pronunciados," Frank said offhandedly, using the common name for Mexico's ubiquitous revolutionaries.

John Grover nodded slightly, his jaws still for a moment as he gazed steadily at the local lawman before clearing his throat to regain Butler's attention. "Someone better ride for the army, Frank. It never fails; even if Mex route armies beat them, they come up over the line like madmen. Especially then."

The nearest army post was northeast of Albuquerque. It consisted of three companies of horse soldiers, little more than patrol force. Years back it had consisted of four regiments of soldiers, both foot and horse. Economizing at the Washington level caused the cutback.

There were other posts. Down along the border there were several; farther eastward there were at least two large, permanent commands. With the exception of the border posts, the large commands were several days' ride from Peralta. If there were a mass invasion from below the border, even if someone from Peralta could reach those border stations without being ridden down by machete-swinging, half-drunk Mexican *bandoleros*, it was unlikely the commands would come to the aid of Peralta when their own part of the world was being swamped with burnings, murders, and overwhelming numbers of wild, undisciplined horsemen from Chihuahua.

"Frank . . . ?"

Marshal Butler eased back off the desk. He'd been thinking of the bullion box Hunter Calkins's riders had found. "Wait," he told the merchant, and at the look on the older man's face he said, "John, if we send for help

27

and the army comes — and nothing happens down here . . ."

Grover considered that possibility. Then he offered his opinion, which was that a false alarm that would bring the army in force was better than doing nothing. Kill-crazy *bandoleros* could attack the town in the night, or at dawn, kill everyone, and burn Peralta to the ground.

Marshal Butler knew John Grover very well. He was not someone who was upset easily. He was also someone who, when his mind was made up, could not be moved. "Give it a day or two," Butler said. "It'll take about that long to find out if there's anything to it. You know this country, John. It's full of people who've got tongues with a hinge in the middle and wag at both ends."

Grover departed. As Marshal Butler watched him cross the dusty roadway, he sighed aloud. The story would spread. By morning, everyone in town and perhaps beyond would be running around like headless chickens.

Events were moving too fast. Hell, it had only been hours since he'd listened to Hunter Calkins. And his visit to Mex-town hadn't been productive, which hadn't worried him very much at the time but now did.

He had to know about the political situation

below the border, and except for word of mouth, which was usually unreliable, there was no way, at least in Gringo-town, to get information. Like most distant South Desert towns, Peralta had no telegraph.

He had supper at the cafe and went up to Jess Hobart's saloon for a nightcap. Everything there was normal: stockmen leaned along the bar, conversation was desultory, and a number of local men around the room were concentrating on poker sessions. Hobart came along with a bottle and small glass, looking complacent as usual.

But that was a mask. No sooner had the saloonman placed the bottle and glass atop the counter than he leaned and said, "There's a rumor, Frank." He waited until the marshal had topped off the glass before continuing. "I think it started with that old screwt who clerks for Mister Grover."

Butler lifted the glass, paused seconds to look straight into the eyes of the saloonman, then dropped his jolt straight down, put the glass aside, and said, "If it's about trouble in Mexico, it started with Grover."

Hobart was not distracted. "Whoever started it, what I been wondering is . . . Frank, since I been in this country I've yet to see one of those damned Mex revolutions that didn't spill over onto our side of the line.

'Specially if the *bandoleros* get their backs to the wall."

Marshal Butler refilled his glass before speaking again. "Jess, if there's trouble down there, an' I sure as hell don't doubt the possibility, so far I got no information about it. And . . ." he paused to down the second jolt, "if there is, it's not going to reach this far north for a while."

Hobart, like John Grover, was a dogged individual. "You can't be sure of that. Somethin' else I heard today . . . there was some of those *guerrilleros* north of town. They was seen crossing the stage road."

Butler forced a humorless smile. Grover again. "Yeah, some freighter saw them. A band, maybe twenty of them. Twenty border jumpers amount to mincemeat if they make trouble up here."

"Not if they're scouts for an army of the bastards," the saloonman said gruffly.

Marshal Butler stoppered the bottle, shoved it and the glass away, and leaned on the counter gazing straight at the heavyset, jowly man. "I can't do it tomorrow. I got something else to do," he said. "But day after tomorrow I'll get up a posse and make a big sashay. If they're still around, I'll find them."

Hobart liked this idea. "An' when you catch 'em, bring at least one back with you. Maybe no one up here knows anything, but those bastards sure do." Hobart leaned back off his counter looking satisfied. "One on the house?" he asked.

Butler shook his head. One was usually his limit, and because of the possibility of looming trouble, he'd had two. "No, thanks. You haven't seen old Hunter Calkins around town today by any chance?"

"Nope. Not today."

Frank accepted that, paid for his whiskey, and returned to the dying day. Down in front of Evinrude's trading and livery yard, three dusty-looking strangers were talking to the proprietor. It must have been a mundane discussion; when Pete Evinrude got even slightly nervous, he swung his arms in fitful gestures.

Over at the saddle and harness works, someone had just fired up a coal-oil lamp. That side of the road got dark sooner than the east side.

Frank Butler went up to the rooming house, declined the hard-looking, hefty proprietor's invitation for coffee in her kitchen, and locked the door of his room after himself.

He stood in shadows at the only window of his room, which faced southward through town and out the lower end to open country. Peralta was a fair distance from the border. There were other places, mostly small villages, between Mexico and Peralta, but none with the size, affluence, or wealth of springtime grazing for livestock and the stockmen who took advantage of it.

If trouble came (and Frank doubted that it would soon, although he would not have stressed that point) he hoped he would have enough time to organize some resistance. From his experience, getting stockmen, their riders, even the people in town, to work together was unlikely as someone raising a lake level by peeing into it.

He began to shed his attire in darkness. Someone over at Hobart's place was playing a melancholy Mex song on a mouth harp. Whoever he was, he was pretty good. Frank listened as he kicked out of his boots, draped his gun and shellbelt from a wall peg, and sat on the side of his rope-sprung iron bed.

He probably should have hung around the Mex-town cantina longer. He knew most of the patrons; with a little tact, he might have pulled information out of them. He knew better than to expect them to volunteer anything, not even when their own welfare would be jeopardized by a raid of border-jumpers.

Chapter Three

THE GIFT OF SPRINGTIME

The marshal was on the trail two hours ahead of daylight. It was a long ride, all of it across Indian country, from town to Hunter Calkins's seasonal headquarters. The Isletas were to the east, the Lagunas due west, the Navajos southwest, and the Acomas farthest east, beyond the Laguna Reservation.

Indians generally avoided contact with outsiders. Butler was well into the big crossroads territory where all tribesmen meandered before he saw any sign of life at all. That was a band of horses in the distance, too far to be recognized as either *mesteños* or perhaps Hunter Calkins's loose stock.

They disappeared like wraiths, went over the far curve of land with nothing but a pale dust-banner to show that they'd ever been there.

The sun was rising, the air blessedly cool

and full of springtime fragrances, when he saw a huddle of squat, ugly buildings in the distance. One reason he'd pushed himself was that he wanted to reach Calkins's yard before the stockman and his riders rode out. If he missed them, as huge and empty as this country was, unless someone had been left behind at the yard who would offer directions, the chances of Butler finding Calkins on his own were nil.

He certainly was not expecting what he found when he rode into the silent, dusty yard with its scattering of unkempt old cottonwood trees, its weathered old mud structures, and its air of desolation. He saw clear evidence that riders had rigged out at the rack in front of the yard before departing.

All but one rider.

Calkins was sitting on his long veranda smoking a scarred small pipe, watching Marshal Butler, as he had been doing for a half an hour as the marshal approached.

He called a greeting as the marshal dismounted at the rack in front of the squatty, massive-looking adobe barn. "Frank! Up here on the porch! What'n hell got you out of bed in the dark this morning?"

The marshal smiled. "Got hungry for some homemade chorizo."

Calkins snorted and leaned to tamp his pipe

empty. "It's not that good. Put up your horse. I'll get some coffee."

They met on the veranda, which, true to southwestern custom, ran the full length of the front of the house and down both sides. Because it was roofed over, it provided shade, a priceless commodity when the long summer came.

Calkins handed the marshal a tin cup of hot java, took another cup back with him to the chair he'd vacated, sat down, and put a quizzical gaze upon the younger man. "Nice day," he said.

Marshal Butler eased down upon the rawhide slats of an old chair. "Yup. Nice day." He tasted the coffee. It was strong enough to float horseshoes. He leaned to place the cup on the veranda railing. As he eased back, he said, "The town's full of rumors."

Calkins's lined, perpetually bronzed face showed little as he replied. "Yeah. That's no surprise, is it? Finish your coffee; I got somethin' to show you at the wagon shed."

The older man rose without waiting for Frank Butler to drain the cup. They went down across the yard to a three-sided log structure near the north end of the yard where there was a dusty top-buggy, two big general-purpose wagons, and a light spring wagon, all with their tongues or shafts up off the ground.

Beyond the spring wagon there was a stone boat with steel runners, a tongue for two horses, and low sideboards.

Calkins stopped, shoved both hands into trouser pockets, and looked down. On the scarred floorboards of the stone boat there was a bundle wrapped first in old blankets, then rolled into stained wagon-canvas. He made a gesture. "Help yourself, Frank."

Butler did not move. "A body, Hunter?"

"Yes. I'll show you," the cowman replied, and leaned to begin the unwinding process. He talked as he worked. "Been out in the weather for a spell. Mex. My riders come onto him a few miles north of town near the road, but there was no horse. . . . There. Ain't real pretty, is he?"

Marshal Butler said nothing. The dead man was young, coarse-featured, and husky. He had little bells on his britches.

"Packer," Butler finally stated. "Gawddammit! If he's who I think he is . . . Some *arrieros* came to town a few days back. One of them got into a pawin' match with a woman named Elizondo. She punched him, and he punched her back. Did a good job of it. She had an eye puffed up like an oak gall, swollen plumb shut."

Hunter Calkins looked from the corpse to the lawman. "She got a husband?"

"Yes, but he's been out looking for *mesteños* for a couple of weeks. I doubt that it would have been him. She's a tough lady, Hunter. You most likely know her brother. Jésus Obando."

Calkins's eyes widened. "Yeah, I know him. Knew his pappy before him. Never knew the old man had a daughter, though."

Butler's expression was sour. "Bullet hole in the forehead, Hunter. Smack dab in the middle."

Calkins returned his attention to the corpse while gently nodding his head. "I noticed. They was facin' each other. Not very far apart either, was they?"

The marshal went to a little wooden horseshoe keg and sat down. "The night after the lady got hit in the eye, she was in bed when someone rode past and pitched some gold coins through the window." As Butler finished speaking he looked up, met the cowman's gaze, and shook his head. "Son of a bitch!"

Calkins turned slowly back to gaze at the dead man for a moment, then turned aside, expectorated, and faced Marshal Butler again. "El Cajónero isn't all we got to worry about. . . . The reason I was still in the yard when you rode in this morning is because the last few mornings when we headed out we come onto horse tracks around the yard. All the way around it. Fresh tracks, Frank. Maybe ten, fifteen riders. No sign of 'em in broad daylight. That's where I sent my riders — to find them tracks, take the freshest ones and follow 'em until they find whoever in hell made them, then get back here."

The old cowman stepped to a stall door and leaned. The dead man on the stone boat was now between them. "Mexicans," he said. "Now, if I got this figured right, it's them lads that buried the bullion box. Maybe they missed the crucifix and maybe they found some tracks down yonder and backtracked 'em to the yard. Maybe a whole raft of things. Maybe they scouted up the yard to find out how many of us is here. One thing I know for a fact, Frank, those bastards are pretty shrewd about scouting up a place before they come at you like a whirlwind. Usually just before sunrise."

Butler looked across the corpse at the cowman. "You think it's those same *bandoleros* who buried the box?"

Calkins flung his arms wide. "Who else? In'ians pass through now an' then, but there's no call for *bandoleros* up out of Messico to be anywhere near."

They exchanged a long look before Marshal Butler stood up and dusted his britches. Then they returned to the long porch, where Hunter

Calkins sighed loudly as he sat down. "I was sittin' here thinkin' before you came along. I been summering down here for a lot of years. Good years and bad ones. I like the desert, always have, but never sat down until this morning to tally things up. I'm not sure I got to do this anymore, Frank. If I had a family, maybe two, three sons, it'd be worthwhile." Calkins grinned. "Got no family, an' that's probably my fault, but that don't change anything. . . . There's trouble coming."

Marshal Butler looked around quickly, but Calkins waved off the question he knew would be asked and said, "Like I said, I been down here a long time. I can feel it. It's in the air. It's nothin' I've seen, exactly, except for that box of looted treasure, but mark my word, Frank, it's coming."

Butler asked the question anyway. "You've heard something's going on down in Mexico?"

"Nope. Out here we don't hear gossip." Again the old stockman grinned. "Until all hell busts loose. That's the feeling I got now." Calkins waved in the direction of the buggy shed. "El Cajónero paid off another son of a bitch, but come right down to it, Frank, all I've ever heard of him doin' was things only Mexicans was interested in an' maybe most of the time he was justified, ghost or not."

"He's no ghost, Hunter."

"You ever see him?"

"No. Have you?"

Calkins chuckled. "No. Never believed in *fantasmas,* but I got riders that sure do." The old stockman shifted in his chair. "Frank. I can feel it in my bones. Real trouble is coming and this time El Cajónero won't amount to a hill of beans against it."

Butler was gazing toward the buggy shed when he asked if Calkins was going to bury the dead *arriero.* The older man replied indifferently. "Yeah. Unless you want him."

The marshal shook his head. "No. Did he have anything on him by way of identification?"

Calkins looked around. "Letters? They can't read nor write. Not one in a hundred can. No, there's nothing. Some Mex money, his handgun that hadn't been shot, that's about it."

Butler arose. "The reason I rode out —"

"All I can tell you, son, is that we've been scouted up. Maybe it's them same *bandoleros* who buried the box. I sure don't know. But I'll tell you this: If it's not, then there's more border jumpers around, and that's what's got me worrying. I'm a little long in the tooth for this."

As they crossed toward the barn for Frank's horse, the marshal was thoughtful. As he was rigging out in the barn, he said, "Grover thinks we ought to send for the army."

Calkins showed little interest. "If those *bandoleros* are scoutin' up the country for a raid, the army'd never arrive in time, an' if those bastards are up here in force, your messenger'd never get past 'em, would he? But you could try."

Butler agreed, led his horse out front to be mounted, thanked the old stockman for the coffee, and left the yard in the direction of Peralta. He rode at a walk, head lowered in thought.

He'd ridden out here hoping for at least a scrap of information. He was now riding back without having learned anything except that Hunter Calkins had a dead *arriero* in his wagon shed. And he was full of foreboding about some night riders he had not yet been able to trace, something else to worry about.

Once, his attention was attracted by a big dust banner off in the distant northeast. Remembering the horses he'd seen earlier in the opposite direction, he speculated that it probably was horses this time too, quite a herd of them.

His attention was distracted from the dust by a pair of blanket Indians sitting their horses like statues about a half or three-quarters of a mile southward. They were watching him.

If there'd been any cover . . . but there wasn't, so they sat out there like statues until he'd put a lot of distance between them. Then they turned back and rode without haste in a south-westerly direction.

Butler thought they were probably a buck and his woman, maybe going to visit relatives at one of the Reservations.

By the time he arrived back in town and had put up his horse at Evinrude's corrals, dusk was coming. There were a few lighted windows and not much traffic. Folks who lived orderly lives were sitting down to supper. There were three saddle animals patiently standing at the tie rack in front of Jess Hobart's saloon, and over at Grover's store the elderly clerk, who was rarely without black cotton sleeve protectors from the wrists to the elbows, was canting apple barrels and rolling them inside off the plankwalk.

Up at the corral yard, where the late-day stage had recently arrived, five or six people, obviously strangers, milled out front as they studied the town. Two of them, elegant individuals with dusty button shoes and little curly-brimmed derby hats, broke away from the others to make a beeline for Hobart's place. One thing about traveling peddlers, they could spot a saloon in a strange town before they looked for either the rooming house or the cafe.

Pete Evinrude came forth from his untidy little combination office and harness room, saw Marshal Butler, and called to him.

"That muleteer from Mex-town's been lookin' for you. He's been in here twice."

Butler nodded his thanks and led his animal out back to be turned into a corral.

He went over to the cafe, which was half full, sat at the counter, and returned greetings with several diners. When the cafeman came padding along in his felt slippers — he'd frozen both feet in Montana eleven years back; leather boots gave his feet hell — Butler nodded for supper and waited until a mug of black java had been set in front of him before looking up.

The cafeman said almost the exact same thing Pete Evinrude had said. "Jésus Obando's been lookin' for you. Acted real serious about it."

The marshal took his time getting the pleats out of his innards, had a second cup of coffee before paying up and departing, and walked out into a fully settled dark night.

Now there were more lights, but most of the business establishments were dark, doors bolted for the night. Also, there were now seven horses standing hip-shot in front of the saloon.

Over at the jailhouse Butler took down his lamp, lighted it, adjusted the wick, and was reaching to hang it from the ceiling hook when a large man walked in out of the darkness and spoke before he'd even closed the door. "I have to talk to you."

Butler went to his desk, sat down, and smiled. "Your wife said she wasn't sure when you'd be back."

The powerfully built Mexican dropped into a chair. "I have not even been home yet," he replied in very faintly accented English. "I have looked for you all afternoon. Frank, all hell busted loose below the border."

Marshal Butler was not surprised; in fact, he was almost relieved. "Revolution?"

Jésus Obando nodded his head. "Santanistas. There's been one pitched battle. They beat a route army under Francisco Otero. All hell's loose down there. Some *bandoleros* came up an' made a pass at Rincón. Scairt the hell out of people. A big band of them."

"Did they attack the town?"

"No, but everyone down there believes they'll be back. Folks are loading up and leaving."

Butler leaned on the desktop. "Did they go back, Jésus?"

"That's why I've been lookin' for you. No! The people down there told me they thought they'd go back, but when they left Rincón they rode north."

Butler sat a moment gazing at his friend. North was where Hunter Calkins had found tracks of Mexican night riders. "How big a band?"

Obando threw up his arms. "They were scairt pee-less down there. One man told me there was no less than three hundred. . . . Drunk, shooting in all directions, riding people down, taking every horse they could find. And women."

Butler's brows dropped a notch. "Three hundred?"

"Well." Obando shrugged mighty shoulders. "An old woman told me she saw thirty. She counted them. The storekeeper where I unloaded said it was at least seventy-five, maybe a hundred." The *arriero* waited a moment before continuing. "Otero's route army numbered no less than six hundred soldiers, mostly on foot but with some lancers. No one knew who commanded the Santanistas, but whoever he was, if he could rout six hundred regulars, you can bet your last dollar he'll have recruits swarming to his *grito* from everywhere."

Butler sighed. "I thought Santa Anna was dead."

Obando stared. "Dead? He's not dead. Old,

maybe, and exiled, but they've turned him out before and he always comes back, and when he does . . ." He made a slashing movement with a rigid finger in front of his throat.

Marshal Butler continued to gaze at the *arriero*. He was silent for a long time. Santa Anna had not been just a *presidente* of Mexico — at least five times — he *was* Mexico. He was remembered north of the border for two bloody triumphs, the first at the Alamo in Texas, the second at Goliad. In Mexico, he was the hero of such places as Tampico and Veracruz, where he had beaten the Spaniards.

"What is the revolution about this time?" Butler asked.

Obando looked annoyed at the question. "It's to bring back the exile. It's not the usual drunken armed mob out for plunder. The *grito* is for Santa Anna's return. Frank, this isn't just another uprising!"

Obando arose to pace once toward the gun rack on the back wall, then to the closed roadway door before resuming his seat. Marshal Butler, who had known the *arriero* a long time, watched his pacing and when Obando was seated again, said, "If they whipped one of those big route armies, won't they drive deeper into Mexico — toward the capital?"

Obando relaxed, considered the scuffed toes of his boots, and shrugged again. "Yes. The

46

genuine *pronunciados* will. They got a taste of victory. They want to overthrow the present government and bring back the cripple. . . . Frank, what we're likely to face is the ones who don't care who sits in Mexico City — the ones who want plunder, all of it they can get. Down there — and up here. How many will that be?" He gestured again. "Who knows, except that it'll be a lot."

Marshal Butler eased back off the desk. He told Obando about the bullion box, got the heavy crucifix from his safe, and let Obando handle it. Then he told him about the first party of *bandoleros* that had been seen north of Peralta, and also about the night-riding horsemen who had scouted up the Calkins ranch headquarters.

As the big Mexican handed back the crucifix and watched Butler return it to the safe, he said, "It must be the ones who rode north from Rincón."

Butler was sitting at the desk again when he nodded. "But they buried that box weeks before hell busted loose south of the line. They were up here before that."

Obando was not impressed. "All right. They came up to hide part of their loot. It'd be safer up here than down there."

The marshal nodded, but did not continue this part of the discussion; he did not believe the *bandoleros* had ridden as far north as Peralta just to bury their loot. They could have buried it miles closer to the border, where it could be more readily retrieved.

That was what was on his mind throughout the remainder of the conversation with Jésus Obando. After the *arriero* had departed, Butler continued to sit in his office staring at the far wall.

He had intended to tell Obando about his sister's swollen eye and the return of El Cajónero, but Obando's news from the south had chased the El Cajónero episode completely out of his mind.

Anyway, as soon as Obando went to Mextown he would learn of the attack on his sister. And by morning all of Mex-town would know about the uprising south of the border.

Butler bypassed Hobart's place, where he usually had a nightcap before heading for the rooming house. Tonight he was not in a mood for socializing.

Like the El Cajónero episode, Obando's news would spread like wildfire. Although stockmen beyond town paid scant attention to legend, this latest uprising in Mexico and its highly menacing aspect would eclipse just about every other concern they had.

Chapter Four

BUTLER'S DECISION

Butler's premonition was correct: news of the bloody explosion south of the border usurped every other consideration among Peralta's inhabitants. Most of the information came by way of Mex-town, from refugees fleeing from the horror and from returning Mex-town people who went south every springtime to visit.

The marshal got Pete Evinrude's nightman to ride for help to the nearest military establishments. He kept his fingers crossed about Hunter Calkins's prediction that a messenger would probably not get through.

Once news of the revolution had spread, Peralta residents, as well as ranchers from over the countryside, began arriving in town to seek out Marshal Butler for information. What he gave them was unembellished fact, which many chose to doubt because it was not as lurid as rumor. The result was confusion bordering on panic.

Butler was over at Jess Hobart's place when the saddle and harness maker walked in. His name was Bart Matthews. He was tall, stringy, lined, and clear-eyed. From things he'd said, folks believed him to be at least sixty. He'd been in business in Peralta for eleven years, and although he'd arrived in the area driving one of the wagons of a Texan trailmaster in the drag of five hundred wicked-horned, slab-sided, and unpredictable fighting longhorn cattle, he'd picked up the harness maker's trade somewhere else. He never said where and folks never asked.

He chewed, drank whiskey, swore a blue streak, and was avoided by every female within a mile of his shop. When he bellied up to the bar and looked from Hobart to the marshal, he smiled with his puckered little pale eyes and said, "Well, it's warmin' up, ain' it?" and laughed before either of the other men could reply. Then he called for a bottle, and when Jess went to get it, fixed the marshal with a steady gaze, said, "It's goin' to get hot, Frank. Hotter'n the hubs of hell," and laughed again.

Hobart set up the bottle and glass. Matthews filled the glass to the brim, raised a hand to grip it, and raised it without taking his eyes off the contents. He was performing the rangeman's proof of manhood, which was not

50

to spill so much as one drop. Nor did he. With his head back he dropped the whiskey straight down, blew out a flammable breath as his eyes brightened, put the glass aside, and leaned on the counter.

"I rode out pot hunting," he said to no one in particular, gazed at himself in the backbar mirror, and sighed. "Time was, gents, when a man could find antelope within maybe five miles of town. I was out all yestiddy and come back with two gawddamned scrawny brush rabbits. Jess, set 'em up."

Hobart went after two more glasses, which the harness maker filled and pushed toward his companions. "Covered a lot of country for them two rabbits. Drink 'em down, boys." Matthews set the example, again without spilling a drop. "Didn't see a single damned In'ian. That's uncommon this time of year when they're visitin' over the countryside. Wouldn't you say, Marshal?"

Butler said nothing. He knew Matthews as well as anyone did, and if there'd ever been a man born sly, it was the harness maker.

"Not a single damned In'ian, gents. No antelope . . . but horse tracks all over hell." Matthews pushed the glass away and straightened up a little.

The marshal asked a question: "How far out were you?"

51

Matthews made a sweeping gesture with one arm. "All over, like I told you. The harder I hunted, the more country I covered. Mostly north and west." He turned his head toward Frank Butler, no humor in his little eyes now at all. "Shod horses, Frank, until I got about as far north as I figured to get, then it was barefoot horses too. More gaddamned barefoot horses than you could count in a month of Sundays. Drove horses, gents. They come from the northeast somewhere. I didn't see no dust, so I backtracked a few miles. Come from the northeast."

Hobart made a tactless remark. "Mustangs, Bart."

The Texan straightened up to his full height and glared. "Jess, I never in my life knew a saloonman who knew anythin' but bottles, an' you just topped the list. I said there was *shod* horses too, didn't I?"

Hobart reddened, and the harness maker turned on the lawman. "Shod horses! A hell of a herd. Someone's remuda bein' drove from northeast on a slant toward the southwest. Frank . . . there's only old Calkins in that direction, and he's got horses of his own along with his cattle. Now, where do you expect someone was takin' all them damned horses, anyway?"

Marshal Butler's eyes widened a little at a

time. Horses! The bullion box. That isolated, insular country around the Calkins ranch. Mexican *bandoleros* in the countryside keeping out of sight. He said, "Son of a bitch," and walked out of the saloon.

Marshal Butler went down to Mex-town. He sat under a gnarled olive tree at a battered wooden table with Jésus Obando opposite him and a jug of red wine between them and told him what he'd just heard.

Obando was filling two thick crockery cups from the jug. Concentrating on what he was doing, he quietly said, "That's a hell of a place for Hunter to be — if they are really going to do what you figure. . . . Right smack in the middle."

They sipped the wine. Obando's handsome wife appeared in the doorway to ask if they wanted to be fed. Obando raised his eyebrows at Butler, who shook his head. "Later, maybe," the *arriero* told her.

She closed the door as Butler said, "That's why they didn't raid Rincón. That's why they've been riding around keeping an eye on folks. Jésus, that's why they buried that loot up here. Take delivery of the horses out where no one'll be around, hand over the loot, and bust their butts getting back down over the line with the horses."

Obando leaned with the tin cup held in both

hands. "They need horses," he said finally. "Every time they bust loose down there, they need horses. Since I was a kid people in Mextown used to say when horses were stolen up here, all you had to do was wait — there'd be a revolution bust out down there." He raised his eyes. "Where'd they come from?"

Butler had no idea, and right now he didn't care. "I've got to stop it."

"Why? It's none of our business. Unless you want to help the central government stay in power down there."

Butler flushed. "I don't give a damn who's in power down there. Any more than you do . . . Hunter Calkins and his riders will be in the middle. They'll be massacred."

Obando dropped his gaze back to his half-empty cup. "Not if they mind their own business. If you're right, the *pronunciados* contracted to buy a big herd of horses. For once they're going to pay for them, which means they don't need Hunter's livestock. He don't have enough, anyway."

Butler raised the cup, drained it, and set it aside. "When did they ever just take horses up here and leave? Not that I ever heard of."

Obando nodded almost imperceptibly. "Now you're talking about something else," he said, and leaned back off the table.

"Raid Peralta in the dawn, kill people, torch

the stores, steal women, and plunder every-thing they can," Butler exclaimed.

Obando said, "Maybe not," in a tone of voice that lacked conviction. Then he smiled. "All right. You want information. I'll see what I can find out. But it may take a while."

The marshal rose. "Thanks for the wine. I wish I could be as easy about this as you are."

Obando also stood up. "I'm not easy about it. . . ."

After they parted and Marshal Butler was hiking back toward Gringo-town, Jésus Obando's wife came out and sat down at the old table where Butler had been sitting. "What is it?" she asked.

He told her, and poured them both a cupful of the red wine.

Before touching hers, she said, "It's their trouble, not ours."

He looked steadily at her. "How can you say such a thing? What happened to your aunt, to other people since we were chil-dren? Those aren't our people, they are wolves. Everybody's enemies . . . I'm hungry, woman."

She rose and walked toward the house with a saucy swing to her hips. He sat a moment longer, then rose, rolling his eyes, and fol-lowed.

★ ★ ★

Because the marshal returned to his office from the south and the harness shop was opposite the saloon northward, Bart Matthews did not see Butler until they met at the cafe. There, the customary droll banter had been replaced by an almost funereal gravity. Butler listened and said nothing. Much of what he heard could not possibly be true, he knew, but that would not stop it from being repeated.

The harness maker came in, sank down beside Butler, and squinted at him. The cafeman came along for Matthews's order and padded away after it had been given, allowing the harness maker to finally say what was on his mind.

"What about them horses, Frank?"

Butler reared back to allow the cafeman to place a platter in front of him. Then he settled both elbows atop the counter, ignored the food, and said, "If they tie in with some other things, why then I think I'd better get up a posse and go find them and have a talk with their owner."

Matthews nodded slightly. "If they're still in the country. Whoever's peddling horses to the insurgents will know he'll be in trouble if the U.S. army gets wind of it. He'd be a fool to hang around. And one other thing, Frank, if you ride out there and the trader an' his crew is out there, more'n likely the

56

Messicans will be too."

Marshal Butler eyed the harness maker wryly. "Do I look like I came down in the last rain?" he said. "While we're talkin' about it, how would you like to ride with the posse?"

Matthews considered the platter placed in front of him before replying. "I ain't as young as I used to be."

"None of us is," stated the lawman.

"Well . . . say, what kind of meat is this?"

Butler, who had just about finished his own meal, gazed at the plate in front of the harness maker. "Mexican mule. Are you going to ride with me or not?"

"Yeah, I'll ride with you. Tonight?"

"Be down at Evinrude's barn an hour or two before sunrise," Marshal Butler said, and rose to depart.

There was more activity in the darkened roadway than usual. Anxious people hunted up the marshal to make nervous inquiries. He made no attempt to placate them, but neither did he tell them all he knew. Eventually, he headed back to the rooming house.

He intended to lead his posse out very early. For years Peralta had had a vigilance committee. It had come to life during earlier times, when it hadn't been just border jumpers who threatened the area. On his way to the rooming house, he stopped at the saloon to pass word

57

by Jess Hobart when the committee was to meet at Evinrude's barn. Committee members were to bring along grub, coats, weapons, and plenty of ammunition.

Inevitably, John Grover heard. While he usually supported such things, tonight he left a warm supper to visit Marshal Butler at his room. He was met by a tired, unsmiling lawman, whose response to the merchant's spoken fear of what might happen if Butler stripped the town of men was to bluntly ask if Grover had a better idea.

Grover had no better idea. In fact, he had no idea at all beyond his whining complaint that Butler would be leaving Peralta defenseless.

"Against what?" Frank asked shortly. "John, if anything happens tomorrow it'll happen a long way from town."

"You don't know that," exclaimed the merchant. "Frank, they're out there. Everyone knows that. You lead the committee out in the morning an' they'll see you leave."

Butler, who'd been leaning in the doorway in his stocking feet, spoke sharply. "The town can look after itself."

Grover blanched. "What'll we have? Some old men, some merchants, some women and kids. Frank, it's your duty to protect the town."

"That's part of what I plan to do, John — stop trouble before it gets here. Not sit around town waiting for it. And there's reason to believe they aren't interested in Peralta."

"Well, just what in the hell are they interested in?"

"I got to be stirring before daybreak, John, and it's late. When we get back tomorrow, we'll know more. Now go home, and if you can't sleep, go over to the saloon. They're passing around stories that'll make your hair stand up. Good night!"

John Grover stood, briefly staring at the door that had been closed in his face, then went down the dingy hallway and out into the darkness, alternately groaning to himself and cursing.

Marshal Butler locked the door, bedded down, and slept like a dead man until his inner clock awakened him in cold darkness, with Peralta silent and mostly dark around him.

Pete Evinrude was down at his barn. Since his main hostler had been dispatched for the army he'd been doing most of the dunging out and feeding by himself, something he was not overjoyed about. When heavily armed, silent men began arriving out front — some with saddled horses, others to get their animals from his barn — Pete ducked inside his smelly little office, felt under a pile of sweat-stiff collar pads, dug out a bottle, took three big swallows to calm his nerves, and returned to his dimly lighted runway to ask questions.

Bart Matthews eyed the agitated liveryman, spat amber, and leaned to whisper. "We're fixin' to invade Messico. Now, keep it to yourself."

Evinrude's arm swung wildly. "What! Are you crazy? We got border jumpers breathing down our necks and —"

"Bart," a large, thick man said from a distance of a few feet. "This ain't no joke!" The heavyset man, Peralta's town blacksmith, was not known for a sense of humor.

Bart Matthews went after his horse, leaving the liveryman and the blacksmith facing each other. The blacksmith, with slack reins hanging from one gloved hand to the big horse behind him, shook his head. "We're goin' on a scout beyond town. As soon as Frank gets here . . . you might speed things up by rigging out his horse for him."

The blacksmith led his horse out front where a dozen men were swinging their arms in the cold predawn, booted carbines under their *rosaderos*. They said very little until one man saw someone hiking southward from the direction of the rooming house, and hissed at his companions that the marshal was coming.

A graying committeeman from Mex-town smiled as the marshal walked up. He was the only posseman who did so.

There were a few grunted greetings as Frank entered the runway for his animal. The waiting possemen checked *cinchas* and surreptitiously passed a couple of bottles around as insulation against the chill. When Marshal Butler led his horse out, turned it once, and swung across leather, the other men followed his example.

They rode northwest through town, making noise only when a shod horse struck stone or when bone-dry leather squeaked.

Evinrude got another couple of swallows from his bottle and went out front to watch them. When Marshal Butler turned westerly across some empty lots, the liveryman wagged his head; damned fools weren't even going in the right direction. Mexico was southward.

The sun was several hours from springing over the east curve of the world. Although there were committeemen from Mex-town among the possemen whose sympathies were obviously with gringo law and order, Frank Butler wondered if there might not be other dark eyes watching him lead his riders out of town.

CHAPTER FIVE

DESPLOBADO

A lithe young man eased up to ride stirrup with Marshal Butler, who recognized him as an occasional helper with the Obando mule train. He had come forward to say Jésus Obando had been unable to ride with the posse because he had two sick mules.

Butler eyed the young Mexican, who had a guileless smile, and asked if Obando had had the trouble with sick animals down at Rincón or on the way back.

The young man shook his head. "No. I was with him. It was a big cargo, an' we used all the mules. There wasn't no sick ones." He showed his smile as he added, "But colic can show up overnight."

Butler nodded and concentrated on his bearings. He knew the *desplobado* — the uninhabited land — well enough, but predawn darkness made a few degrees of drift entirely possible, and he wanted to go far enough northward to get among some fat little round hills. From the top of any of them he would be able to see for many miles southward in the direction of the Calkins yard, and elsewhere.

Bart Matthews, astride a big, rawboned *grullo* horse, rode up to make a vague gesture with an upraised arm. "Them tracks come from the northeast, but this far out they dropped more southerly."

Butler would not be interested in tracks until after sunrise. He explained his reason for heading more northerly and the older man drifted back among the others, not rebuked but for a while content to ride in silence.

There was almost no conversation. By the time the eastern world was firming up with a kind of fish-belly color, the riders had covered roughly two-thirds of the distance they had to travel to reach the area of the hills.

With improved visibility, they were able to scan for movement. There was none, which did not mean eyes weren't watching them; there were always watchers, mostly with four legs, but unless they dove into holes in the ground before the riders came along, they were unheeded.

As they came to the area of the low hills, some half-wild cattle, roused no doubt by reverberations in the ground, sprang out of their beds and fled. The possemen watched them, and one man laughed as he said, "Takes generations to breed the longhorn out, don't it? Look at 'em run."

Another posseman, probably with a bad experience in mind, dryly said, "Better away from us than at us. Must not be any wet cows among 'em."

They stopped behind a round swell and swung to the ground while Butler climbed to the top. It still was not very warm, but it would be shortly; sunlight was exploding in all directions.

Butler squatted, tipped down his hat, and waited with the patience of an Indian until he saw movement. It was neither mounted men nor cattle; it was dust. It was made thin by distance and sun brilliance, but it was unmistakable.

The large blacksmith grunted up the hill and sank to one knee as he said, "You expect Mister Calkins is movin' cattle?"

Butler had no idea, but the longer he sat up there watching, the more it seemed to him the dust was moving too fast for cattle. "Horses," he stated, and the blacksmith immediately altered his earlier opinion.

"Yep, sure as hell. It's a pretty big herd of 'em, wouldn't you say? Mister Calkins don't have that many horses, does he?"

The marshal shook his head without replying. The dust was dispersing, getting thinner as it settled. Whoever was driving those animals had evidently stopped. He tried to remember if he'd heard of springs or water holes northwest of the Calkins place.

From the base of the hill, someone whistled. Frank and the blacksmith rose to look down there. Several men were pointing eastward. The stage road was several miles away in that direction. Otherwise there was nothing for a great distance, then it was other cattle outfits who, like Hunter Calkins, brought herds to the South Desert for the springtime and early-summer feed.

What held the interest of the men at the base of the knob was a band of horsemen. Butler could not even guess at their number, because they were riding bunched up, but he thought it was at least ten, maybe fifteen. He and the blacksmith went back down to the others. By his estimate the oncoming riders were at least two miles distant, too far to make any definite judgment except that they were riders.

He led the way among the hills for a mile, then halted when Obando's young mule-train swamper waved an arm. The riders were angling more southerly now; they would not approach the country where the possemen were hidden from their view by a particularly thick hill.

Butler watched them, and decided they were *bandoleros* before they were close enough for a positive identification. They rode *la jinetta*, the way men rode whose stirrups were rigged like their *cinchas*, in a center-fire position.

Someone swore softly as the riders loped past about a half mile southward. If any of them looked in the direction of the thick low hill that hid the possemen, no one saw it. Butler's impression was that, whoever they were, they had a definite destination in mind and were in a hurry to get there. The riders were heavily armed. Some even carried the ubiquitous machete of Mexico.

Butler corrected his earlier guess by making a head tally. "Twenty-two," he said aloud. He remembered what Grover's freighter had said about seeing riders like this crossing the stage road north of town.

The riders disappeared down one side of an arroyo and reappeared up the opposite side. They began angling still farther southward, and Butler swore under his breath. They were heading in the direction of the big dust banner he'd seen earlier.

If they got there they would undoubtedly be in the company of another party of horsemen. Bart Matthews spoke around a cud in his cheek. "Marshal, we should've caught 'em when we had the chance."

The blacksmith, who had growled at Matthews back in Evinrude's barn, growled at him again. "We ain't no army. Those fellers was carryin' everything but cannon."

Butler swung into the saddle, sat a moment until his companions were also astride, and set a course almost due south. The posse held to it until the sun was high enough to warm the world. Then it swung due west in the direction of the Calkins yard. The marshal hoped it would appear to watchers that the posse was coming from the direction of Peralta.

There were long periods of silence. The possemen had reason, finally, to be wary and watchful. Before they had rooftops in sight, they had all fairly well worked out in their minds that the *bandoleros* had passed the Calkins place well to the north.

Butler's personal opinion was that the big cloud of dust he'd seen earlier had been made by men driving a large band of horses, probably to a rendezvous with the *bandoleros*.

They were passing through a thornpin thicket strung out down a wide arroyo when they heard two gunshots. Frank raised his arm to call a halt.

There was a fierce fusillade, then silence.

67

A grizzled older man astride a too-fat bay horse stood in his stirrups, wrinkling his nose like a dog as he pointed westward, and sat back down without saying a word.

Butler gestured for the harness maker to go up the side of their arroyo on foot. Matthews swung off and, trotting like an Indian, scrambled up the slope. His footing crumbled under him several times, making him turn the air blue, before he dropped flat and lay motionless for a long time. As he turned to scramble back down, he didn't have to raise his voice to be clearly heard.

"Dust. Couldn't make out much. It's a hell of a distance off, but sure as hell it was a pretty hot fight for as long as it lasted."

He was panting when he reached his horse.

Butler led off down the arroyo through underbrush that had thorns, little round dusty-looking leaves, and wiry limbs growing in all directions. The men alternately watched the uphill sides of the arroyo and the passageways through the brush. Their horses, with no interest in anything but avoiding thorns, pretty much picked their own routes.

It was hot in the arroyo, but where the land began to lift, the brush to thin out, there was less heat. The men halted just short of leaving the underbrush, with a clear view of Calkins's yard.

There was not a sound down there, not even from using horses in the corrals. Someone plaintively asked if Calkins kept dogs. Butler said he didn't; he'd scorned the use of dogs although most stockmen in the area would not be without them. Longhorns had a tendency to avoid round up by closing their eyes and running full-tilt into thickets of thornpin where riders could not get at them or rope them. They could best be choused out by dogs.

Nevertheless, old Hunter Calkins's antipathy toward dogs was deep and of long standing.

Butler sat studying the yard with both hands resting on the saddle horn. The ragged old cottonwoods had shadows only around their bases, which meant it was close to midday. He told the others to remain out of sight; a man could not appear as a threat if he rode into the yard alone.

The possemen watched him leave the underbrush behind and ride at a steady walk down into the yard. Nothing happened. No one appeared.

He tied up out front of the barn, looked inside down the cool runway, saw no horses in the stalls, and lingered as he eyed the saddle pole. Every saddle was gone. He walked in the direction of the corrals, where layers of shod-horse tracks lay over each other.

He went around from behind the barn to the house, where an impression of desolation touched him even before he got to the veranda.

One of the rawhide-strung chairs on the porch was overturned.

He pushed on the door, which swung open without noise. It was easily ten degrees cooler inside than outside. The place smelled as it usually did, of coffee, pipe smoke, and fried food.

Everything looked normal until he went to stand in the kitchen doorway. The kitchen was a scene of chaos. Cooking pans on the stove had remains of a meal in them. Two nearly empty whiskey bottles were on the table along with scattered dishes and eating utensils. Canisters had been overturned, scantlings from the wood box carelessly scattered. Hunter's old hexagonal-barreled hunting rifle, which usually hung from a hook on the back of the door, was gone. His old chore coat had been flung down. And, as though whoever had been here had searched for something, drawers had been yanked out and dumped.

In the old stockman's spartan bedroom, it was the same. Plunderers had left havoc in their wake. They had also left something else: blood on the bedroom floor and a thin track of it from the bedroom to the parlor.

Butler returned to the porch, signaled with

his hat, and remained out there until the posse-men arrived, tied up, and trooped to the house. He jerked a thumb for them to go inside and make their judgment.

Charley Rivas, a pockmarked, barrel-chested short resident of Mex-town came out first. He stood a moment looking westerly, then scanned the northward range too before saying, "*Caramba, jefe;* what did they do with him? Maybe we shouldn't look." Rivas turned to Butler. "Didn't he have riders?"

The marshal nodded. "Yeah. That's what I'm trying to figure out. He usually had five or six riders, vaqueros and Indians."

Rivas hitched at his britches and went down off the porch in the direction of the bunk-house. He kicked the door inward, cocked his handgun, and waited a moment before spring-ing inside, gun up and moving. The bunk-house was empty. The possessions of its inhabitants appeared undisturbed.

Butler walked to the bunkhouse with other possemen joining him. There was no sign of violence, but the same feeling of abandonment existed as in the main house.

Bart Matthews went out to the tiny bunk-house porch to squint in all directions before raising his voice slightly to the men inside. "We better go west, find out what that shootin' was about. Mister Calkins might be out there bleedin' like a stuck hawg."

Now Marshal Butler was sure they had been seen. The fierce gunfight had occurred to the west. He led his possemen due north and kept them riding in that direction for an hour, until they were far beyond sight of the yard. Then he turned abruptly westward.

If watchers had been hiding somewhere in the vicinity of the yard, the band of armed riders from Peralta going north might at least have puzzled them. The best the marshal could hope for was that the watchers returned to their companions to report that the possemen had been fooled into riding in the wrong direction.

The marshal actually had little hope that this would happen. But this plan was better than going west, as they no doubt would be expected to do, and riding into an ambush.

The blacksmith was riding with the harness maker, their mutual animosity forgotten, at least for now. The usually loquacious harness maker was quiet.

Butler glanced around when Charley Rivas came up alongside and said, "Do you know where Vasquez Spring is, *jefe?*"

Butler eyed him and shook his head. "West of here?"

"*Sí*. Not very far. Maybe four miles," Rivas replied.

"I had a wife; she was Laguna-Acoma." Rivas shrugged. "She took me to Vasquez Spring when we were courting. It's a very private place." He paused briefly, then said, "What is past is past, no? She died in childbirth four years ago. I never came back here. You understand, *jefe?*"

"Yes. What about that spring?"

"It is the only water between Calkins's sump holes and the wells of Laguna. Unless a man has been there, he wouldn't find it. Without the guidance of God, *jefe,* he could never find it."

Butler straightened around in the saddle, squinting southwesterly. "This morning when we saw that big dust —"

"*Jefe,* that's what I thought. The dust was close to Vasquez Spring."

The marshal was quiet for a moment, still looking southward and westerly. Eventually he said, "Can you lead us there?"

"Yes."

"Can you do it without someone seeing us coming?"

"No, it is very dry and barren country long before you get there. But I was thinking back at the yard . . . maybe two men could sneak up there in the night." He smiled broadly. "Three or four gunshots should stampede the horses of anyone camping there. Men on foot out here have many miles to walk to find more horses." He smiled broadly again. "If *bandoleros* or bad gringos try to reach the Lagunas' horse herds . . ." He made a stiff-fingered motion across his throat and continued to smile.

Butler sent Rivas ahead to scout, and for the first time since leaving Hunter Calkins's yard, his spirits rose a little.

The heat stabilized at a level that was less than comfortable, but Butler's committeemen were either natives or had lived on the South Desert long enough to develop a tolerance.

He didn't worry much about the men; he worried about the horses. The smallest horse along, probably close to eight hundred pounds, had lots more bulk to be cooled than any of the riders.

He believed Rivas, had no reason not to, but if for whatever reason his information was incorrect, or if Vasquez Spring was dry this year. . . .

Chapter Six

CAUGHT!

They rode without haste. For one thing, Butler was not as eager to find men and horses as he was leery of ambushes, a *bandolero* specialty. Also, it was hot enough to make even walking horses sweat, so he wanted to favor the animals as much as he could.

Rivas returned from his scout grinning. He called in Spanish to Jésus Obando's mule-train swamper before swinging in to ride with Frank Butler. Then he switched to English.

"Three dead men. A vaquero and two Indians," he reported, and pointed ahead with an upraised arm. "That was what the fighting was about we heard this morning."

Butler asked, "Tracks?"

"Everywhere, *jefe*. Shod horses. Some seemed to come from the west, others from the southeast. Maybe those dead ones belonged to Hunter Calkins. They would come

75

from the ranch. Those shod-horse marks from the southeast were maybe theirs. It wasn't an ambush, but I think they saw a band of riders coming and went north. There are plenty of marks of running horses to the rocky place where they fought. Someone took their horses." He shrugged. *"Bandoleros."*

Everyone listened in total silence until the scout said, *"Jefe,* they know we're coming. They got to know."

The old man on the fat horse groaned aloud and called to the harness maker. "You was right, Bart, we should've busted out on 'em back yonder from behind that fat hill."

No one else took this up. Everyone was less interested in what might have happened than in what was going to happen.

While they sat motionless, listening to the scout, a solitary horseman came out of a distant thicket and sat like an Indian facing them. Rivas's eyes were fixed on the stranger as he quietly said, *"No Indio, señores . . . Gringo!"*

Butler and the horseman sat facing each other. The stranger was clearly not going to advance, so the marshal quietly told the others to stay in place and eased his animal ahead at a steady walk.

The horseman swung to the ground, placed his animal between himself and Frank Butler, and let his gun lie gently across the saddle seat. He did not cock it.

Butler halted about twenty yards away and raised his gloved right hand. The stranger did the same thing, so Butler kneed his horse ahead.

They were close enough to see each other in detail when the dismounted man spoke with a faint Texas accent. "That'll do, mister. Keep both hands on your saddle horn."

Butler's hands, already on the horn, remained there as he studied the stranger, a medium-size, lean individual with skin the color of old bronze and narrowed gray eyes. His clothing was stained, faded, and worn. The gun lying casually across the saddle seat had long since lost all its blueing.

The horseman made a slight smile and nodded as he said, "You the law, are you?"

Butler's answer was curt. "You see the badge."

The man with the weapon acknowledged the response with an almost imperceptible nod of his head. "And them boys back yonder, they'll be your posse riders?"

"Yes. And who are you?"

"Names don't matter, Marshal. I got a friend with me over in the brush. We knew you was comin' right after you left that ranch yard down yonder. When you rode north it didn't fool no one, but it gave us enough time to figure things. The gent with me'd like to talk to you. . . . Marshal, don't look back, don't make a move that'd make me shoot you. The boss don't want to kill you or your posse riders. He just wants to talk a little. You understand?"

He understood: The Texan and whoever was waiting to talk to him in hiding were not the only men out here. The thicket from which the stranger had emerged was probably full of them.

Butler said, "Call him out," and waited until a second horseman came from the thicket. This one was taller and heavier. He was also quite a bit older than the young stranger. He had a full beard shot through with gray, bushy dark eyebrows with the same combination of colors, and a mouth like a bear trap, which even his smile as he walked his horse toward Frank Butler could not disguise. Whoever he was, Butler read him to be as hard as steel as he approached.

When he was drawing rein, the rider with the gun introduced him. "This here is Mister Jacob Cartwell, Marshal. You'll be . . . ?"

The marshal ignored the man behind the horse and looked straight at the older man. "Frank Butler, marshal of Peralta."

Jacob Cartwell came closer before dismounting and standing at the head of his horse, one rein dangling. He continued to smile — with his mouth, not with his eyes.

"You're ridin' around lookin' for them folks from that ranch back yonder."

It was not put to Butler as a question, but he nodded as though it had been. "Hunter Calkins and his riders, Mister Cartwell."

"Well now, Marshal, they was sneakin' around. We got a big herd of horses. The men sneakin' around spyin' on us got the horses real nervous. I expect you'll know it's one hell of a chore tryin' to mind three hunnert head of loose stock even when they ain't bein' spooked." Jacob Cartwell's smile remained in place. The little gray unsmiling eyes fixed on Marshal Butler were both sly and menacing. Cartwell relaxed his stance as might a man who felt he had the upper hand, which at the moment he certainly did have.

"We got them boys at the camp, Marshal. Unfortunately, the old gent put up a fight an' got bloodied a little. He'll be all right. . . . But three of his riders figured to sneak away, so we had to run them down. They commenced firing. . . . A man's got a right to defend himself, don't he? Well, we saw you boys stop over where them three riders is lying.

"I wanted to explain all this to you, Marshal. We're livin' in lawless times. I'm a horse rancher. Just like any other businessman, I got the right to protect myself an' my interests. If them damned fools hadn't tried to sneak away . . ." Jacob Cartwell shrugged mighty shoulders and continued to smile.

Behind him, Butler could hear a faint murmur among his waiting riders, most of whom had done as the rangeman had done — dismounted and swung their horses to provide protection.

Without taking his eyes off the big bearded man, the marshal spoke quietly. "Why did you take Calkins and his riders? This is their range, Mister Cartwell. They got every right to be out here."

"Sneakin' around like damned diggers, Marshal, givin' my loose stock fits? You got any idea what'd happen if they'd stampeded my herd? From the looks of this country, Marshal, I'd be lucky to get half of 'em back if I rode for six months huntin' them."

Butler glanced in the direction of the nearby thicket, but did not see anyone. He swung his attention back to the lounging Texan before addressing Cartwell again. "You killed three men who had a lot more right out here than you have. Suppose you tell me *why* you shot them. It wasn't for scaring the horses, because they were a long way from Vasquez Spring before they were killed." Butler watched the big man's smile fade. He probably should have been warned, but he wasn't. "Where are the Mexicans, Mister Cartwell?"

The menacing gaze hardened. "What Messicans?"

"The *bandoleros* from Mexico who bought your horses. They're going to take them south, aren't they?"

Jacob Cartwell looked at the lounging Texan, whose calm, hard gaze had not left Frank Butler. "Paul, you seen any Messicans out here?"

The Texan wagged his head slowly. "No sir. I sure ain't," he said.

Butler felt color coming into his face. He gazed steadily at the bearded man. "We saw *bandoleros* this morning riding toward your dust. In Peralta, folks have seen others. Out a ways, acting like they didn't want to be noticed. Mister Cartwell, you know there's a revolution in Mexico. When there's a demand for horses down there, the price gets damned high. You aren't the first horse trader who's figured how to get a sackful of greenbacks out of this. Only in your case it's not greenbacks, is it?"

Cartwell had lost the initiative. He was also close to losing his temper. "What the hell are you accusing me of?" he snarled. "Marshal, whatever we done we done to protect ourselves and our interests. That's allowable under the law. Any law I ever run across, anyway." As Cartwell spoke, his confidence grew. "Only reason we're keepin' Mister Calkins and his riders is because they been troublesome. We don't figure to stay in this country any longer'n we got to, but while we're here, we're goin' to protect ourselves. You can make anythin' out of that you want to, we're still goin' to do it."

The one named Paul lazily leveled up his six-gun and cocked it. It was not a loud sound, but it was certainly an unmistakable one.

Jacob Cartwell was quiet for a long time, looking from Marshal Butler to the band of possemen a fair distance behind him. Finally, in a quieter voice he said, "Marshal, you put me between the rock an' a hard place. Get down off your horse!"

Butler remained in the saddle, hands lying atop the horn as he looked stonily down into the bearded man's face.

Cartwell let out a long breath, almost a sigh. He hooked both thumbs in his shellbelt and stared at Frank Butler. Without addressing the marshal, he raised his voice a little.

"Stand up, lads!"

The thicket from which Cartwell had emerged shed dust as armed men appeared. Butler was surprised only by the number of them. At least fifteen, every man with a gun to his shoulder facing the distant, stunned possemen. There were more *bandoleros* among the strangers than gringos.

Butler smiled slightly without a shred of humor as he addressed the big bearded man again. " 'What Messicans,' " he said, mimicking Cartwell.

The Texan spoke softly. "Mister, you get down off that horse unless you want me to blow you out of the saddle and my friends yonder to massacre your possemen. Get down! *Now!*"

Butler swung to the ground. When he faced Jacob Cartwell, he was surprised at the actual size of the man. Cartwell was almost a head taller than he, and easily twice as broad. An imposing figure under any circumstances, in the present situation he was not just impressive, he was intimidating.

Paul spoke again. "The gun, Marshal!"

Butler dropped it without taking his eyes off Jacob Cartwell. "You're going to have damned near as many prisoners as you got horses."

Cartwell's hard gaze showed a trace of irony as he replied. "It won't be for long, Marshal. When our business here is finished, we'll set all of you loose . . . on foot. After that, if you don't die out here, you can try to find us." Cartwell's bleak smile reappeared. "The Messicans will be back down over the border. Us, well, you won't even be able to track us. . . . Marshal, you made a bad judgment back at that old ranch. Now, turn around an' tell them possemen of yours to shed their weapons — all of them — an' walk over here leadin' their horses." Cartwell held up a large hand. "This is where you'll get salted down with lead if anything goes wrong. Don't let 'em make any mistakes if you want to see the sunrise tomorrow."

Butler turned slowly. Without a doubt they would kill him and his men. He'd already seen evidence of that where those three Calkins riders had been riddled.

He did not have to raise his voice. "Put down your weapons. All of them. Walk over here leading your horses. Don't think, just do it. You can see the ones in the brush. There never was a man or a horse that could outrun a bullet. Slow, put down your guns."

The longest moment of total silence and stillness any of them had ever lived through followed Butler's order, until one man broke it. In monumental disgust, Bart Matthews said, "Son of a bitch!" and flung down his weapons.

The other possemen followed the harness maker's example. When Matthews began

84

walking forward leading his horse, the others followed that example too.

Jacob Cartwell stood wide-legged, keen eyes missing no detail. His Texan range rider turned his Colt slightly from Frank Butler to the advancing possemen. When the possemen halted a couple of yards away, the old man who rode the bay horse made a sniffing sound and looked coldly at the marshal. "Nice kettle of fish," he said sourly.

Cartwell studied them over a long interval of silence, then told Paul to check each of them for hidden weapons. It took more than fifteen minutes, and by the time Paul was finished the watchers in the thicket had lowered their long guns and were leaning on them as interested spectators.

Paul found a boot knife on Obando's swamper, flung it away with a curse using his left hand, and using his right hand brought the youth to his knees with a vicious blow to the soft parts.

Bart Matthews growled and moved to help the injured man. Paul drew his six-gun without haste, pointed it, and cocked it. Butler held his breath.

Jacob Cartwell growled. "Put up that damned gun and finish searchin' them."

The Texan obeyed, but from this point on his search was more thorough and much rougher. When he finished, Cartwell gave him another order. "Get on your horse. Bring up the rear. Use your gun if you got to; otherwise just herd them along." He made a motion for Butler to get back astride. As the possemen all did the same, Cartwell warned them: "The marshal told you a fact: No one ever outrun a bullet."

He waited a moment looking from prisoner to prisoner, then went back toward the big thicket where someone handed him the reins to a large, muscled-up sorrel horse. He mounted as he spoke curtly in Spanish, then nodded for Butler to lead out heading west.

The day was not insufferably hot, but a month from now there would be no mercy from a lemon-yellow sun that could fry an egg on a flat rock.

Cartwell rode in the lead. Riders emerging from the big thicket made a loose surround. Two *bandoleros* rode with Cartwell, one on each side. The three men talked, Cartwell alternating between border Spanish and English with a facility that made Butler suspect he too was a Texan. Certainly he was not a stranger to the border country, and that was something Butler would remember.

They passed about a mile of countryside identical to the land the possemen had been riding over most of the day. Then a subtle change occurred: the land became more rocky; some of the rock fields had boulders as tall as a mounted man. Here there was less undergrowth, the heat was more intense. But no one paid attention to that.

West of Cartwell's camp on the farthest fringe of the boulder field, horses were scattered over a considerable distance searching among the rocks for something to eat. There were riders out there to prevent a drift. Closer to the lowest part of the field of big rocks there were several raffish cottonwoods and a fringe of greenery that covered a distance of roughly a hundred feet in all directions.

It wasn't actually a spring. It was a sump. There was water in a natural rock basin about thirty feet across. The water's motionlessness suggested it was a pool; but the water was cool and had no green scum.

The camp was typical, except that it had no wagon, which was customary on long drives of large herds. But there were several pack animals, large Missouri mules. There also was saddlery and camp equipment scattered indiscriminately where rocks had been removed from the edge of the pool.

There was just one man at the camp when Cartwell rode in with his captives. He was a pudgy, cockeyed Mexican whose straight black hair hung down his forehead. He was not one of the *bandoleros;* he was Cartwell's camp robber, someone who helped with chores, from scouting up dry brush for cooking fires and helping with meals, to bringing in hobbled using horses each morning before sunrise. He was not a young man.

The riders who had surrounded the possemen lingered at the camp only until the prisoners had been dismounted, their outfits dumped, and their horses driven out where the loose stock grazed.

The Texan remained, as did a solemn Mexican with a hint of gray at the temples. He was a typical *bandolero.* On the inside seam of each trouser leg had been sewn soft leather. His sombrero was tipped up fore and aft; his face was lean, hawkish, and russet tan. He wore two six-guns on the same shellbelt, and although there was widespread disdain for men who wore two belt guns, this man looked and acted as though trying to impress and intimidate people was not part of his nature.

Cartwell had the captives sit down, called to the cockeyed roustabout for coffee, and, while removing his riding gloves, looked far out where his riders were being joined by the men who had returned with him. From off to one side the unsmiling, hawk-faced Mexican spoke in Spanish.

"The trouble is not out there. It is here."

Cartwell nodded almost indifferently and did not look at the *bandolero* as he grunted down into a sitting position facing Marshal Butler. His mood was different from what it had been at the ambush. He even smiled at the lawman and offered a crooked little Mexican cheroot, one inhalation from which was like being kicked in the chest by an army mule.

Butler declined, watched the bearded man light up, and waited.

The two-gun *bandolero* turned his back, went to a horse, swung up, and loped in the direction of the widespread grazing horses. Butler watched him go; so far he had identified two men who were unmistakably deadly: Cartwell's Texan and the cold-eyed, two-gun Mexican.

Chapter Seven

A DEAD MAN

There was another man just as deadly, but it seemed that his character was different. Cartwell seemed not to see the world in blacks and whites like the Texan and the two-gun *bandolero,* to whom a decision was followed by action.

As he sat facing Marshal Butler smoking his little cigar, Cartwell's gaze was unfriendly, but more speculative than menacing. He removed the little cigar to ask a question.

"Back yonder you said somethin' about me sellin' horses for somethin' other than greenbacks. What did you mean?"

Butler did not hesitate. "I meant that bullion box the *pronunciados* buried up here. Full of gold and silver that was most likely raided from churches in Mexico."

Cartwell considered that for a moment before asking another question. "Did you see such a box, Marshal?"

To avoid making a statement that would point to Hunter Calkins, Butler replied ambiguously. "I wouldn't know about such a box if there wasn't one, would I?"

Again Cartwell paused in thought before speaking. He gave his head an irritable little shake. "This gawddamned country's supposed to be uninhabited."

The marshal smiled a little. "Yeah. That's why you an' the Mexicans figured to rendezvous here. I sure can understand that. And most of the time you'd be right. But not in springtime, when the stockmen arrive from up north for the early feed and Indians from the Reservations are out and about. Still, if you'd figured the meeting farther south, you most likely wouldn't have run into trouble. There are no free grazers down there, and it's a few miles closer to the border."

Jacob Cartwell considered his cigar, which had burned down. He killed it by smashing it against the ground. "Closer to the border those sons of bitches would have come in the night, stampeded my horses southward into Messico, an' before I could get rigged out they'd be safe an' I'd be ruined." Cartwell raised his eyes. "What I should have done was ride over here myself and look around."

"Didn't you?"

Cartwell's gaze showed hard irony again. "No. I left it up to Paul. He found the Calkins ranch but said he saw only one old man and two riders."

Butler's reply was curt. "Not two riders. Five or six."

"I know that now. Well, it'll be finished by morning."

"You got the box?"

Cartwell nodded. "Got it, an' those border jumpers'll leave at sunup in the morning. With just a little luck, they should be close to the border by evening." The big, bearded man looked around where possemen were glumly listening. "Three hundred horses raise a lot of dust." He smiled everywhere but around the eyes; they were calculating and cold. "If you an' old Calkins hadn't come out here, Marshal, things would have worked out. They'll still work out. You're not goin' anywhere until the Messicans are gone with the horses an' me an' my lads strike camp. After that, you got one hell of a walk before you get anywhere."

Several riders loped in, and Cartwell went to talk to them. Butler went over where Hunter Calkins and two of his riders were sitting. The riders were stoically dejected. Calkins had a torn mouth, swollen and purple, and bloodshot eyes. He'd obviously taken a pretty hard shellacking.

He watched Marshal Butler approach, eyes fixed and solemn. It was hard to understand him because of his grotesquely swollen mouth, but he said, "Well, rode right into it, didn't you?"

Butler hunkered. Calkins hadn't done much better or he wouldn't be here either, but the marshal ignored the sarcasm to ask how the old stockman felt.

Calkins gingerly touched his torn mouth with a blue bandanna before replying. "Like three of them bastards overhauled my running gear." He lowered the bandanna, looking for blood. There was some, but not very much. "They got into the barn; come up on the blind side where the barn cuts off the view. Got inside, and when the riders came back, threw down on them. They robbed the house. Lookin' for a cache they said I had. Cache? I got no cache. They worked me over, but I couldn't tell 'em anything else: I had no cache. Then they herded us all over here, an' some time in the night three of my riders got clear and made a run for it."

Butler nodded. "We saw them."

Calkins jutted his jaw. "That feller Cartwell is talkin' to — that lanky Texan? He's the one led the search an' come back grinnin' like a preacher. He talked loud, I guess to scare me an' the two riders I got left. It worked. When he told Cartwell what happened out where they run my riders down, it was enough to make a man's hair stand up."

Butler looked around. He was not surprised to hear of the Texan's brutality.

Later, more horsemen loped in from watching the horses and a meal was prepared. Very little was said. Cartwell and his riders seemed to want this interlude to end, as did the *bandoleros,* though for different reasons. When the *bandoleros* headed south, their responsibility for three hundred horses would be beginning, Jacob Cartwell's would be ended.

Before dusk, nighthawks were sent out, to be relieved after midnight. One man would remain awake in the camp, Winchester across his lap, while the others bedded down. Jacob Cartwell sat hunched like a bear, smoking a cigar.

Rivas approached Butler in dying daylight to tell him that the young swamper the Texan had hit in the stomach was spitting blood.

Under the watchful eye of the man with his back to an upended saddle and the Winchester across his lap, Butler went to look at the youth, who smiled wanly. He did not look very well. Butler hunkered with Rivas beside him and several other possemen nearby.

The harness maker said, "It'll pass. I been

hit in the guts and kicked too. Spit blood for a day or so, then it passes."

There was nothing Butler could do. Like the others, he hoped Bart Matthews was right.

He wasn't.

In the chill of predawn, Rivas knelt beside Marshal Butler's bedroll and said, "He's dead. Obando's swamper is dead."

Butler sat up as the gun guard growled at them. "Hey, beaner, go on back to your blankets and stay there. You — Marshal — lie back down an' don't stir until daylight. *Move, beaner!*"

Rivas faded off in the direction of the youth who had died in his blankets.

Butler regarded the man with the Winchester. He was thin and had a prominent Adam's apple. He was one of those weathered, lean, lined men whose age was indeterminate.

From a short distance, Hunter Calkins spoke without rising up. "That makes four," he told no one in particular.

The sentinel snarled for silence and got it, but for Marshal Butler and others who had heard the rancher, sleep was not possible.

Butler had both hands folded beneath his head as he looked at the endless and indiscriminate scattering of stars. Gunshots sounded. First, one solitary muzzle blast then, only seconds later, a second one.

Men sprang from their blanket rolls fumbling for weapons. Someone yelled at Cartwell and got back a string of hair-raising profanity. "Who the hell's out there? Who's not in their bedroll?"

A nasal voice called back. "Paul ain't here, Mister Cartwell."

Butler watched men converge on an empty bedroll and look elsewhere when they were convinced the murderous Texan was not there. The man's absence was not unusual; men who rode horses most of their lives and drank black coffee just naturally peed a lot.

Except for the gunfire.

Cartwell strode among his captives looking for a second empty bedroll. There was none. He stood looking down at Butler for a long time before speaking. "Who is he?" Cartwell snarled. "Did someone come out here with you we didn't see?"

Butler shook his head.

Cartwell lingered with a murderous look and might have said more, but one of the aroused *bandoleros* came up, plucked the big bearded man's sleeve, and took him away.

The thoroughly capable-looking two-gun Mexican said something to Cartwell none of the captives could hear, but the bearded man's reaction was very clear even from a distance. He turned and bawled for everyone except the dog robber to take Winchesters and go find the Texan.

Not everyone was enthusiastic, particularly among the *bandoleros*, who were rarely confident in darkness.

Rivas sidled over beside Marshal Butler and leaned to hoarsely whisper, "It's him." The scout hunkered to say more but the nighthawk walked up and swung his Winchester. Rivas ducked, took a glancing blow, and returned to his bedroll waiting for the Texan to follow. But he didn't; he stepped close to the marshal, who was rising to stamp into his boots, and pushed the muzzle into the lawman's side.

"Tell you something, Marshal. I ain't the only one been on guard. Any more funny business from your possemen and we're goin' to start shooting."

A man's shout in the middle distance was taken up by another man. The guard stepped back and raised his head. Jacob Cartwell's unmistakable bull bass called back. A number of men, both range riders and *bandoleros*, were converging on the spot where the outcries had originated.

The captives ganged together like sheep, with Hunter Calkins growling and grumbling under the cold eyes of two *bandoleros* who seemed to Marshal Butler to be on the verge of shooting.

He went over to the stockman. "Leave it be," he said. "Those *pronunciados* are nervous enough."

Calkins glared at Butler. He evidently was still incensed that the posse he'd thought would liberate him had instead ridden into an ambush and been captured.

Men were returning from the northward night. There was now no talk among them, but their footfalls sounded loud.

Rivas eased up beside Butler to speak again. But as before, there was an interruption. The men in Cartwell's wake were edging toward the nearly dead fire carrying something.

The scout was beside himself, which Butler did not notice. If others did, they paid no attention. The men at the coals were lowering something to the ground. One of the *bandoleros* knelt to stir twigs in among the coals. Smoke rose, a fairly respectable fragrant cloud of it, but until the Mexican leaned and blew, there were no flames. When they came, though, they burst out all at once as though the fire had been doused with coal oil.

Until increasing heat drove the onlookers back a little, Frank Butler was unable to see the object Cartwell was staring at. Calkins saw it and softly said, "Good riddance. There wasn't no call for him to hit that young Messican like he did. No call at all."

Marshal Butler stared ahead. For a moment one of the guards barred his way with a carbine held across his body in both hands. Then the man relented, shrugged, and stepped aside.

Calkins had been correct. It was the Texan named Paul. Firelight swayed across his limp body and face. He had the expressionless, totally composed features of the dead. The look people said was "peaceful" and that wasn't peaceful at all. It was simply the mask of death. No peace, no anger, no resignation. Just death.

Butler was staring at the fatal wound when Jacob Cartwell rose to his full massive height and snarled. "Find him! Saddle up and don't come back until you got him!"

A number of men walked out into the gloom and came together with the hawk-faced, two-gun Mexican. What he told them must have favored Cartwell's command, because they did finally go after horses.

Cartwell put a fierce look on Frank Butler. "There's somebody out there. You knew the son of a bitch was out there. You knew he'd sneak in here tonight."

Butler shook his head. "Whoever did that sure as hell didn't come out here with me."

Cartwell's gaze dropped to the corpse. "In the dark, for Chrissake, *right between the eyes!*"

There was a brief flurry of activity and noise as men got astride and headed northward, fanning out as they went. The two-gun Mexican was in the lead.

Cartwell abruptly walked away.

Two of his riders were gazing steadily at Marshal Butler. One of them was a thin man with a whiny Texas drawl. He said, "Well, now, this spoils things, don't it? There's someone out there, ain't there, Marshal? Them Messicans ain't real brave in the dark. Me, I was figurin' we'd see the last of the Messicans about sunup when they rode south behind the remuda, an' the rest of us'd ride out of this damned country. It was supposed to be done clean and quick. We'd fetch over the horses, they'd meet us an' take 'em south. One day, at the most. Maybe like Jacob said, half a day. An' then we come onto that old stockman an' you. Nothing's gone right since. . . . Fred, ain't that right?"

The other man inclined his head without saying a word. He was staring at the dead Texan, made more visible now as the fire steadily brightened. All he said was, "Jake, lend a hand pullin' him back a ways. He'll cook beside the fire."

Butler turned away. Cartwell hunkered among his riders with a bottle. Whatever they got out of their bottle did not appear to have a solacing effect on them.

Rivas waited until Marshal Butler was close

enough to hear a hoarse whisper before saying, "Through the forehead, in the center?"

Butler stopped. Rivas waited, but not very patiently. When Frank nodded his head, the scout returned to his bedroll to pass the word. The possemen listened, but their eyes were fixed on the area away from the hot fire where their captors were converging.

There were not as many as there had been before the two-gun *pronunciado* had taken men out to ride down the killer of the Texan. In fact, they were outnumbered by their captives, but with a distance of about a hundred and fifty feet between them, and with all the guns in the hands of their captors, no one with the sense God gave a goose would attempt anything.

The riders returned, dismounted, and cared for their animals as the unsmiling Mexican with a gun on each leg approached Jacob Cartwell and his riders. As the Mexican hitched at his belt, he said, "I think he came from this camp."

Cartwell stared for a moment, then made a scoffing sound. "Not on your life," he retorted. "Ask the guards. No one walked out yonder except Paul."

The *bandolero*'s dark eyes remained on the larger man. "What would you expect the guards to tell you?" he stated in a thin, faintly hostile tone of voice.

Cartwell paused a moment, then turned to his men. "Bury him. Come daylight we'll find that son of a bitch. Unless he's got wings, he left tracks." Cartwell turned abruptly and walked away, leaving the hawk-faced *bandolero* looking after him.

One of the rangemen softly said, "Hell's bells. Dig a grave in the dark? Why not just pile rocks atop him. There's plenty of them around."

No one took that up even after the tall Mexican walked back in the direction of the *bandolero* camp. The old man with the bay horse sniffed. "You fellers think you'll find that gunman's tracks? Let me tell you somethin' about trackin' folks. By daylight that man'll be fifteen miles away an' you'll be ridin' over his sign, which will be where he *was*, not where he *is*."

The rangemen ignored the old man and went after digging tools.

Marshal Butler went over where the coffeepot was atop two flat stones and got himself a cupful. Bart Matthews joined him, got a cupful, and stood like a forlorn stork gazing at the corpse as he said, "You like to know what Charley Rivas told me?"

Butler tried the coffee; it was too hot, so he lowered the cup. He could guess what Rivas had told the harness maker, but he asked anyway.

Bart looked into his tin cup as he replied. "El Cajónero," he said without looking up, acting as though it embarrassed him to mention The Undertaker.

When Butler did not scoff, Matthews finally raised his head. "He tell you that too?"

He hadn't, but the marshal knew it was on Rivas's mind. Butler's response was quietly given. "First off, how would El Cajónero know we were out here? Secondly, you got to believe there is such a person, and Bart, that's an old legend. El Cajónero was settling scores over a hundred years ago, according to the legend. Did you ever know anyone who lived over a hundred years? I never did."

Matthews pointed. "Right between the eyes," he said, lowering his arm but continuing to gaze at the dead man. "Every story I've heard about El Cajónero, that's his mark. No matter where else he shoots 'em, there's always one smack dab between the eyes. Accordin' to folks in Mex-town, that's his mark."

Butler tried the coffee again. This time it could be swallowed, but it lacked a lot in terms of being worth drinking. "Since the El Cajónero legend's been around," he told Matthews, "there've been lots of men shot between the eyes. Even in the dark a man wouldn't have to be a good shot to do that at close range."

Matthews said no more on the subject of El Cajónero. He moved to another topic. "After those *bandoleros* head for home at sunrise, we could maybe make it back to the Calkins place for rest an' water before it gets too hot. Then lie up until evenin' and head for town. Maybe make it by morning."

Butler flung the coffee into the fire, where it made a furious hissing sound. Then he leaned to place the cup atop a nearby rock and straightened up before speaking again. He did not tell the harness maker that he had a bad feeling about the end of this trouble; just nodded a little absently and returned to the area under guard to await sunrise.

For a long time, the men digging a grave made the only sounds. They did not finish their chore until there was a gray smear along the horizon.

CHAPTER EIGHT

A STRANGE NIGHT

When Frank Butler was kicking out of his boots, Jacob Cartwell strolled over smelling of whiskey. He stood glaring down at Marshal Butler for a moment before speaking. "That *bandolero* thinks it was someone from camp who snuck out and shot Paul."

Butler answered without looking up. "Maybe it was. Their camp is separate from this one."

Cartwell seemed to be turning that over in his mind before he hunkered down to speak again. "That idea crossed my mind."

Butler glanced around. "They're not real friendly."

Cartwell agreed. "Haven't been since they come up here, but that never bothered me until now."

"They outnumber you," Butler said, wondering whether driving a wedge between Cartwell and the *bandoleros* might be a good idea. The *bandoleros* had shown leashed hostility to the captured possemen too.

If there was a fight the captives would not be in a good position no matter who won, and would very likely be in a worse position if the *bandoleros* won.

Cartwell faced Marshal Butler. "Bein' outnumbered . . . I got a proposition for you, Marshal."

Butler finished with the boots, set them beside his bedroll, and waited.

Cartwell got slightly more comfortable before continuing the conversation. He offered Butler another of his little crooked stogies. Every time he'd done that he'd had a scheme in mind. Butler declined as he'd done before, and waited for the big bearded man to light up and begin speaking.

"Well now, Marshal, there's more *pronunciados* than I got riders."

Butler waited until ash had been tipped off the little cigar. He had already said that.

"But between my crew an' your possemen, we'd outnumber 'em enough to make 'em have a little respect, wouldn't you say?"

Butler glanced around where men were digging a grave and other men were restlessly moving. The flames were beginning to diminish a little. The marshal looked longest at the bedroll with its blankets pulled up over the head of Jésus Obando's dead swamper.

Jacob Cartwell scowled darkly. "You lost your tongue?" he growled.

"No . . . Mister Cartwell, this isn't our fight. You —"

"You damned idiot," the big man snarled. "You think that colonel or whatever he is wouldn't take the horses, and the box of trinkets he traded me for 'em, an' leave your bones along with mine out here for the buzzards?"

Butler spoke as though there had been no interruption. "You got yourself into this mess."

Cartwell leaned a little as though to emphasize his next words. "That two-gun Mex don't like you."

"Seems to me, Mister Cartwell, he don't like any of us."

The big man leaned back slightly and looked down his nose at Marshal Butler. "That's my point. An' they outnumber us. An' I know for a fact there's not a man among them who wouldn't open fire if that leader of theirs told them to. Let me tell you somethin' I learned about Messican revolutionaries. . . ."

"I've been down here a while too, Mister Cartwell."

"Then you know the whole bunch of us is settin' on the edge of a very sharp knife. I'm offerin' you the only chance you got — if trouble comes."

Butler looked steadily at the big man. "It's already here."

". . . You mean Paul?"

"Yes. And now we're back where we started fifteen minutes ago." Butler moved to pull back his blankets. "I'll tell you something else. You said everyone would fan out and run down whoever shot your Texan." Butler shook his head. "Did you see the look on that tall Mexican's face when you said that? He was thinking, Like hell we will; come sunrise we'll round up the horses and get the hell as far south of here as we can."

Butler leaned to lower himself into his bedroll. The bearded man sat like a big Pima squaw, saying nothing until the marshal was bedded down. Then he shoved up to his feet and shook his head. "You don't have it right yet, do you? If there's trouble, you an' your friends are goin' to be like roosting birds. I'm offerin' you a chance to at least make a fight of it."

"In exchange for what, Mister Cartwell?"

"Why, for gettin' turned loose. Give you your horses and let you go."

"And our guns, too?"

The big man hung fire for two seconds, then offered a conspiratorial smile as he replied.

"Your guns, too." He stood waiting for the lawman's reply.

Butler gazed upward. "What about the bullion box, and Hunter Calkins with his two remaining riders?"

"Calkins and his riders can go with you. The bullion belongs to me. That's what the *pronunciados* paid me for my horses."

Butler slid his gaze past the big man's shoulder in the direction of the eastern sky. He couldn't be sure, but he thought there was a thin streak of gray over there. "Mister Cartwell, it's damned if we do an' damned if we don't. Either way, our chances of riding away from here like we rode in are about as good as the chances of a snowball in hell."

"You ain't got no choice," the big man stated, showing no trace of his earlier smile. "With me you got a chance; with the insurgents from Messico you don't have. Marshal, it's on your head. You're goin' to get a lot of folks killed if you're not careful."

The abrupt, startled call of a sentry interrupted them. "It's a rider," the man said. "Coming from the east."

Jacob Cartwell hastened to his bedroll for a Winchester and roused the men nearest him. Out at the *bandolero* camp there were sounds of activity, but visibility did not reach that far.

Not far from Butler the stolid town blacksmith roused up and raised his head to look around. He listened for a moment, then began to struggle out of his blankets, cursing as he did. "What is it this time?" he called. "Why'n't you damned fools just let a man sleep. Plenty of time tomorrow to . . . Frank?"

"What."

"What is it?"

Butler did not reply. As he irritably climbed back out of his bedroll and reached for his boots, a man using Spanish cried out again, this time from farther to the west.

"It's the killer!"

Someone with a drawl yelled back. "Shoot the son of a bitch!"

But there was no gunfire, not even after Cartwell led his rangemen in search of the pair of agitated Mexican sentries. Both sentries pointed in a different direction and swore they'd heard the killer out there, walking his horse, making a very distinct sound.

As other armed men appeared, someone asked what the killer had looked like. Neither of the sentries could say. One man explained that he had been too distant. The other man mumbled something that sounded like agreement.

Men roused from sleep began to grumble. The two-gun *bandolero* arrived, expressionless and silent. While the others spoke and argued and gestured, the hawk-faced man walked alone out into the night well beyond the camp.

Then the annoyed rangemen and the *bandoleros* began to heap scorn on the sentries for rousing everyone over what was probably an animal in the underbrush among the big rocks. The men went trooping back toward their blankets, muttering and cursing.

Jacob Cartwell was about to take his men back, too, when the two-gun Mexican appeared, walked up close, and blew out a ragged breath. In Spanish he said, "There was someone out there. On a shod horse. I could feel his tracks once I found the first ones. Very fresh; the earth was still crumbling." The man waved one arm. "He rode from east to west. Maybe half a mile out." The man lowered his arm. "At a walk. It wouldn't be the one who shot your man, Señor Cartwell. By now that one is ten miles away." The Mexican looked steadily at the big bearded man. "What is it? Are you trying to do something, maybe?"

Cartwell replied in English. "What the hell kind of talk is that? Not a soul left our camp. Go count the horses."

The Mexican stood gazing at the big man for a while, then walked off in the direction of the *bandolero* camp.

Cartwell glared at the Mexican sentries before also turning back. Frank had heard most of the distant conversation; the voices of the upset men were loud in the deathly still early hours.

Nearby, a voice hissed at him. "Marshal, I told you!"

Butler sighed, sank down with his back to the speaker, and watched Cartwell and his riders return to their dying fire for coffee or something stronger. It was getting chilly.

There were nighthawks out, but the excitement at the camps had evidently not disturbed the horses, because there was no sound from their grazing area.

The anxious sentries were replaced, but while that alleviated the fright of some Mexicans who had been guarding the camp, it kept other men in both camps wide awake, particularly the *bandoleros*. Several of them squatted by a tiny fire talking and waving their arms, visible in Cartwell's camp as animated silhouettes.

Charley Rivas spoke in Spanish to one of the *bandolero* guards who came over to get hot coffee. The man ignored everything until he was squatting with a cup in his cold fingers, then turned toward the lumpy bedrolls and answered in Spanish.

"I can tell you, friend, I saw the man. Not close, but distant and moving. He was riding a big black horse."

"What did you see of the rider, friend?"

The Mexican tasted the coffee before replying. "He was large, compadre. A big man. In the dark he seemed to be dressed in black, but the distance . . . and the darkness." The man sipped more coffee.

Rivas had a question: "You said you didn't see anyone?"

The Mexican shrugged. "I didn't think Colonel Esparza wanted anyone to be seen."

"You're afraid of him, friend?"

This time when the *bandolero* heard the sound of the scout's voice, his teeth shone. "Let me tell you, horseman, he is a man to be feared." The *bandolero* finished the coffee and rose holding his Winchester.

As he was turning away, Rivas said, "Listen to me, companion. Did you ever hear of The Undertaker?"

The Mexican stopped and half turned. "The Undertaker?"

"El Cajónero. In our town, he is a legend. For over a hundred years. All anyone sees is a large man on a black horse. *Fantasma,* friend. He rides slowly past. In town he throws gold coins into the houses of people who have been hurt. My father knew of him, and he said his father also knew of him."

The *bandolero* stood looking in the direction

of the bedrolls. The only sound over there came from the speaker. He said, "What are you talking about?" The question hung in the air. "You think you can scare me?"

"No. I just told you; the man you think you saw fits the description of El Cajónero, the way people have seen him for a hundred years."

Another voice joined in. The harness maker said, "Hey, vaquero, he told you the truth. What you saw out there was El Cajónero, sure as hell."

The Mexican hoisted his carbine and walked northward, back out where he was supposed to have been all this time.

Bart Matthews told Rivas, "Charley, that one's goin' to be wide awake until daylight." Matthews softly chortled, but the scout was not amused.

"How," Rivas asked softly, "could El Cajónero be out here? How could he know that Texan killed the swamper — unless he is a ghost?"

Matthews got back down inside his bedroll and said no more.

Coyotes, possibly drawn by the smell of food but just as possibly making their nocturnal sortie, barked and sang east of the gringo camp. No one paid much attention until one of Hunter Calkins's riders, a flat-faced man with small black eyes and lank black hair, poked his head up and said, "Acoma."

Over in the *bandolero* camp no one heard him, but in the rangemen's camp heads came up off the ground as men turned in the direction of the moving, yapping sounds.

Marshal Butler was not convinced. He would concede that Indians could imitate animals, sometimes sounding more believable than the animals themselves. But coyotes ranged and foraged at night. Indians didn't. Not as a rule anyway, and not without a very good reason.

The stolid blacksmith groaned, then swore a blue streak. He probably wasn't the only man trying to sleep, but he seemed at the moment to be the only one who fervently cursed this night for its constant interruptions.

The sound of barking kept moving, which was another thing that made Marshal Butler believe the scavengers were indeed four-legged. When coyotes hunted food at night, they did so by scent. They made wide sashays over a countryside. Their yapping helped the bands to keep track of one another.

Calkins's flat-faced rider said no more. No one else did either, after the blacksmith pulled a blanket up around his ears and tried one last time to sleep.

Butler remained awake. Even if there had

been Indians out there, it would make no difference. They had learned over generations not to become involved in other people's problems.

Eventually he thought he detected activity over in the *pronunciado* camp. He remained perfectly still listening until he was sure of it.

The *bandoleros* were stirring.

Among the bedrolls around him, other men also showed signs of awakening. It was cold, as cold as it would get until the next morning at this predawn time. Jacob Cartwell's cockeyed dog robber was hunkering at the stone ring to make a fire.

Butler waited. It was warm inside the bedroll, and there was no need for him to roll out yet anyway. If the riders from Mexico were preparing to leave with the horses, as far as he was concerned they could do so. Their departure would eliminate one source of trouble.

The cockeyed man had his fire burning and was leaning to fan it with a misshapen old hat when someone called from the middle distance in Spanish. Butler could only make out something about horses. Whoever the speaker was, he was agitated.

Moments later other excited voices erupted, also speaking Spanish. The cockeyed man at

116

the fire stopped fanning and looked around, one eye probing the dim distance, the other making an indifferent, rolling sweep. The Mexican got to his feet, hesitated briefly, then scuttled over near Jacob Cartwell, who was coming out of a deep slumber. Butler could not make out what the swamper was saying, but Cartwell must have been motivated by it; he came up out of his blankets growling and reaching for his boots first, then his shellbelt.

Others stirred, including Butler. Over at the *bandolero* camp there were howls and curses. In Cartwell's camp men stamped into their boots looking into the dying night, where the *bandoleros* were calling back and forth beyond their cooking fire.

The old man who rode the fat bay horse shuffled over to Butler and squinted as he said, "Now what? Somebody wake up with a Gila monster in his blankets?"

It had to be more than that, but Butler ignored the old man. The shouting *bandoleros* seemed to be south of their fire. When they called, it sounded as though they were distant from one another.

Jacob Cartwell strode up scowling, coarse hair jutting from beneath his hat. "Their saddle horses are gone," he told Marshal Butler. "Damn!" Cartwell narrowed his gaze but said no more.

Everyone stirred, mostly only as far as the cooking fire, where they stood with their backs to the heat looking over where the *bandolero* fire glowed.

The scout was warming his backside when the town blacksmith said, "Now, what the hell?"

Rivas replied matter-of-factly, "Their using horses are gone," and got a wide-eyed look from the men around him. Someone asked how he knew this, and the scout answered irritably. "Didn't you hear 'em hollerin' in Spanish?"

No one answered.

Jacob Cartwell gave his shaggy head a bearlike wag of annoyance and left Marshal Butler to go to the fire. His swamper was on the far side with smoke in his face; everyone else seemed to be standing over where there was no smoke. He filled a tin cup and handed it to the big bearded man, swung his hat at the smoke, which was making his eyes water, and finally retreated until the fire was burning hot enough for there to be no smoke.

Bart Matthews came up to stand with Marshal Butler. They were silent as they listened and looked. They were joined by Charley Rivas, who said, "I told you, Marshal."

Everyone looked at Rivas, who flung up his arms and rolled his eyes before speaking again. "El Cajónero."

Chapter Nine

A DAY TO REMEMBER

The Mexican colonel arrived at Cartwell's camp with several sets of rawhide hobbles in his hands. Without a word, he held them up to be examined. None of the hobbles had been cut or torn; all had the rawhide buttons free of their little loops.

Colonel Esparza's gaze, even in poor light, was hostile. "Tell me again all your men were here," he challenged.

Cartwell, a man unlikely to be intimidated even by someone wearing two belt-guns, looked the officer in the eye and made a gesture. "Go see for yourself. Feel inside the blankets. Go count our horses. Look for one with sweat."

Esparza looked at the other men, then turned slightly to glance over where the captives and their guards were standing. He asked two of the guards in Spanish if anyone had left. Both men shook their heads.

Bart Matthews spoke. "You ever hear of El Cajónero?"

The tall, hawk-faced *bandolero* stared at the harness maker. For a moment he seemed unwilling to answer, then he said, "What are you talking about?"

"The Undertaker. Everyone in Peralta knows of him."

As before, Esparza regarded the speaker as though he would not reply before making a statement dripping with scorn. "The Undertaker," he said in English. "Who is he?"

"He's a legendary horseman who goes around settlin' scores."

This time the tall man showed clear derision when he replied. "The gringo's Robin Hood?"

"No. Folks don't set a lot of store in him in Gringo-town, but they sure do in Mextown."

The tall man turned his attention back to Jacob Cartwell. "Do you believe in this ghost?" he asked.

Cartwell said he'd never heard of him and didn't believe those old Mex ghost tales anyway.

The *bandolero* relaxed a little. In the background his men could be heard calling back and forth in the distance. He held up the hobbles again as he said, "A ghost didn't turn

120

our saddle horses loose last night. How could a ghost unbutton them?"

No one answered. The dog robber came fawningly around with a cup of coffee for the Mexican colonel, who accepted it without looking at the man who had brought it. He held the cup down as he addressed Jacob Cartwell.

"Now we have to wait until daylight, catch horses from the ones you brought. That means we won't be able to leave until the middle of the day."

Cartwell nodded. "Couldn't be helped," he told Esparza, whose reply was curt.

"Maybe not. For your sake, I hope not."

The Colonel walked away as the dog robber asked Cartwell in a whining voice what the Mexican had meant. Cartwell brushed the obvious threat aside with a growling comment. "We're supposed to shake in our boots. Get breakfast started."

Dawn arrived, and visibility improved. In the distance, *bandoleros* were trying to talk their way up to the loose stock. To the amusement of the men watching from around the stone ring at Cartwell's camp, including the captives, this did not seem to be going very well.

It was inevitable that of the three hundred horses, there would be at least one caught.

That horse would be ridden by the *bandoleros'* best roper who would run down and catch more horses until all the *bandoleros* were mounted.

It happened about like that, but the border jumpers were not finished until the sun was climbing and the chill was diminishing.

Cartwell had his riders roll their blankets and bring in their using horses. His clear intention was to leave. Neither Butler nor any of the other captives was unhappy about this until Cartwell smiled across the breakfast fire at Butler and said, "We'll drive your animals along for a mile or two. You can walk after them." Cartwell swilled his tin cup empty before adding, "Them *bandoleros* most likely won't have any more trouble, but just in case, we'll leave you boys behind for them to waste time on."

Butler looked steadily back at the larger and older man. "Our guns . . . ?"

Cartwell shook his head. "Now you know better'n that, Marshal. We aren't goin' to ride off an' leave you behind us with guns."

Two men went after the horses and pack mules. Jacob Cartwell lingered at the fire. Something was on his mind.

Hunter Calkins took his remaining riders over to their bedrolls, where they sat down and palavered. Old Calkins was shrewd and wily; he'd lived with all, or at least nearly all, of the treacheries that existed on the South Desert.

Butler watched Hunter and his men sit down to talk, and had a moment of misgiving. Anything Calkins did that would fire up either the *bandoleros* or Jacob Cartwell could get them all killed.

Cartwell spoke, bringing Marshal Butler's attention back. "This here undertaker," he said. "What that Mex said is true. Ghosts don't go around unbuttoning hobbles. They ain't got fingers for that kind of work. . . . Marshal, that's a living, breathing man out there, ain't it?"

Butler was slow answering. "You heard Bart here. All I got to say is that I never heard of a living, breathing man who was over a hundred years old ridin' around with a gun."

Cartwell's thick brow creased. He looked at the harness maker. "You ever see this undertaker?"

Bart said, "Never have, but I've seen some of the gold money he tosses into the houses of folks. Nothin' ghostly about it. It's real money."

Cartwell finally said what was bothering him. "Is he still out there? I don't like the idea of him bein' behind us when we leave. Ghost or no ghost, he's got a gun."

Charley Rivas had something to add to what Matthews had said. "I'll tell you something. El Cajónero don't bother folks who haven't made trouble for the folks of Mex-town over in Peralta. Well . . . once in a long while he does, but mostly the stories of him over the generations are about settling scores with the enemies of the folks in Mex-town."

Butler suddenly recalled something. He called over to Hunter Calkins. "You remember where that Mexican *arriero* was shot, Hunter, the man who blackened the eye of Jésus Obando's sister?"

Calkins did not hesitate. "Right between the eyes. You saw that."

Cartwell's eyes widened as he looked from the distant stockman to Marshal Butler. "Like Paul?"

Butler shrugged, but Bart Matthews said, "Exactly. The legend says that's El Cajónero's mark. He's used it for about a hunnert and fifty years."

One of Cartwell's rangemen was rolling a smoke. When his fingers stopped moving, he raised his head to stare at the harness maker, then looked down to finish with the cigarette and pop it between his lips without lighting it. He said, "Boss, that ain't no ghost, it's someone who shoots pretty good in the dark."

Jacob Cartwell sat a long time gazing across

the fire ring in silence. Beyond him, over at the camp of the *pronunciados,* they were bringing in the horses they'd caught to be rigged out. A wisp of faint smoke rose above their dying breakfast fire. Eventually Cartwell blew out a ragged sigh and shoved up to his feet as he said, "You're dead right," to his smoking rider. "That son of a bitch's flesh and blood. I think I'll go see if I can talk the colonel into ridin' out with us and tracking down this ghost that sneaks around at night shootin' people."

He left them sitting around the coals with fresh morning warmth beginning to soften the marrow in their bones. Rivas rolled his eyes but said nothing until a taciturn, graying Mextown posseman made a short statement. "If those *bandoleros* got any sense they'll turn Cartwell down, get astride, get behind their loose stock, and not even look back for ten miles."

Charley Rivas smiled. "It won't matter if they all go looking. They'll never find El Cajónero." He spread his hands, palms down. "No one ever has, have they, and they've been trying since my grandfather was a boy."

Soon Jacob Cartwell returned to tell them Colonel Esparza had refused. He was leaving as soon as he could strike camp. If the gringos wanted to go manhunting for a ghost, he wished them well, but his intention was to be as many miles south of Peralta in the direction of either Angostura or Rincón as he could get before sundown.

Bart had a question. "Did they find the horses that got loose last night?"

They had, all but one.

An hour later, with the sun high and still climbing, the *bandoleros* completed their gather, lined the loose stock out southward, and left amid shouts and clouds of dust.

Cartwell's riders, as well as the unarmed possemen, watched them go. Now the tense situation between the two groups was even more pronounced. Jacob Cartwell detailed two rangemen to stand guard, then ordered the captives to go to their bedrolls and stay there.

Butler expected Cartwell to strike camp later in the day, but Cartwell did not. He seemed uncertain for the first time since Butler had met him.

One of the riders rode out on a scout and returned with a small pronghorn, which the cockeyed man fell upon with a skinning knife while Cartwell and the scout squatted nearby to talk. The scout had found shod-horse tracks from east to west, as had the Mexican colonel. He had also found something else. He leaned to use a finger to draw two letters in the dust: HB.

Some time later, Jacob Cartwell hunkered

down facing Marshal Butler. He jerked a thumb over his shoulder. "That big grumpy feller, what does he do for a living?"

"He's town blacksmith in Peralta."

Cartwell lowered his arm. "I thought so. Something I heard a few days back. What's his name?"

"Hans Bechtold."

Cartwell's bearded features creased into a triumphant and malevolent smile. "Call him over here."

Butler was mystified, but he obeyed. When the unsmiling big man came over, Cartwell told him to sit down. He obeyed and gazed without a shred of amiability at the other large man.

Cartwell said, "You're Hans Bechtold?"

The blacksmith nodded his head in silence.

"You're Peralta's blacksmith?"

The blacksmith nodded again without speaking.

Cartwell seemed to be enjoying himself. "Pretty common for blacksmiths to stamp their initials on shoes, ain't it?"

This time the town blacksmith did not nod. "What about it?"

"Well, blacksmith, that ghost rider was riding a horse whose shoes had your stamp on them." Cartwell's eyes crinkled. "Pretty hard shoein' a ghost horse, ain't it?"

The blacksmith snorted. "No such thing as a ghost horse."

Cartwell slowly inclined his head without taking his narrowed gaze off the blacksmith. "These here shoes wasn't real old. Your initials stood out even when the shoes was used over dusty ground . . . HB. Name the last half dozen or so folks you shod horses for."

The blacksmith looked at Frank Butler as if for help, but Butler had been caught as off guard as Hans Bechtold.

"Blacksmith!" snapped Jacob Cartwell with his right hand atop the saw handle of his holstered Colt.

"Well, I got to think back. I shoe a lot of horses, mister, along with warping tires onto buggies and repairing stage-coaches and —"

"Gawddammit, *name them!*"

The other large man gazed at the ground for a moment. "Well, there was Jess Hobart's buggy mare."

"Who is Jess Hobart?"

"Feller who owns the saloon in Peralta."

"I'm not interested in driving horses. Who else?"

"Pete Evinrude. He's the liveryman an' trader. I shod three horses for him a week or so back. He rents horses out, mostly saddle animals I think, but some teams too."

Cartwell's face changed slightly. "You know

who he let have any horses lately?"

The blacksmith gazed stolidly at the bearded man and shook his head. "They come an' go. I got my own work to worry about. Don't recollect right offhand seein' anyone ride out the last week or so. Me an' my helper been busy putting new running gear under one of the stages that busted hell out of things when it straddled a big boulder."

"Who else? Think. Think hard, blacksmith. Who else?"

"The feller who runs a mule train down in Mex-town."

"Dammit, horses, not mules."

"It was a horse. Big seal-brown."

"Who else?"

"Some fancy-lookin' feller passin' through. Nice big black thoroughbred horse."

Cartwell's countenance underwent a swift change. "Big black horse?"

"Well, tall, not very heavy. But tall an' black."

"What was the feller's name?"

"I told you, he was passin' through. I never asked his name, an' if he told me I forgot it. When strangers come along I do the job, take their money, an' move on to other things."

For a moment Butler thought Cartwell was going to swear, then he checked himself and said, "What did the feller look like?"

"Small, bones like a woman, small and sort of delicate-looking. Maybe twenty-five. No more'n thirty. Wore real thick glasses. Thick as the bottom of a whiskey bottle."

Cartwell stared at the blacksmith for a long while, then rose, dusted off, and said, "Keep thinkin' back. I'm lookin' for a big black horse. You shod him not too long ago."

The blacksmith looked. "Got to be black?"

"Yes. He was black last night. The fellers who thought they saw a rider in the dark would have noticed if he'd been gray or maybe sorrel."

Cartwell shot Marshal Butler a long look, then walked away leaving the blacksmith gazing at the lawman. "What was that about? Hell, lots of smiths mark their shoes."

"He's trying to settle his mind about whoever rode out here and shot his ornery Texan."

"Well, hell, that don't have to be new shoes, Marshal. Lately I've been having trouble orderin' blank cold plates through Grover's store, so I been working down tines off hay rakes. They're real fine spring steel. They'll outwear any cold-rolled plates five to one."

Butler glanced over where Cartwell was talking to his riders. If the blacksmith had told Cartwell what he'd just said, it would have let the air out of the big bearded man's sails.

The blacksmith returned to his guarded area looking puzzled.

Cartwell had expected to be told the name of the owner of a tall black horse right up until Bechtold had said the horse was a narrow thoroughbred. Now, as he was talking with his riders, the man he'd sent out earlier to bring in the saddle and pack stock rode in bareback, driving the other animals in front. Cartwell's other men went to catch and tie the animals.

The day was getting warm. In another hour or two it would be hot, and today there was no sign of one of the high veil-like overcasts that kept the heat down.

Butler went to the sump to wash. While he was there one of his possemen came along, sat on a rock, and said, "Marshal, I got a gun."

Butler froze for two seconds, then slowly turned with water dripping from his chin. "Where'd you get a gun?" he asked.

"It belonged to that feller they buried, that cranky Texan." The old man showed nearly toothless gums in a wide smile. "It was on his shellbelt when they was fixin' to roll him into the hole. One feller was workin' the buckle loose an' the other feller was down in the hole waitin' to settle the feller out flat. The gun fell out of the holster. I was standin' nearby, an' the feller out of the grave called

131

me over to lend a hand at lowerin' that son of a bitch. He clum down an' told me to roll the feller so's they'd catch him. I did, and while they was layin' him in the hole I stuck the gun inside my shirt an' offered to help 'em fill the hole. I scuffed dirt in where I'd picked up the gun, but I don't think they missed it. Maybe they figured it fell in the hole."

As he finished speaking, the old man reached inside his shirt. Butler stopped him. They were in plain sight of the camp. "Leave it be," he exclaimed. "Go back over to my bedroll and be damned careful nobody sees you shove it inside my blankets. Real careful; the mood they're in right now, they'd kill you sure as hell."

The old man departed looking pleased with himself. Butler sat down on a rock to towel off with his shirttail — and wait for his heart to resume its normal cadence.

One gun wasn't enough, but with a little luck it could be. At least it was better than no gun.

Cartwell and his riders were occupied rigging out the livestock. They spoke among themselves, but not very much.

The last thing they did captured the attention of their captives. Three men dug in the ground beneath the area where Jacob Cartwell's bedroll had been. Because the ground was soft in that spot, it required only a few minutes to exhume what was clearly a bullion box. It was the kind stage companies used, with metal corners and both a heavy hasp and curved bolt where the lock would go.

Bart Matthews breathed a soft curse as the rangemen carried the box to the right side of a big mule and boosted it to the *alfoja*. It was a snug fit, and they had to put more weight on the opposite side to balance the load.

Cartwell saw them watching, and threw a grin over his shoulder. "We'll leave your horses at the old ranch down yonder."

He was in a good mood, and in Frank Butler's opinion he could afford to be. Hunter Calkins, standing nearby, softly said, "There's a damned fortune in that box. Worth more money'n any of us is likely to see if he live two hunnert years."

One rangeman went after the posse horses. He did not bring them all the way back to the camp but only bunched them for driving. Down where he left them, the horses milled a little but made no effort to scatter. They would still be down there when the Cartwell crew got astride and rode toward them.

Cartwell's men had more trouble with the posse's guns than they'd had with the bullion box. One man complained, and Cartwell placated him by saying they'd carry the weapons only until he was sure the men on foot wouldn't find them for a couple of hours. Then he turned toward Marshal Butler with his smile showing again.

"Good luck," he said. "Wait until it cools down, or your tongue's goin' to be big as a flour sack before you get down there to water. . . . Marshal?"

"What."

"If you run across El Cajónero, give him our regards. I don't know what he thought he was doin' last night, but except that he cost me a good man, he's welcome to anything that's left. . . . I forgot; ghosts don't eat or drink, do they?"

The big man let out a booming laugh. It was the first time Butler had heard it, and although he did not know it, this would also be the last time.

Evidently Jacob Cartwell, despite his earlier anxiety about the night rider who had killed his range-riding Texan and his interrogation of the blacksmith, had decided to get away as quickly as he could.

As Butler watched them depart, he thought that in Cartwell's boots, he'd have done the same thing: take a chance on the mysterious night rider catching up in open country with no chance of getting close enough to use a gun in broad daylight.

CHAPTER TEN

SHANKS' MARE

With the immediate anxiety lessened, Butler's possemen grumbled. They had to bury Obando's swamper and were not happy about it, even though they knew they could not walk away and leave him lying there in his bedroll. But they didn't dig a grave as Cartwell's men had done; they arranged the body properly and began carrying big stones to build a typical desert pyramid of them to mark the last resting place of a human being.

When the old man said something about the gun he'd put in the marshal's bedroll, all work stopped. The blacksmith looked darkly at Butler as he said, "Why didn't you use it? Sneak up behind Cartwell and shove it in his back?"

Butler started to speak when a thin, unkempt posseman replied to the glowering blacksmith. "What's the matter with you? One gawddamned gun against all them other guns?"

Neither the blacksmith nor anyone else kept this discussion alive. They went back to piling rocks. When they finished and grouped around the fire ring of blackened rocks, Butler said, "Never mind anything but your canteens. We'll come back for the rest with a wagon."

A man spoke tartly. "Wait for nightfall, when it'll be cooler walking."

The marshal eyed them coldly. "And give Cartwell a six- or eight-hour head start?"

Another posseman argued. "The hell with Cartwell. Far as I know, all he done was trade horses to some Messicans."

Hunter Calkins turned on the speaker in a fury. "You son of a bitch — he had three of my riders killed. That don't count?"

The stockman's fighting stance brought quiet. Frank repeated what he'd told them earlier. "Canteens and let's go."

It was cool, and would remain that way for most of the morning. As Butler arose after stuffing the six-gun into the waistband of his trousers, several sharp flashes of sunlight off metal caught and held his attention. They had come from the direction Cartwell had taken, but a considerable distance away.

When Charley Rivas walked up, Butler jutted his jaw Indian-fashion. "Looked like Cartwell dumped our guns."

Rivas, who had seen no flashes, squinted eastward. "How far?"

Butler answered while still looking out there. "Hard to tell in the morning when the air's as clear as glass. Could be a couple of miles, could be maybe twice that far. You ready to go?"

Rivas nodded. He had the canteen from his saddle slung over one shoulder. Other possemen walked away from their belongings, and the hike began. Once they were clear of the boulder field, walking was easier. Unlike the *bandoleros* and Cartwell's rangemen, Butler's possemen were from town and were accustomed to walking.

They made fair time and talked very little as they continued the hike. For the first time since being ambushed they were able to speak their minds, and although, as Butler had expected, there were a few cutting remarks about being led into that damned ambush like greenhorns, most of what was said had to do with what had happened after the ambush.

Hunter Calkins sank to the ground when they paused to rest. "I was hoping," he muttered, "they'd stop for the night at my yard."

No one bothered to point out that Cartwell would be well past the Calkins place before nightfall, but one townsman had something else to say.

"You got horses out here somewhere, Mister Calkins?"

Everyone hung on the stockman's reply except his two remaining riders, who ignored the question. Their silence might have provided the answer if anyone had been looking in their direction.

Calkins grimaced. "We turned out yestiddy, left one horse for someone to use to fetch in fresh animals."

Charley Rivas said, "In the barn?" Calkins nodded and Rivas spat, saying "There wasn't no horse in the barn when we come through."

Calkins was not surprised. "They choused him off. Y'know, you got to hand it to Cartwell; he had this pretty well figured out."

Not everyone would have agreed.

They resumed the trek under steadily increasing warmth, with surefire heat to follow. They had covered most of the way to Calkins's yard when one of the Mex-town possemen farther back said, "Look! South along that lift in the land . . . look at that big rock at the bottom of the rise and follow out straight up it. . . . See him?"

They did not all see him at once, but eventually they all did: a solitary horseman facing northward. There was no shelter, or he'd probably have used it. He was in plain view but a long distance southward, not close enough for the posse to determine anything except that it was a man on a horse.

He disappeared back down the far side of the low lift of land.

For an hour more, until they were close enough to the Calkins yard to see trees and shade and buildings, they speculated about the horseman. The general opinion was that he had been one of the Indians who were abroad this time of year.

When they got into the yard, everyone scattered for water and shade. Several possemen with blisters removed their boots and trickled water over their feet.

Butler went to the main house with Hunter Calkins. The stockman's two riders went to their bunkhouse and did not emerge for a long while. They had food cupboarded in there, but nowhere nearly enough for all the possemen.

The harness maker and the blacksmith stood in pleasant barn shade, quietly talking with two other men. It was Matthews's opinion that they could overtake Cartwell if they walked all night and were quick about it. The only person receptive to this was one of the younger townsmen; but when the others scoffed, he eventually changed his opinion and Bart Matthews said no more.

Hunter bawled for them to come up and

be fed. Butler stood by the door until the last man had gone inside, then let the door swing closed and strolled alone out back, where there was a big old stone trough. He shed his hat and shirt, scooped water with his hat, and dumped it down over his head. He did that four times, then sat on the edge of the trough for the sun to dry him. He'd had an errant thought back yonder where they'd seen that "Indian" atop the land swell. The more he dwelled on it now, the more possible it seemed.

If that hadn't been an Indian . . . As far as he knew, the only other riders southward were the *bandoleros*. They were hastening to Mexico to deliver horses to other insurgents.

But maybe not all of them were.

Pronunciados were often professional brigands. At the least, they were lawless people whose purpose in taking up arms had nothing to do with politics or oppression. They were peasants, usually landless or starve-out gourd and maize growers in a land where lack of rain made people destitute in greater numbers than revolutions ever did.

Somewhere eastward, riding along with a bullion box full of treasure, was a small party of rugged but probably relaxed rangemen who had shrugged off most of their anxiety the farther they got from Vasquez Spring.

Butler felt almost drowsy from the effect of his dunking and drying, but one part of his brain plodded along with its thoughts.

The two-gun *bandolero* officer, Colonel Esparza, had left no doubt in anyone's mind that he had ice water for blood. Marshal Butler also thought he was extremely crafty. If he was as amoral as Frank suspected, he would not have forgotten the laden bullion box. It did not require as many men as he had with him to keep the horses trailing southward through open country. In fact, once the animals understood that was the direction they were to travel, it would require only a few men to keep them heading that way.

The old man who had hidden the gun came around the corner of the barn, stopped as though surprised to find anyone at the trough, then made a gummy smile as he came over to remove his sweat-stiff old hat and doused his head with water. But he did not remove his shirt. After shaking off the residue, he leaned on the trough, eyed the marshal briefly, eyed the gun lying nearby, and made one of his sly remarks. "Gun didn't do us no good after all, did it?"

Butler agreed, still gazing southward. "Nope. Not yet, anyway."

The old man dropped the subject. "Mister Calkins is goin' to send his riders out to see if they can catch some horses on foot. Sure would help if we could all get astraddle, wouldn't it?"

"What I'd like to know is where they dumped those guns," Butler told the old man, and gestured with a naked arm. "They got to be out there somewhere. Didn't seem to me it was this far, but distances fool a man in this kind of weather."

The old man straightened up off the trough, nodding and squinting northward, then easterly. "If it ain't too far," he said. "Tell you what, Marshal; while you fellers is restin' in the shade, I'm goin' to track Cartwell a ways. Not too far, mind; at my age, a man's legs ain't all they used to be."

Butler offered no objection and sat watching the old man walk away, disappear around the north side of the barn. He was shrugging into his shirt when Hunter Calkins's two Indian range riders appeared, looked impassively at Butler, and strode past with lasso ropes looped around their shoulders. They were youngish men, probably born and raised in this empty land, with the stamina and powers of observation that Indians usually had.

Some possemen began trooping back into the yard. Watered and fed, like horses they were now ready to settle in shade and let the process of digestion work uninterrupted.

Calkins came around to the trough, nodded at the marshal, and pulled a wood plug from a hollow sapling log that came out of the ground beside the trough. Water came. He saw Butler watching and pointed. "Dug-well out yonder a piece. When I first trailed into this country, there wasn't no water anywhere." He shifted position and nodded toward the raffish-looking old unkempt cottonwoods. "Any time you see trees like that, water's not far below. They won't grow anywhere else." He gazed at the lawman a moment before speaking again. "I don't like the idea of leavin' those lads of mine lyin' out yonder in the sunlight. They was good men."

Butler understood. "Bury them, Hunter. If your men bring in some horses, take a wagon and go back there and bury them."

Calkins nodded. "I don't like leavin' you. This fandango ain't over yet. Well . . . if they bring in some horses, maybe you fellers can ride the rest of the way. That'd be my contribution." Calkins continued to regard the larger and younger man, his expression pensive. "Remember we talked about runnin' livestock out here?"

Butler nodded.

"When I was settin' up there in them damned rocks, I had plenty of time to do a little figuring. After we trail north at the end of the season down here, I won't be back."

Butler's eyes widened.

"I'm too old for all these shenanigans. Not just *bandoleros,* for all of it. Workin' cattle at the marking ground, eatin' every meal out of the same fry pan, worryin' about losin' cattle to hungry In'ians. And the long drives down and back." Calkins screwed up his face. "You want it, Frank?"

"Want what?"

The old man waved his arm. "All of it. The land, the buildings, the consarned snakes and scorpions, the border jumpers, the South Desert in summertime." He let his arm fall to his side. "When I pull out this summer, I'm not coming back. Wild horses couldn't pull me back. If you want it, it's yours. Course, I got no deed to the land. Like everyone else who run cattle down here, I free-grazed. Land ain't worth two bits a section anyway. After I leave, all you got to do is ride out and move in."

Calkins hiked over to the barn and went in. He found loafing and sleeping possemen inside, in as much shade as they could find.

Marshal Butler was still standing like a stone when the old gummer returned sweating like a stud horse, red in the face and dry as a bone. He brushed past Butler, sank over the trough, and drank until fresh sweat burst out under

144

his shirt. Then he reared back to fling off water and said, "No more'n a mile northeast." He held up an old Colt from which all the blueing had disappeared years earlier. "My own gun," he croaked, and ducked to briefly guzzle more water. The second time he straightened up, his legs were near to trembling; but he'd have died on the spot before he'd have mentioned it.

"Shellbelts, carbines — mile or so northeast. They dumped 'em as they was passin' a big stand of thornpin."

The old man shuffled inside the barn, where it was ten degrees cooler, and found a horse stall with reasonably clean straw. He dropped his hat and sank down. Even a startled rat half as large as a house cat that sprang out of the straw nearby and scuttled wildly away did not disturb the old man. He was asleep almost before his eyes closed.

Marshal Butler went around front to announce the old man's discovery. The announcement aroused interest, but no one made any move to spring up and go find the abandoned weapons.

Not for an hour, anyway. Then most of the men left the yard with Hunter Calkins, who would be able to identify the thornpin thicket if anyone could. Two men who remained behind had swollen and blistered feet. They went to soak them in the trough for the second time.

Butler and Charley Rivas sat comfortably on the main-house veranda. Rivas had convinced another man from Mex-town, an old friend of his, to bring back Rivas's guns. He promised the man a bottle of whiskey when they returned to Peralta. As he dryly told Marshal Hunter, he had done more walking on foot today than he'd done since he could remember, and made a gesture to indicate that his short, compact body had not been intended for walking.

Butler half listened. When Rivas ended his justification for not leaving the yard, Butler said, "There's something you could do, if they bring in horses."

Rivas turned wary eyes. "Not go back after our things?"

"No. Scout southward. Make a big sweep, but be careful."

"Why?"

"That 'Indian' we saw?"

"Yes."

"If it wasn't an Indian, if it was a *bandolero*, it could be the two-gun soldier coming back to hit Cartwell from behind in the night and take back the bullion box."

Rivas's brow got two deep creases. "You think it was?"

"I don't know. That's why I brought this

up. But be *coyote;* those sons of bitches will shoot you."

Rivas straightened around in his chair. After a moment, he asked a question. "But why do we care? That loot most likely was stolen down in Mexico anyway. Why can't Cartwell and the *bandoleros* settle this among themselves?"

"Because, Charley, this isn't Mexico. If they get Cartwell up here, who else'll they get? He's the only reason they didn't attack Peralta. They needed Cartwell's horses. Now that they have them, I wouldn't bet a plugged centavo they won't raid ranches and towns on their way south, and I won't bet they won't come back. Never mind, I'll get someone else."

Rivas sighed, settled deeper into the chair, and stared out where the others had gone and where a faint, milky haze was settling as the afternoon advanced. Eventually he said, "All right, I'll go. But I can't do it on foot."

CHAPTER ELEVEN

A BAD NIGHT

It was an hour or so before evening when Calkins's riders approached behind a cloud of dust in the wake of a band of horses. Each man had caught one animal. After that they had widened their search until they had found other horses. They were driving them toward the yard when re-armed possemen and old Calkins saw the dust and hastened to open the corral gates and form two lines. But the horses knew where they were being driven and entered the corrals in a dusty rush, making no last-minute attempt to veer off and break clear.

Possemen lined up looking in at the animals. It was late in the day, and their saddles and bridles were back at Vasquez Spring, so their gratification at being able to ride again was a little less enthusiastic than it otherwise would have been. But Charley Rivas snaked out a horse and, with the loan of an outfit by Hunter Calkins, left the yard riding southward. His last remark to Marshal Butler was that in his particular case, the dying day would be in his favor.

Rivas's departure required an explanation. After Frank had finished, the harness maker said, "Why'n hell would they come back? They got the horses, which is all they come up here for."

"The bullion box. It's full of gold. Things plundered from churches down in Mexico."

Even Bart Matthews was silent after that announcement. They left the area of the corral, all but Calkins's vaqueros, who remained down there to pitch feed to the animals.

Out front, with the heat diminishing a little, possemen discussed saddling up and tracking Cartwell. The idea was sound, but the timing wasn't. Darkness would arrive shortly.

Calkins took two men to the main house to help him make supper. Butler and the other men remained down near the barn. Some of them, after what they'd been through over at Vasquez Spring, were content to remain where they were. Oncoming dusk supplied them with an excuse for staying where they were at least until sunup. But it wasn't the only reason; they were tired all the way through.

The harness maker was one of those individuals who had an ingrained restlessness. He'd been like that all his life. He took Marshal Butler aside to talk. On one thing he thought everyone should agree: Cartwell had not deviated from his easterly course after leaving the sump back yonder. He probably would not do so until darkness forced him to make camp. If that was correct, no one had to wait for sunup to run him down — all they had to do was get astride, locate his sign, and ride steadily in that direction until they found the son of a bitch.

Marshal Butler watched the sky change color as he stood apart with Matthews. He said nothing, so the harness maker spoke in support of his idea, this time using considerable profanity.

"What the hell do you figure to accomplish settin' here, for Chrissake? Or maybe you don't really want to go lookin' for that old son of a bitch."

Butler's ambiguity, up until they'd seen the spying horseman, had been grounded in his belief that Jacob Cartwell was perhaps not worth the trouble of capturing him. The worse thing he'd done was condone what the Texan and others had done when they'd run down and killed Calkins's riders. Otherwise, the laws he'd broken or bent were not the kind that got consideration in frontier courts. Neither would they sit very well with the folks in Peralta, who could be counted upon to look down their noses about Butler's leading his riders into that ambush.

It wasn't consideration of this humiliation that prompted him to answer the harness maker. It was the possibility of *bandoleros* returning to plunder and probably kill Cartwell and his riders.

He'd already committed Charley Rivas. He said, "Calkins won't be going with us."

Matthews answered predictably. "What difference does that make? We don't need him."

"It might make a difference if those *bandoleros* come back in full force. But I doubt they'll do that. Someone has to stay with the horse herd."

Bart Matthews looked puzzled. "Sounds to me like you're havin' trouble makin' up your mind."

Butler's reply seemed to confirm this. "If I knew for a fact the *bandoleros* were coming back, I wouldn't hesitate, not about Cartwell but about *pronunciados* running wild north of the border."

Matthews rolled his eyes. "The law," he said. "The gawdamned law. While we're standin' out here arguing, I'll bet you a hatful of new money those *bandoleros* are coming back. Marshal, at least let's make a scout. Just you an' me. When everyone's bedded down, let's the two of us . . . I know where the tracks are. We saw them where we found the guns. I can lead you to them with m'eyes closed. You ready?"

Butler nodded.

When they returned to the yard, dusk falling, there was a poker game going over on the little porch of the bunkhouse. Other possemen were on the veranda at the main house with Hunter Calkins. No one heeded their return. The possemen who saw Marshal Butler in the yard were disinclined to look at him or approach him, an attitude that made it abundantly clear that they were not likely to respond favorably to an invitation to go night-riding.

Eventually most of the possemen bedded down. Calkins came down off the veranda where Butler was sitting, stoked up his foul little pipe without a word, fired it up, and spoke around the stem. "I'll go out with a wagon in the morning, bury those lads, then go on over to the spring an' fetch back the saddles and whatnot you boys left over there. . . . Frank? If them *bandoleros* do come back, they may have in mind returnin' to my yard."

"They already plundered you, Hunter."

The stockman removed his pipe, tamped it with a callused thumbpad, and spoke softly. "Yeah. An' they come away convinced there wasn't anything."

Marshal Butler turned slowly. "There is?"

"Well, it's not exactly a cache, but you can't run a cow outfit, pay your riders, settle up with the store in Peralta, and a few other things unless you got some money, now, can you?"

Butler settled back to briefly ponder. The *bandoleros* had done their damnedest and had found nothing. The chances of their returning to the yard seemed very remote. On the other hand, men like Hunter Calkins had to be stubborn as a Missouri mule to even be down here, and anyone that stubborn who got an idea in his head was not going to listen to someone else's logic.

He saw a lanky shadow materialize over in the front barn opening, and straightened up as he said, "All right. Let the possemen lie over for another day. For a fact, they're worn down."

"An' what about your notion of those Messicans goin' after Cartwell?"

Butler replied, "It's what you called it, Hunter — a notion."

He left the old stockman smoking his pipe in the dusk and met Bart Matthews inside the barn where two saddled horses were tied. He asked where the two booted carbines had come from.

Matthews's teeth shone in darkness as he replied, "Where do you think; from the guns we brought back. That's your Winchester. We goin' to stand around and talk again, or get astride?"

They led the horses out back, swung up and, with Matthews ahead, struck out on a northeasterly course at a dead walk, which was possible to hear in the yard but wouldn't be heard by most of the weary men, who were sleeping.

Hunter Calkins heard it as he was knocking dottle from his pipe and looked up, but there was nothing to see in the increasing darkness.

There was a moon, barely deserving to be called one. It shed less light than the stars, but as Frank rode he wasn't convinced moonlight, especially bright moonlight, would be an advantage.

When they reached the thornpin thicket where the guns had been found, the harness maker did not even hesitate. He reined almost due east, making only an occasional sashay around swales or other thickets. He said nothing for an hour. Then, as he drew rein and grunted down from the saddle, he jutted his jaw and began leading his horse left and right

154

until he found what he was looking for. He got down on all fours and remained that way for a couple of minutes before rising, teeth showing in the gloom. As he mounted, he pointed. "Like I figured, damned near straight east."

Farther along, Butler thought that if Cartwell had encamped, there should be light from a supper fire. But not if he made a dry camp, which most camps were in this country.

He thought of Charley Rivas. If Charley returned to Calkins's yard and found Butler and Matthews gone, he might swap horses and try to find them.

Not everyone would do that in the dark when they were dog-tired, but Rivas might.

Matthews halted with an upraised hand. There was no reflected firelight, but there was the sound of horses, faint but unmistakable. Butler straightened in the saddle. It could be Cartwell, and it could also be the *bandoleros*.

He had good reason for expecting the worst: If Cartwell had kept on riding, he should be much farther ahead. Without any indication that he had made camp, Frank accepted the probability that the riders up ahead in the darkness were *not* Cartwell and his riders.

Bart Matthews looked worried. "They maybe struck camp after eatin' and lettin' the animals rest for a spell."

Butler made an estimate of the distance and swung to the ground, pulling out his carbine as he did so. "Cartwell would be another five or six miles ahead, Bart."

Matthews also dismounted with his saddle gun.

The horse sound was made by mounted men. Loose horses did not move in close order in a straight line, even when they went to water. In darkness, if they moved at all, it would be in a meandering, wide front.

Bart lowered his voice as he spoke. "You don't expect there's someone else out here besides the Messicans an' Cartwell, do you?"

Marshal Butler did not reply. He looked for something to tie his horse to, waited briefly for his companion to do the same, then led off in a brisk walk.

The sound came from nearby, and that too bothered the harness maker. "Hell, if they know which way Cartwell went, they should be a lot closer to him, shouldn't they?"

Butler said nothing. Maybe they should be. Then again, if that "Indian" the possemen had seen earlier had been watching Cartwell, not the posse riders, and had tracked Cartwell from the same discreet distance, the riders up ahead could be covering the same ground after meeting their spy Butler and Matthews were covering now.

In any case, Butler was concentrating on following by sound. As the distance widened between where the horses had been left and the horsemen up ahead, he lengthened his stride.

He did not want to get up among the riders, just close enough to identify them. Two men on foot would have to be insane to attack only the Lord knew how many armed mounted men.

The sound in the eastward distance abruptly stopped, but only briefly. Then fidgeting horses made a different kind of sound.

Butler looked for shelter. There was none. The countryside where he and the harness maker now were had no underbrush that would conceal a man.

He and Matthews sank to the ground, carbines shoved ahead. A man's voice, slightly raised, carried well enough to be heard farther back, but the words were indistinguishable. Bart said they were in Spanish. Butler was unable to make that good a guess.

The invisible riders up ahead in darkness stepped to the ground. Most of their movements were recognizable by sound until they practically ceased; then Butler led off in a belly crawl to get as close as prudence allowed. He wanted to hear what was being said, and in which language it was being said.

Matthews, straining ahead, crawled over a

Gila monster. The ugly, fat, lizardlike creature hissed to let Bart know what had happened. Without wasting a second, Matthews rolled violently sideways. Gila monster venom was deadly.

Butler twisted to look back, saw his companion wielding a steel butt plate to stamp something, and reached to touch the harness maker for silence. He might as well have tried to influence a rock.

Only after the Gila monster was pulp did Matthews stop pounding it. He used the barrel of his carbine to fling the creature away. As he settled forward, he said, "Subbitching Gila monster," and held his vest away from his body to show where he had been bitten, then sat up, unbuttoned the vest, and examined the shirt and skin beneath. The bite had not quite penetrated the vest.

Butler eased flat down to rest a moment, until his companion, who clearly was deathly afraid of Gila monsters, recovered. Matthews was rebuttoning the vest when he raised his head.

Butler sat up. There was not a sound up ahead in the middle distance. His heart sank. Their horses were one hell of a distance back. Now all thought of creeping up to identify the horsemen yielded to the fear that Bart's pounding on the ground had warned the men up ahead, whoever they were, that someone was behind them.

He made a curt gesture for the harness maker to follow, got into a low crouch, and ran. That sound, too, would carry. The alternative was to lie there where an enemy might find them. They had no friends out here.

They had crossed open country to get up where the Gila monster had been. They ran hard back across this land now, making no attempt to conceal what they were doing. Later, they might wonder about a Gila monster being abroad in the night. At the present moment, they were concerned only with reaching their animals and getting back to the Calkins yard.

Matthews called ahead and gestured northward, where there was sheltering underbrush. Butler did not deviate from his direct course until he heard horsemen. They were coming fast, making more noise than they'd made when riding at a walk.

He veered in the direction of the nearest thicket, which was slightly uphill, and ran harder than he'd run since childhood.

Matthews looked over his shoulder, saw moving shadows, and shot past Butler to dive headfirst into the first thicket. His face was torn by thorns, but he did not even feel the pain or the blood as he squirmed around to face down the gentle slope.

Butler made an equally swift but less impromptu entrance; he belly-crawled among the bushes at ground level and had a little more difficulty turning back.

Matthews said, "If it was daylight, they'd hang our hides out to dry."

But it wasn't daylight. The riders, what appeared to be at least eight or ten of them, rode past in a lope, some with carbines balancing on their hips, others bending down as far as they dared, trying to find tracks.

Butler swore and said, "They'll find the horses."

Matthews was mopping blood off his face with a soiled cuff and said nothing until he'd finished. Then, as he watched the last rider fade in darkness, he spoke. "Yeah. An' if they wait another hour or so to start back, it'll be light enough for them to see our tracks." Matthews was struggling to rise and free himself from the undergrowth as he spoke.

He turned looking for a way either deeper into or through the thicket, and found nothing like that at all. As he faced forward Marshal Butler rose, hooked the Winchester in the crook of one arm, and stood listening.

There was not a sound until a night-roosting brush wren, which had used up every iota of

160

its courage after the two men invaded its hideout, made several squawks and rose almost straight up before whirling and flying away as swiftly as it could flash its wings.

Butler picked thorns off, glanced at his companion, and quietly said, "You look like you been through a meat chopper." Then he leaned to peer along the front of their thicket for a passageway.

What they eventually found was an ancient deadfall tree of some kind, probably the victim of a desert drought a hundred years earlier. It was lying across their path with underbrush growing around it. The wood was as hard as iron. In a country where it rarely rained, wood tended to petrify, in contrast to the way wood rotted into oblivion in areas with plentiful rain and snow.

Butler got behind the deadfall, leaned his carbine, and helped Matthews shove past underbrush to also settle low with the ancient log in front.

Safe, at least for the moment, they sucked down huge amounts of chilly night air. Neither of them had exerted himself in the last forty years as he had during the past half hour. For Bart Matthews, it had undoubtedly been more than forty years.

He was mopping his face again when he said, "Gila monster! What was the blasted thing doing crawling around in the night?"

Butler was watching and listening. His reply was offhand. "Waiting for you. Why in hell did you climb atop the thing?"

Matthews straightened up very slowly, stopped mopping his face, and glared. "A man always crawls atop them things," he stated. "That's how you smother 'em. Didn't you know that?"

Butler settled against the old log. "If they find our horses —"

"What'd you mean 'if'? I just hope they ride far enough easterly for the lads in the yard to hear 'em."

Butler blew out a long sigh before speaking again. "Did you get a good look at them?"

"Sure. I always run over uneven ground with my head turned back," exclaimed the harness maker in a voice of purest sarcasm. "*Bandoleros,* Bart."

Chapter Twelve

SURPRISES!

After resting they rose and went cautiously along the front of their thicket. If there was an opening, they did not find it.

They heard horsemen approaching from the west, this time in a walk, fled back to their deadfall, and crouched behind it. When the riders appeared, riding bunched up, making the usual little musical sounds of men who wore spurs and used rein chains, Bart rested his chin atop the old log and waited until they were close enough to be seen. Then he swore with relief, because the horsemen were too far south to find their tracks even in daylight.

Frank Butler verified the identification when one of the distant, vague moving shadows said something in Spanish. The marshal interpreted, although the harness maker understood Spanish well enough.

"He said they wasted time, that we were

probably Indians sneakin' around in darkness to steal horses."

Matthews's relief was palpable. Their saddle animals had not been found!

A sharper, more incisive voice reached them. This time the harness maker interpreted. "By Gawd, you was right. Did you hear him? He said now it'd more'n likely take them an extra hour to overtake Cartwell."

Butler was settling against the log when one of the distant shadows mentioned something that had evidently been brought up before. He said that if Cartwell had hidden the bullion box to come back for it later, they would have ridden themselves tender for nothing.

This time the man with the unpleasant voice was sharp. As he was snarling at the previous speaker, Bart Matthews leaned and whispered. "The two-gun colonel, sure as hell."

The horsemen did not pick up their gait, so evidently they did not believe this diversion would really cause them much trouble.

The marshal and Bart Matthews watched the shadows pass from sight, heard their voices become more distant before either of them noticed a revealing stain of pale light stealthily brightening the land, outlining, among other things, their tracks.

This time when they left the deadfall, they were less interested in cover than they were in reaching their horses quickly. They knew without a shred of doubt that at least some of those *bandoleros* would come back, tracking them.

The question was *when* would they come and how fast. The closer it came to daylight, the easier it would be for someone to track them. Butler trotted. Matthews did likewise, occasionally looking back. They were close to the place where they'd left the horses when Butler slackened off long enough to point southward.

The *bandoleros* had ridden past their tethered animals too far south to see them in the dark. Their tracks proved it.

The harness maker's only comment was to say it was about time someone — or something — lent a hand.

Butler dropped down to a steady walk. When he saw the horses they were looking northward, ears up, heads high. They did not look to the east until they heard Bart speaking. They were only slightly the worse for standing all night.

Neither the lawman nor the harness maker wasted a lot of time freeing the animals and snugging up their cinches. So far there was no sign of pursuit. But sunrise was close, and their tracks would stand out like a sore thumb. And they still had a fair distance to cover to reach the Calkins yard.

The thicket that had prevented their horses from being seen earlier was not particularly wide, and it straggled from west to east. It was not as abundant or as flourishing as the thicket had been back by the deadfall log.

Matthews paused to skive a sliver off his cube of molasses-cured before mounting. He waited until Butler was twisting the stirrup before he said, "Well, we come out here to find 'em, an' we sure as hell did, an' they was border jumpers."

Matthews turned his back, twisted the stirrup, and had his left foot in the air when a voice spoke in Spanish. "Stay on the ground. Don't turn around. Keep both hands in front where I can see them."

Both the marshal and the saddler did not breathe for three or four seconds. The surprise had been complete. They slowly put their feet down, stood like statues, and held their hands up in plain sight.

The voice from the thicket sounded youthful but calm. "Now the guns," it said in English. "One hand at a time. Good. Now kick the guns away." When that order had also been obeyed, the voice lightened even more, became almost amiable.

They heard him pushing out of the thicket behind them. He remained back there.

"*Tontos,*" he said. "Fools." He paused and added, "Like children. Of course we found the horses. But we have enough horses; we wanted the owners of the horses. Turn around!"

They turned.

The *bandolero* was indeed young. Butler recognized him from Vasquez Spring. They had never spoken, but this was one of the men who had gone out to catch loose stock and use it to rope other horses for their companions. He was lean and wiry, the kind of individual who could get the customary Mexican *riata,* all sixty feet of it, the full distance in a perfect throw.

He did not look antagonistic, but rather wary and capable. The gun in his right fist was stone-steady. He hadn't cocked it, but he could do that and get off a shot as long as he stood twenty feet from his captives. Neither the lawman nor his companion had any intention of trying to close the distance.

He smiled at them. He was a handsome youth with a very nice smile. "They will be along, hombres. You didn't count them when they rode back." The youth's smile remained. "That's why they rode in a bunch. You had to be watching. If you hadn't got back to the horses, you had to be hiding somewhere watching."

Butler finally spoke. "Do you know what's behind you?"

The youth laughed. "Yes. All those men on foot at that old ranch. Mister, you can't scare me."

Butler smiled back. "All right. Then tell me; why didn't the colonel ride a wider line and intercept Cartwell, instead of coming in behind him and having to trail him in the night?"

"If you are lucky, mister, you'll know why. If you are unlucky you never will; so I'll tell you, because I don't think you are going to be lucky. Yesterday our scout saw a band of armed riders coming from Peralta. We had to cross in front of their course in the night. To be safe, we did this much farther west than we liked. But" — the young *bandolero* shrugged — "maybe those men from Peralta are worried because you've been gone so long and are looking for you. I think they will ride into the yard of that old ranch. By then, mister, we will be too far eastward behind Cartwell to be worried. Now you know."

The young man shifted position with all his weight on one leg. He shot a quick look eastward where his companions would appear. Butler and Matthews looked in that direction too.

There was no sign of riders.

Matthews, who had been silent up to now, made a sly smile, spat aside, and addressed the youthful *bandolero,* "Friend, suppose the men from Peralta cut your sign. Suppose they followed it instead of heading for the Calkins place?"

The younger man eyed Matthews before speaking. "I don't think so," he said in the same calm, almost amiable tone of voice. "They would cross our tracks in the dark. Even if they saw them in the morning, it wouldn't make much difference. We would be too far away."

Butler had completed his judgment of their captor. If the youth had a soft spot, Butler had not found it. He was calm and confident, something not often encountered in men his age. He also held his gun as though he would use it.

But Butler made the effort anyway. "You should have stayed with the horse herd. By now you'd be miles away, not far from the border. Now you're in a country full of stirred-up folks. That makes your chances of getting home a lot worse."

The dark eyes went back to Marshal Butler. "It's worth the risk," he stated. "We've been promised twice the usual share of loot from the box we brought to the rendezvous at that rocky spring to trade for the horses." After a moment, the smile returned. "Mister, it's never hard to raid up here. I've done it six times so far. Everyone runs like sheep." The youth threw another quick look eastward. There still was no sign of riders.

Butler said, "They've had plenty of time, vaquero. Maybe they decided to go on after Cartwell and leave you behind."

This time the youth flashed a wider smile. "No. They will come. Colonel Esparza is my father."

Some little wrens fled out of the thicket behind the youth. Butler and Matthews noticed, but the young *bandolero* couldn't as long as he faced his captives.

Matthews shed his cud, spat lustily, and hooked both thumbs in his shellbelt while gazing at the youth. He stood hip-shot as he spoke. "What is your name?"

"Elias Esparza. Yours is Matthews and his is Butler. He is the marshal of Peralta."

"Elias, you're young. Your past is still ahead of you."

The youth's dark eyes showed amused irony. "You can't bribe me. You don't have as much as my share will be."

Butler and Matthews felt the fresh presence before they saw the man. There wasn't much they could make out except that he moved in underbrush without a sound, a foot at a time, softly twisting with the wiry thornpin limbs. After he passed, they returned to their original position without a sound.

Butler spoke to hold the *bandolero*'s attention. "If they're coming, where are they? It's been half an hour."

The youth's confidence was undented. "They will come. Not all of them. Then I'll catch up when they find Cartwell and the box."

"*If* Cartwell has the box."

"He has it, friend. Two men crept back to the rocks at the sump hole to watch. They saw him load it on a big mule before he rode away."

"Why didn't they get it at the spring?"

"Because we wanted him to carry it away from there for us. Carry it past that old ranch. East of here there are miles of empty land. That's where we'll catch him."

Matthews replied, "Partner, it's broad daylight, and Cartwell's got some pretty savvy riders. You'll be lucky if you get close enough to see him before he sees you. You go any closer and some of you will get killed."

The youth listened, then gently wagged his head. "I don't think so, gringo. The colonel knows more than anyone about things like that. I'll tell you: he means not to challenge them and make a fight. He means to ride far around and make an ambush for them to ride into."

Twenty-five feet behind the youth, a gun was cocked. Elias's smile congealed, his eyes widened, his breath came short. In his world there was usually only a second or two after a gun was cocked that the trigger was pulled.

A deep voice said, "Drop the gun, *muchacho!* I don't tell you twice!"

The weapon fell almost soundlessly to the sandy ground.

The invisible man spoke again, this time to Marshal Butler. "Take it. Get his gun. Tie him and leave. Don't stand there!"

Butler stepped ahead, picked up the gun as Bart Matthews pushed the youth to the ground, and used his own belt and bandanna to bind him, with his face in the dirt. When they finished and rose, there was no sign of the man who had been in the underbrush. Matthews swore, but Butler turned toward the horses.

They left the youth without even so much as a backward glance.

The sun was climbing, and the chill was leaving. There was not a cloud in the sky, hadn't been for a couple of months. The horses were restlessly fidgeting when the men arrived.

Butler walked out for half a mile to favor

the horse that had been standing all night. Then he boosted the animal into a rocking-chair lope.

Bart caught up and called across the intervening distance. "We should have brought him with us. If he's the head Mex's son, we could have swapped him for something."

Remembering the face and eyes of the head *pronunciado*, Butler doubted that. What bothered him was what he had heard about more riders from town being in the area. He had the best posse riders with him at the Calkins place. What had been left in town had been men like Jess Hobart the saloonman, flighty Pete Evinrude from the trading barn, and others not much better.

If those Mexicans succeeded or failed in their attempt to get the bullion box, their next move would be to head south as fast as they could, and if they angled southwesterly they very well might ride downcountry smack dab into those other riders from town. And that, Butler told himself, would be like setting weasels loose in a henhouse.

They had Calkins's rooftops in sight when Matthews said, "Was that feller in the bushes a Messican? I couldn't tell from the way he talked."

Butler had no idea, nor did he want to dwell on their release from captivity right at this moment. But of one thing he was certain: who-ever that had been was no novice at slipping through thornpin thickets.

Someone in the yard raised a yell. He had seen the two riders approaching from the northeast. Another man freed a horse from the rack in front of the barn and loped to a meeting. Butler recognized him easily, even at a considerable distance.

Charley Rivas whirled in beside Marshal Butler to say, "Nobody knew you was gone until daybreak. I come back before that to tell you that redskin was a *bandolero* like you thought, and to tell you I stalked 'em until I was sure — they're going after Cartwell. That scout they got out ahead went like a honeybee to Cartwell's tracks. But about the time I was starting back, there was a big pa-laver, and instead of tracking Cartwell, the whole band went straight north."

Butler knew about this. "There's riders coming from town. Their scout saw them. Otherwise the border jumpers would have gone after Cartwell in a straight line. They cut north to keep away from the town riders. By now they're on Cartwell's tracks again."

In the yard, refreshed posse riders clustered. Matthews leaned his back on the tie post and told the whole story while Butler went to the main house to tell Hunter he'd be paid livery rate for the use of his horses. But Hunter was not there. Neither was either of his two riders.

Butler rummaged the kitchen for food to fill his *alforja* with, then dallied a moment between swallows from a whiskey bottle on the drainboard before returning to the yard.

Men were rigging out in the barn and out front of it. One of them met the marshal at the tie rack and told him that old Calkins and his two riders had left the yard about dawn in a wagon with digging tools.

The old man who owned the fat bay horse came along, saw Butler's weapon in its holster. Then he saw the other gun, the one the old man had acquired at Vasquez Spring, in the lawman's waistband. He asked for it. When Butler handed it over, the old man wagged his head. "Risked my danged life, an' for all the good that done I might as well stole a piece of cheese or something."

The old man walked off with straw in his hair, to which he seemed oblivious. It probably would not have bothered him even if he'd known it was up there.

CHAPTER THIRTEEN

UNDER AN OVERCAST SKY

There was a chill in the air as the riders left Calkins's yard. Butler watched for sign of the Peralta riders without seeing them or their dust. But he might not have seen the dust anyway; even the South Desert had moisture in the early-morning air.

He sent a man to look for them, and if he found them to bring them along. Bart Matthews spoke as he watched the horseman ride away. He mentioned the man they hadn't been able to see clearly back where they'd been rescued from the youthful *bandolero*. Butler rode along watching the country ahead as he listened. He knew what the harness maker was going to say as he finished his harangue, and said it first.

"El Cajónero?"

Matthews was in the act of hunting through his pockets for his plug of molasses-cured. He stopped searching to cock his eye. "You think so?" he asked.

Butler smiled at him without answering.

He did not lead them directly to the *bandolero*'s tracks. Instead, he angled over where they'd left their animals the night before.

The young *bandolero* was gone. So was his handgun and his horse. Matthews sat his saddle, studying the ground. He spat and said, "Didn't expect him to be here anyway, did you?"

Butler hadn't, but without mentioning it in order to avoid having the subject of El Cajónero brought up again, he did not speak until he'd read everything from the marks on the ground he could make out. As they were moving again, he said, "We're too far behind now, Bart."

Matthews was in a contrary mood this morning, the result, no doubt, of weariness. His reply was curt. "Maybe not. They ain't machines. Neither are their animals."

The other possemen were fresh, as were their Calkins horses. Unshaved, rumpled, soiled-looking, but not as tired as the man leading them.

When they'd been on the tracks for half an hour, Rivas rode up and volunteered to scout ahead. Butler nodded. Charley Rivas was proving to be worth his weight in gold.

Without explaining why, Butler also sent a rider northward to seek a sighting of anyone he could find up there. Of one thing he was dead certain; whoever had saved his bacon last night hadn't been a *fantasma*. He'd been flesh and blood, with an audible voice and a gun that made a noise when he cocked it.

Bart was riding with the blacksmith. They had never been particular friends, but after being at Vasquez Spring together, they'd developed a kind of mutual toleration. But the blacksmith was not a talkative man and Matthews was, so they only rode together for a short while before the harness maker dropped back to mingle with the other possemen.

Butler led off in a slow lope, the kind of gait horses could maintain for miles. A slow lope covered a lot of ground, especially in the morning before the heat arrived.

But the possibility of overtaking the *bandoleros* was remote, unless they'd halted during the night to rest. Once they heard the two-gun man's son relate his story, they would know there were riders somewhere on their backtrail. They already knew there were other riders somewhere southward. While this party posed no particular threat, if they were still down there after the *bandoleros* overtook Cartwell and got the bullion box before fleeing southward toward a rendezvous with the horse herd, they might encounter more trouble than they could handle.

Butler dozed in the saddle until a man named Elwell, whose normal occupation was driving stages, rode up, pointed ahead, and jarred Marshal Butler awake by saying, "I can't make out whether that's Charley. . . . See him north a ways settin' on that sidehill with a big thicket behind him?"

Butler did not see the horseman at once, not until he'd blocked in individual areas to be examined minutely before duplicating the search elsewhere. When he finally saw the rider, the man was moving toward a higher roll of land. As Butler watched, the rider rode up top it and disappeared down the far side.

Elwell, a man of sound judgment and hardy appearance, said, "I'll tell you what he ain't, Marshal. He ain't Charley an' he ain't a Messican. Charley would've signaled. A Mex would have been straddlin' one of those saddles with the big saddle horn."

Behind the lawman a posseman spoke dryly in voice almost of resignation. "Fine. Now we got someone else taggin' along. I'm wonderin' how many friends he's got cached in that arroyo he went down into." The man paused before finishing. "You reckon news of that damned box of bullion has spread? If it has, sure as hell two-legged buzzards'll be gathering."

Butler slackened to a steady walk for a couple of miles and led off in another slow lope after that. The heat was increasing. He wanted to cover as much ground as possible before it was too hot to push the animals.

The men behind him were muttering, eyeing the gentle high roll of land where the mysterious rider had disappeared. This time of year Indians were abroad. Some gruff older man farther back scotched the notion of Indians' being after the bullion. He said Indians might steal your horse, your weapons, maybe even your blanket roll if you weren't in it, but they didn't care a damn about the kind of things in that bullion box.

None of the possemen were entirely placated, even though the man had clearly spoken from experience.

They passed the place where Butler and Matthews had heard the *bandoleros,* the place where Matthews had used his butt plate to kill the Gila monster. They were following tracks made by a large party of horsemen into country as desolate as any on earth, without anything but the tracks they rode beside to indicate human beings had ever been here before.

But they were riding a well-defined trail.

The *pronunciados* were riding over earlier sign left by the passage of Jacob Cartwell and his companions.

The environment did not change much. There was less underbrush, but the land had erosion gullies, some of which were deep enough to conceal a man sitting on a tall horse. There was mumbling about bushwhackers, and while Frank did not believe the men they were hunting would be diverted from their quest, not even long enough to set up an ambush, he nonetheless cut out and around the deepest gullies.

A rider appeared in the middle distance loping in their direction. Not a word was said, although every eye was on him until he was recognized as the scout, Charley Rivas. Then a posseman spoke doubtfully about the possibility of Charley's having seen anything so soon. Like Butler, his companions had done some basic arithmetic and decided that unless the *bandoleros* had halted for several hours in the night, they were still a long way ahead.

Unless they had located Cartwell; that would change everything. But so far, there was no sign that this had happened.

Charley dropped to a walk at a hundred and fifty yards, loosened in the saddle, and spoke when he knew he could be heard. "Gunfire," he exclaimed, twisting in the saddle to wave eastward. "Hell of a long way off, but no mistake, it's gunfire." He dropped his arm and gazed at Marshal Butler. "They caught up with him sure as hell. But from the sound, they didn't catch him by surprise."

Charley did not return to scouting; he led off in a lope with the others following him. They unexpectedly came upon the roofless ruin of an old adobe jacal. It had one fairly large room. There was now no indication people had ever lived here, but leached-out ash filled the interior and told its own story. Someone had made the walls thick enough to turn bullets and arrows, then had made the roof of fireproof sod. But soddies inevitably sprouted weeds and grass on their roofs. After a few years of reseeding, there wasn't an inch of the roof that didn't have thick growth on it. And after the rains, the roof covering cured on the stalk. One firebrand up there would make a furious blaze that would heat and weaken the sod, and the roof would collapse inward.

It had happened before many times. But outlying inhabitants of the South Desert still built their homes like that, because there were no other freely available materials.

Butler looked briefly for the well. In a place like this, no one could survive without water. He hesitated before leading off again.

Charley widened the gap between himself and the posse riders again. They had reached the farthest point of his earlier scout.

The heat should have continued to increase. The reason it didn't was that another of those high, thin veils was aloft, the kind that presaged rain in other places but rarely brought anything more than a slight decrease in the day-long heat on the South Desert.

From this point on, conversation was infrequent and short. Visibility was excellent, which should preclude any surprises. But this far east, while the land flattened so that movement could be discerned at a great distance, there were more of those deep arroyos. Maybe they did not conceal ambushers, but that was nothing a man wanted to bet his life on.

They rode at a steady walk. Out ahead Charley Rivas was doing the same, head moving, eyes never still, carbine across his lap.

When they heard intermittent gunfire, it seemed to come from the far curve of the world. It was faint, but it was also distinct.

Someone commented to the effect that the *bandoleros* had lost their dark-night advantage, that what they should have done was wait for nightfall to attack. The harness maker snorted at that.

"With us behind them an' for all we know them lads from town south of them, not to mention ol' Cartwell in front? If they'd been smart, they never would have come back at all!"

That prompted a thin-voiced posseman to ask for an estimate of the value of what the bullion box contained. Butler ignored the talk behind him. He was watching Rivas and the country they were passing through. The harness maker offered his opinion, which was based on little more than scraps of talk he'd heard. But it held the attention of the men around him.

"Jewels, piles of 'em, and gold pieces from Mex missions. Y'know, the kind of gold ornaments they keep in their churches. An' lots of gold money. Hell, I'd guess it figures up to more'n the President of the United States makes all his four years in the White House."

The possemen were impressed enough to ride along in thoughtful silence for a fair distance. Then the stage driver named Elwell called to Matthews. "How do you know it's that much?"

Matthews was ready. "Ask Frank. He knows."

But no one called ahead to Marshal Butler, because Charley Rivas had come to a dead stop up ahead and was holding his carbine stiffly over his head, the age-old sign of an enemy sighted.

Slouching possemen straightened; a few unshipped carbines and held them across their laps. Someone swore softly, making sounds everyone could hear. Even hoof-falls did not break the hush as horses plodded over an eons-old thin layer of dust that soaked up sound.

The gunfire had stopped. It hadn't been very loud before, but now there was nothing to break the deathly hush of infinity.

Butler stood in his stirrups, scanning in front of the scout. There was nothing to see, no movement, no break in the geography, just endless miles of the *desplobado*.

As he sat down Charley walked his horse back, leaning to reboot his Winchester as he approached. He reined to a halt, looking as solemn as an owl. "When the shooting stopped about a mile or so ahead, there was some riders come out of an arroyo. Too far to count 'em. They was bunched up. But they sure looked like *bandoleros* to me."

The significance of this escaped no one. The *bandoleros* had won their skirmish with Cartwell; otherwise they wouldn't have ridden up into plain sight.

An additional scout ahead would clarify things. But Butler did not suggest it, not only because it would be dangerous for Charley Rivas, but also because if their presence had not been detected, he did not want that to happen now.

He asked Charley about the nearest arroyo. Without answering, the dark man turned, kneed out his animal, and led the way on a slightly northward course to the edge of a deep gully.

The gully was too steep and had banks of crumbly earth, so they went upcountry for almost a mile before they found places to slide down without having the horses upend beneath them.

Charley left them on foot this time, carrying his Winchester. Everyone else piled off, but no one loosened a cinch, because they did not expect their animals to stand idle for a while.

Butler walked down the arroyo southward. The other men hunkered for relief from the heat, which was greater in the almost airless gully than it had been atop the plain. In this kind of place, the faint overcast worked in reverse: it still partially blunted the sun's rays, but without any air stirring, it also made the deep gully uncomfortably hot.

Butler turned when he heard someone coming. The harness maker, his turkey-lined neck red and his shirtfront getting darker by the moment, came up and waited to be addressed. But the lawman said nothing as he resumed his walk with the harness maker at his side.

They encountered Charley Rivas where he had plowed his way up the crumbly bank. After four or five landslides that carried him back down, he had finally reached the plain above. He had heard them coming and was facing around as they appeared below. Sweat was dripping off his chin.

"Whatever happened up there is over. Before the damned overcast come, I could see for a hell of a distance." Charley wagged his head, as much to throw off sweat as to show disgust. "Now all I can see is someone on horseback now an' then. But sure as hell they're plundering."

Butler asked if they had a scout out. They had. Charley pointed southward.

Butler considered. If the colonel had a scout watching the southerly land, he probably did not know Butler's posse riders were west, or behind him. He should have known; but if he had seen no one so far, he might have thought that pursuit from the west was far behind.

Matthews had an idea. "He ain't worryin' about someone comin' up behind him. He's worryin' about there bein' open country southward so's as soon as he can load that box, and anythin' else they take, they can head for a rendezvous with the fellers drivin' the horse herd."

Charley thought that was probably close to the truth. "He sure as hell knows about them riders from town. They was way south riding in the direction of the Calkins place. He won't want to blunder into them."

Butler asked about arroyos to the south that could be entered from where they now were without having to go up onto the plain. Charley shook his head. "There's deep places, but we got to cross open country to get to them. They'd see us sure as hell."

The marshal tilted his head. The sun was off center, but not by very much. At least five or six daylight hours still remained. He looked down to see the scout and harness maker watching him. "How many are there?" he asked the scout.

Rivas frowned. "A guess? Maybe ten, maybe a few more. An' maybe a few less. I couldn't count 'em. If you're thinkin' about pitching into them an' they see us coming from this far off, it's goin' to end up as a horse race. In this heat . . ." Rivas wagged his head.

Butler did not like the idea of remaining in hiding until nightfall, but if there was an alternative that wouldn't get some of his possemen killed, he did not know what it was. Those *bandoleros* would put up a stiff fight. Without question they were very experienced at running fights. Their horses were a long way from being fresh, but desperate men wearing Chihuahua spurs would rowel the last breath out of anything they rode.

Butler was thwarted, and it did not sit well with him. Neither Rivas nor Matthews had a suggestion. Whatever decision the marshal made now, right or wrong, was going to follow him to his grave.

Matthews seemed to understand. He grimaced. "Between a rock an' a hard place," he said. One moment later, a solitary gunshot sounded. There was no echo, but within moments other shots sounded, a furious fusillade that sounded to Marshal Butler like wild firing.

Charley twisted around. For a long time he seemed transfixed. Then he said, "They're callin' in that scout. They're runnin' around like ants. Something sure as hell happened."

For a long while Charley had nothing more to report. The marshal and harness maker fidgeted in the arroyo, unable to climb up or even to guess what the sudden eruption meant.

Finally, Charley rose up slightly to look below. "I don't know what happened, but they're all on the ground now. Looks like they're all together. No one's looting anymore."

Butler asked if the horses had been stampeded, and Charley shook his head. "No.

Whatever the shootin' was about, it wasn't to run off their horses." He swung forward, still up off the ground like a lizard, both arms bent to support his upper body. He looked elsewhere, left and right, considered the turmoil up ahead, then went back to studying the land. Eventually he twisted around again.

"This arroyo bends around up north a fair distance. I can't tell how far it goes after it bends to the east, but if it goes very far, Frank, an' they don't put someone up there to watch, maybe we could lead the horses up yonder. Where it bends around, maybe it'll go as far as the country north of where they are." Charley rolled his eyes. "I wouldn't bet on any of this, but right now damned if I can see anything else unless we squat down here until dark, then try to find 'em again."

Matthews's spirits revived. With typical enthusiasm, he looked at Marshal Butler. "If it's all we got, Frank, it beats hell out of stayin' down in here and sweatin' off ten pounds. An' just maybe . . . Charley, what are they doin'?"

"Nothing, Bart, milling around."

Butler told the scout to slide back down and turned to go back where the possemen were waiting and sweltering. When he reached them, he explained that there might be a way to get closer to the *bandoleros* without being seen — providing the arroyo went far enough eastward. When the men gathered up their reins, he told them to lead their horses, not to ride them. He did not want to risk some sudden rise at the bottom of the arroyo that would expose their heads and shoulders.

CHAPTER FOURTEEN

THE PASSING OF TIME

One blessing was that as they moved north-ward it seemed to get cooler. By the time they reached the place where the dry wash bent around eastward, moving air, sluggish but at least not still, seemed to slide down the faint tilt of the land.

Butler walked in front with Charley Rivas directly behind him. There was no conversation. For one thing, the walls of the easterly arroyo had washed down over the years, making footing uncertain. They eventually encountered boulders, too, probably at one time well beneath the surface of the ground, which had been uncovered and tumbled down by rainfall. But what eventually prompted Butler to send Charley ahead was the way fill dirt had raised the depth of the arroyo, in some places dangerously high even for men walking their horses.

Butler's private opinion was that while the arroyo would certainly take them closer to their goal, it might not take them close enough.

Charley stayed well ahead. Butler saw him pause several times when he encountered more boulders, but his progress was steady. The farther he went, the more Butler's spirits rose. His best estimate was that the possemen would have to cover at least a mile before they would be north of their goal, the place where the bitter fight had occurred.

Charley dropped his reins again and crawled up the southern slope of the gully. He lay prone there for what seemed a very long time before returning to the others.

"Not much farther," he told them. He picked up the reins and led off again.

Butler asked what he'd seen. The scout replied without stopping or even looking back. "Closer than I figured. Another hunnert yards an' we'll be within carbine range north of the camp."

"What's down there?"

"A mess. Horse riggin' scattered all over, bedrolls been searched and scattered."

"How many men?"

"Five," the scout replied. Then he added, "Five hobbled horses with Mex saddles, more hobbled out a fair distance tryin' to find somethin' to eat. Some of them I remember from back at Vasquez Spring. Most of 'em, in fact. And mules."

Charley halted again where the south wall of the arroyo slanted. As he was starting to claw his way up, he looked over his shoulder at the watching possemen. "Dead men too. Couldn't make out how many because they're among all that other junk, but I saw two plain as day."

The riders squatted as they waited for Rivas to return.

Elwell the stage driver drained his canteen and upended it before slinging it back across the horn of his saddle. "They better have water," he said, and settled in horse shade to build a smoke.

Butler was pondering five Mex horses down there. There had been probably twice that number of riders with the *pronunciado* colonel. He was not particularly uneasy; even if they had discovered the stalking possemen, five of them wouldn't be able to do much. Nor did it seem reasonable to him that the two-gun Mexican officer would send only five men to do what even his entire force would be hard put to accomplish — unless they had already departed with the bullion box!

Butler was waiting when Rivas slid back down, brushed himself off, and wagged his head. "Something's wrong," he told them. "The box is setting right where someone lifted it out of a pack bag. There's a couple of fellers with carbines keepin' watch. . . . Unless they're waitin' for their friends to return, I got no idea why they haven't ske-daddled."

"Chasin' whoever fired that solitary shot," Matthews said, referring to the missing *bandoleros*. Butler saw the sly, triumphant look on the harness maker's face. When their eyes met, Bart winked slowly.

He did not say it, because he didn't have to. *El Cajónero!*

Butler speculated. It wasn't a trap. *Pronunciados* were very skillful ambushers. No rebel officer like the two-gun colonel would send half his men away if he wanted to stage an ambush.

The explanation came to Butler like a blow on the head. He hunted Charley Rivas down where he was among the other men drinking from a canteen. "Those fellers in the camp," he said. "What are they doing?"

Rivas handed the canteen to its owner before replying. "Waiting, I guess. Waitin' for their friends to come back. Sitting around like dog-tired men sit."

Butler said, "It don't make sense, Charley. Those are the same men who don't even sleep in one place more'n they can help, and with one eye open."

Charley gazed at Marshal Butler impassively and shrugged.

The shrewd-eyed harness maker stared at the lawman. "What is it, Frank?"

The marshal ignored Matthews to ask Rivas another question. "Where are they sitting?"

Charley looked puzzled. "I just told you, sittin' around like —"

"Around *what?*"

Before Rivas could answer, the harness maker used the term he seemed to favor above all others when he was surprised. "Son of a bitch! Charley, could you see past 'em?"

"Past 'em?" the scout retorted. "Sure, for a hunnert miles."

"No, dammit! *In front of 'em?*"

"No, not right in front of 'em. What difference —"

"Frank," exclaimed the harness maker. "Sure as hell!"

Charley looked from one of them to the other. "What the hell are you talkin' about?"

Marshal Butler answered. "They've got a wounded man in front of them. That lone shot we heard — someone got hit. Some of them went busting out after him. The others are sittin' down there keeping a vigil."

Charley's face cleared slowly. The men close

by were like statues. Only one of them, the old man with the fat bay horse, seemed to have understood. "The colonel!"

For ten seconds there was absolute silence. When the idea settled among them, they still did not have anything to say.

Elwell hunkered down, leaning on his carbine. "All right," he said quietly. "Maybe. What I'd like to know is . . . didn't none of *us* get around in front of them and shoot him." Elwell looked up. "One of his own men?"

Butler felt Bart Matthews staring at him and refused to raise his eyes. "It don't matter," he told them. "What matters is, are they demoralized enough to give up?"

None of them believed that was possible. Several shook their heads, while the others simply stood gazing at Marshal Butler as though surprised he'd even ask such a question.

"If not," the marshal told them, "then we got to get this over with before the other ones come back." He followed this statement by turning back to hobble his dozing horse, check the slide of his carbine, and start toward the slope Charley Rivas had used to get out of the arroyo.

The other possemen walked ahead to join him, but Charley stopped them all by moving in front and holding up a hand. Charley climbed back out of the gully alone, flattened for a moment or two, then turned to gesture slowly. "Sittin' ducks," he said softly. "Only two don't have their backs to us. Be quiet. They'll hear the least noise."

Charley swiveled back around. The *bandoleros* hadn't moved since his earlier sighting of them. Why they were sitting like that didn't make sense to the scout, until he thought about it.

The longer he watched, the more it seemed they were sitting around someone who was on the ground. He did not reproach himself for not figuring this out earlier. He rarely thought about what had been or what might have been, only about what *was,* which in this instance simply meant some tired Mexicans sitting on the ground.

Where Butler breasted the slope a few yards east of the scout, a *bandolero* was sitting on the ground, carbine between his knees, either gazing disconsolately southward or sleeping.

There was another sentry, but he was south of the camp by at least a hundred and fifty yards. He did not look behind him in the direction of the seated men or the area farther back. As Butler watched, the closer sentry leaned his Winchester against one leg and proceeded to roll a cigarette.

For a moment Butler gave no signal; he

waited until all the posse riders were fanned out along the upper lip of the arroyo on both sides of him, spaced at irregular intervals. Then he spoke quietly to the sentry a few yards ahead. The man hadn't been asleep, or he wouldn't have reacted as he did. He jerked straight up and sat perfectly still. The possemen thought he was probably trying to make up his mind whether or not to be a hero.

The *bandolero* very slowly turned his head as far as it would turn, which was not far enough to see who was directly behind him. He didn't have to see that far anyway; he knew an enemy was back there.

Butler spoke again in a tone that wouldn't carry all the way to the seated *bandoleros*. He said, "Put the carbine down very slowly. Now the Colt." After he had been obeyed both times, Butler said, "Lie facedown with your arms shoved straight out in front of your head."

The *bandolero* found his tongue as he was stretching out. "Don't shoot," he said in English.

Butler asked a question. "What happened down there? Why are those men sitting like that?"

"The colonel, someone shot him. It is a very bad wound."

"Where are the others?"

"Chasing the man who shot him."

Butler gestured for his companions to aim before he called to the seated *bandoleros*. Two of them leapt up, twisting with weapons in their hands. Matthews yelled, "Son of a bitch!" fired, levered up, and continued to fire. The noise was deafening while it lasted. One of the *bandoleros* got off a shot. The bullet plowed dirt fifteen feet in front of the man as he was falling.

When silence returned, two men were sprawled in death; the others had not moved. They remained on the ground, arms rigidly above their heads, unwilling to so much as try to see who was behind them.

The marshal prodded the prone sentry to his feet. The man looked straight at Butler. His eyes widened. The last time he'd seen this gringo, he'd been unarmed and on foot many miles to the west. The sentry ranged a slow gaze along the ragged line of other armed men and let his shoulders sag. He muttered something bitter under his breath in Spanish. No one was interested enough to ask what he'd said.

As they were approaching the camp, the stage driver said, "It was too easy."

Matthews replied curtly. "It ain't over yet."

Butler's deduction was correct. The two dead *bandoleros* and the ones who had been captured had been keeping a vigil beside the soiled, bloody blankets of a man whose face and upper body were protected by a small canvas shelter his companions had erected to keep light out of his face.

Butler stood, Winchester in hand, gazing down. Several possemen were going among plundered saddlebags and bedrolls, but most of them crowded up to look at the wounded man.

The colonel stared back, his face as expressionless as it had been most of the time at Vasquez Spring. But his hawkish features seemed more slack now, more tired or at rest.

Butler sank to one knee, let the harness maker hold his saddle gun, and leaned to study the wound. The bullet had struck the Mexican below the breastbone, in the soft parts that offered little resistance. Someone had tried to stanch the flow of blood, and in fact had succeeded; otherwise there would have been even more blood on the old blankets.

Butler rocked back. He knew where the most serious puncture would be — in back — but he made no attempt to roll the colonel over.

Elwell and Charley Rivas took the captives aside. They and the other possemen were more interested in when the other insurgents might return than they were in a man whose life was leaking out of him a drop at a time.

Not for some time did anyone remember the southward sentry who had been close to the limit of carbine range. Eventually, a search was undertaken, but he was not found.

CHAPTER FIFTEEN

WATER!

Marshal Butler remained with the colonel after other possemen drifted away through the camp, which now resembled a small battle-field.

There were those two dead men Charley had discerned earlier, but although the possemen hunted, they found no more men, dead or alive. That was puzzling, because all the horses belonging to Cartwell and his riders were still hobbled and picking feed a short distance from camp, along with those taken from the possemen.

The two dead men had been riddled. It seemed likely they'd made the same mistake the possemen had made when they'd originally been ambushed west of the Calkins place — they had felt safe.

The *bandoleros* had lived up to their reputation. They had plundered everything in

203

sight, including the pockets of the corpses. Ironically, the only article that had not been moved after being taken off the pack animal was the bullion box. Even now it remained where it had been placed.

Marshal Butler caught Bart Matthews's attention and asked him to look for some whiskey. There had to be some. Two bands of hard riders had tarried at this place; at least one or two from each band would have had some aguardiente, tequila, or pulque. Bart Matthews located two bottles. One was half empty. The other had been broken by a bullet. Matthews took the half-empty one to Butler and put a dispassionate gaze upon the man on the bloody blankets.

The colonel watched everything Butler did. When the marshal leaned to raise the officer's head and tip the bottle, the colonel swallowed twice, then muttered, *"No mas."*

Butler eased his head down, put the bottle aside, and said, "We can rig a horse sling and —"

"No," breathed the dying man, showing the first hint of a smile Butler had seen on his face. In Spanish he said, "Listen, companion, where a man dies is not as important as how he dies." The colonel's black eyes remained clear, even though his color was fading and his body was flattening gently. "How did you do it?" he asked in English, but before Butler could reply, the colonel reverted to Spanish. "I think it will fail. That has bothered me since they sent me up to get Cartwell's horses. They don't understand; they want to get drunk, ride good horses, shoot people, and set fires. They don't want a new government and freedom, they want to plunder. That's all they care about. . . . It will not succeed with men like that. Lean closer."

Butler complied.

"That bothered me even before we came for the horses. On the way back . . . when the revolution collapses down there, the *federales* would hunt me down and shoot me. . . . You understand?"

The marshal thought he did. "You remembered the bullion box."

"Yes . . . the bullion box full of gold and jewels. So I came back. If I got what was in the box I could take the men I'd brought up here, go somewhere north of the line where *federales* and *rurales* could not come, and we could make a settlement and . . . Is it evening?"

Marshal Butler did not reply for a while. He watched the hawkish features softening away from the inner ferocity that normally held them in their fixed, hard expression.

The colonel's eyes widened. He looked

straight at Marshal Butler, straight through him as though he did not exist. Cords in his neck stood out. He pushed hard to raise his upper body with braced elbows and called in Spanish to all the men who had come north with him. But only the captives heard him say, *"Vámonos muchachos, esta gente no nos quiere en es tierra! . . . Vámonos!"*

Butler caught him, eased him down gently, and continued to sit a few moments before rising and turning away. Hans Bechtold, the Peralta blacksmith, was standing nearby, and as he gazed at the dead officer he said, "Marshal, what did he say?"

"He said, 'Let's go, they don't want us in this country.' "

Bechtold showed no expression as he replied. "The son of a bitch was right." Then he turned and walked away with Marshal Butler gazing after him.

Charley Rivas came up to say they had found boot tracks going southwest and the harness maker was tracking them from horseback. "Looked like maybe three or four got away. Why the beaners didn't ride him down, I got no idea."

Butler knew why. He pointed to the bullion box, which was what the *bandoleros* had come for. They cared for nothing else after acquiring it, he explained, except getting as far away

206

as they could, fast.

Charley Rivas shrugged. None of this interested him very much. He pointed out where the animals were. "They're tucked up. If we don't get back to water, we're goin' to have trouble."

Butler agreed, so Rivas said he'd have all the animals brought in and readied for the return trip. Butler asked which way the harness maker had gone, and Charley pointed. "The tracks go southwest. You can't miss them." Then he said, "You want us to wait?" looking as though this was something he did not approve of.

The marshal saw the stage driver and one of the Peralta possemen from Mex-town hauling rocks to pile atop the dead rangemen. "I'll be back directly," he told Rivas, and went after his horse.

Charley had been right; even without shod-horse marks to follow, the marshal would have had no difficulty. Boot tracks were imprinted in the ancient dust. As he rode slowly, it seemed improbable that Jacob Cartwell and his fleeing rangemen could elude Bart Matthews. The land was open and empty, with scatterings of stunted underbrush and dusty caliche soil, the kind that bloomed with an incredible assortment of flowering growth after the infrequent heavy rains, and that otherwise was like the back of the moon — pure desolation.

But there were the erosion gullies, the result of torrential desert rains that could dump several inches of rain in one night.

Anything moving and taller than the stunted stands of underbrush was visible for a considerable distance as long as daylight lasted. But the marshal saw nothing. It worried him. He could not prolong this hunt; the men back at the camp would be getting impatient. Still, he did not want to leave it up to the harness maker to make his way back alone.

His horse had been plodding along at a sedate pace. Then a vagrant scent arrived, and it threw up its head — and Frank saw the rider.

He loped until the horseman also saw him — or heard him — stopped, and turned. It was Bart Matthews, beard stubble and all. When they met, the marshal shook his head. "Time to head back," he said, and when Matthews started to speak, Butler growled at him. "To hell with them. The animals need water. We got to reach it before morning."

Matthews swung a long look around before pointing to the ground. "Not very much farther."

Butler was adamant. "We're going back, and you're coming with us." He gestured.

"They're out there, sure as hell, most likely watching us right now from some gully — with their guns aimed. Bart, we're goin' back. Let this damned country take care of them."

Matthews said nothing until they had the possemen in sight. They were standing with the rigged-out animals ready to ride. Matthews was fishing for the nubbin of his chewing tobacco when he said, "The colonel dead?"

"Yes."

Matthews cheeked his cud before speaking again. "Where are those other *bandoleros?*"

Butler made a guess. "Somewhere out yonder watching us."

When they reached the waiting men, someone passed the word to mount. Charley Rivas led off back the way they had come, and without a word the other men followed him. The old man who had been riding a fat bay horse was now straddling an animal that had shrunk, mostly from dehydration but also from more hard use than it was accustomed to.

The old man did not seem any different, except that his face was hairy now and his clothing was filthy. He still had the extra gun he'd hidden at Vasquez Spring sticking in the front of his britches. Some wag said if that old gun went off, it wouldn't make any difference. Everyone laughed except the old man, who acted as though he had heard nothing.

The day was nearly spent. Both horses and riders welcomed evening and, after that, a darkness that was barely brightened by starshine. The moon had not thickened appreciably, nor would it for a long time. But footing was no problem, and since they did not ride out of a steady walk, progress was slow.

There was not a man among them who could not have slept on hard rocks. Some dozed in the saddle. They did not complain or suggest stopping to rest. Somewhere behind them were skulking *bandoleros* whose interest by now was narrowed down to the bullion box. They had lost everything else, and by now they would probably see no point in concerning themselves with the revolution, only with those who now had the bullion box.

The animals began to lag despite the coolness. Because progress was slow, Frank worried that the animals would be exhausted before they got to water.

Charley Rivas loped ahead for a mile and hunkered beside his horse until he could hear the others. Then he did the same thing again.

It was going to be nip and tuck; they all knew it. They began to have a very valid reason for staying awake. A man on foot in this country without water could not last more than two or three days, even with an obscuring veil during the day.

At daybreak, the exhausted men like scarecrows atop hoof-dragging, head-hung horses rocking along in a kind of dull stupor, Marshal Butler called a halt.

Charley Rivas was riding toward them from the east. When he was close enough to be heard, he said, "Hey! It don't make sense, but there's a water wagon up ahead."

They gazed at Charley as though they thought he was out of his mind or had seen a mirage. He turned in beside Marshal Butler and pointed. "Beyond that low land swell."

Someone growled. "You're crazy, Charley. Ain't no water closer'n the Calkins place."

Rivas stopped smiling, booted his animal into a lope, and with every eye on him, set out for the distant roll in the land and disappeared down the far side of it. The old man on the bay horse raised his reins and clucked at his animal like a farmer. He left the others behind without saying a word or taking his eyes off the land swell.

Butler spoke to the harness maker, who was directly behind him. "We're goin' in that direction anyway."

Matthews nodded his head but growled. "Out of his damned head."

To the surprise of the posse riders, four horsemen appeared on the rim of the land swell waving their hats. Somebody back where the dust was thickest said, "I'll be damned."

The marshal made them walk their horses. Not until he was riding up the low roll of land and recognized two of the waving men, Jess Hobart from the Peralta saloon and Pete Evinrude from the livery barn in town, did he begin to hope.

Atop the low land swell they saw the four-horse hitch and the big old wagon down the far side. There were six or seven men down there, including Charley Rivas. They had flung down four large wooden tubs to be filled from the spigot at the rear of the wagon's big steel-bound wooden stock tank.

For the next fifteen minutes there was enough noise to wake the dead as men swore at greedy horses, fought them away from the tubs, made them wait, then let them drink again.

The paunchy saloonman was red as a beet and profusely sweating, and it was still cool. He met Marshal Butler to one side and, while mopping his forehead with a large white bandanna, he said, "We got to the Calkins place. There was a pitchfork stuck through a piece of paper on the tie rack. It said you were riding dying horses, for us to fill old Calkins's water wagon and head east on the tracks we'd find north of the yard." Hobart stuffed the white cloth into a trouser pocket and watched men and horses at the tubs. "I never worked so hard in my life. It took most of the damned night to get that thing filled from the well. . . . Frank, you look like hell."

Butler nodded. "I feel like hell."

"What happened? Folks in town is fit to be tied. You left town with the whole damned posse. Rumors was all over the place: In'ians got you. *Bandoleros* wiped out the posse in an ambush. You fellers ran toward the border chasin' some *pronunciados*."

Marshal Butler walked down to one of the tubs leading his horse, leaving the saloonman staring after him. The horse, which had been one of the first to drink earlier, drank now with deep gulps and quit of its own accord. Butler was leading the horse away when he was intercepted by the harness maker.

Matthews smiled and asked in a challenging tone, "You a believer now?"

"Believer about what?"

"The water being out here."

Butler's brows dropped a notch. He regarded the older man for a moment before speaking. "Bart, if it rained tomorrow you'd say El Cajónero made it happen. Someone left a note in Calkins's yard for the riders from town to fetch water to us. It could have been anyone. Maybe Hunter Calkins. Maybe one of his riders. Maybe —"

"Maybe the angel Gabriel, but my money's on The Undertaker. I'll tell you something else: We was in that arroyo behind the colonel's bunch. Whoever shot the colonel was a long way around in front of us, somewhere east of the *bandoleros*. Don't seem reasonable one of his men would shoot him, but someone sure as hell did."

Butler's brows drew together. Before he could speak, Matthews said more. "The colonel's son had us flat-footed and dead to rights. . . . There wasn't no one around, was there?"

Butler walked away, leading his horse.

The liveryman, Pete Evinrude, met Marshal Butler as a meager amount of food was being shared, most of it the result of rummaging the Calkins place. Pete was his usual nervous self, but he was smiling as he said, "Is it true you got a bullion box full of loot, an' that some gringo trader dickered three hunnert horses for it to a Mex guerrilla?"

Butler ignored the question to ask one of his own. "When did you fellers from town reach Calkins's yard?"

"Last night."

"Was Calkins and his riders there?"

"Yes, but we didn't visit much. They was dog tired. They not only buried three riders,

214

they also went out to some spring and fetched back a lot of pack harness and saddles and whatnot."

"Which one of you found that note on the tie rack?"

"Jess Hobart. He got up to pee in the middle of the night and saw somethin' white, went over to the rack, and there it was. That note. Y'know, Marshal, it seemed sort of spooky. No one saw whoever stuck it there. Jess routed us all out, we hitched horses, pulled the wagon close to the dug-well out a ways, and made up a bucket brigade. I never handed up so many buckets in my life."

"Where was Hunter Calkins?"

Evinrude shrugged. "I never saw him. I don't think him or his riders heard us. They was dead tired when they left us to bed down."

Butler watched the activity for a while, then squatted in front of his horse. He'd wanted to put his mind at rest: If that had indeed been El Cajónero who had shot the colonel, he'd had to have ridden hard to get far enough east of the possemen to do the shooting, and he couldn't have done that and get to the Calkins yard too. Even a horse with wings couldn't have covered all that ground, unless it had lungs made of leather. And there was one other thing: the colonel had been hit in the body, not between the eyes.

Even if there was such a thing as El Cajónero, he'd have to know the easterly *desplobado* very well, better than anyone Butler had ever talked to. Even if he had been spying on Frank Butler's posse, which he certainly had to have been doing in order to come through the brush and ambush the colonel's son, it would have required more stamina than most men had, and an equal amount of stamina in the horse he rode. If that kind of stamina could be found in a horse, it sure as hell couldn't be found in a man over a hundred years old.

There were other reasons why most of this could not have been done. But all those reasons could not erase the fact that *it had been done!*

Butler was still hunkering when Jess Hobart walked up. Still sweating like a stud horse, the saloonman sank to one knee, fished in his pockets, and said, "Pete told me you acted like us bein' out here with the water wagon was some kind of mystery." Hobart brought forth a crumpled scrap of paper with three tine holes in it. He laboriously smoothed it on his knee and offered it to the marshal, then settled back to wait.

The words were painstakingly printed, which was not unusual in an area where illiteracy was common and even those who could write could not do it well.

The wording was exactly as Hobart had quoted it earlier. When Butler looked up, the beefy man said, "No mystery, Butler. Hell, anyone who knew there wasn't nothin' but scorpions and snakes out here, and who knew you lads had rode this way, would know you were goin' to be ridin' a bunch of wrung-out horses before you got back. It wasn't any mystery you'd need water."

As he was returning the paper, the lawman asked a question. "Why didn't he hang around, Jess? Why didn't he ride in when you first reached the yard and *tell* you we'd be in trouble?"

Hobart's years as a saloonman had taught him several hard-and-fast rules, and one of them was to avoid arguments. He did that now by saying, "Frank, it don't matter. Suppose he hadn't come along? Where would you be right now? . . . Walkin', most likely."

"But —"

"But hell," exclaimed the saloonman, shoving up to his feet. "You know what Bart's saying?"

"I can guess."

"He's sayin' this is the proof El Cajónero isn't no myth. Bart told us about some other things." For a moment the paunchy man stood regarding his friend. Then he shook his head as he made one parting remark. "Whoever he is, or whatever he is, partner, instead of scoffin' you ought to be sayin' a prayer of thanks to him."

Butler went down to get something to eat. Some men welcomed him. Others, like the harness maker and Charley Rivas, looked stonily at him.

Finished eating, the men tanked the horses again and struck out for the Calkins yard. The wagon, which had been down on its axles coming out, rode well up off them on its return.

There was still a slight overcast, which helped to keep the countryside cooler than it otherwise might have been. But as Butler eyed it he told the stage driver he'd seen skies like that in the Peralta country for a lot of years and not once had they brought rain.

Elwell was indifferent. Tanked up and fed, he had only one desire: fifteen hours of sleep. And maybe, afterward, an hour of soaking in the barber's zinc tub out behind the tonsorial parlor. Then a meal that'd make the Mexican cafeman's eyes pop out of his head.

They rattled into the yard in midafternoon. Calkins and his riders were gone, but the wagon they'd used the day before was in front of the barn where the possemen could sort through for their belongings.

Men led their animals out back to be fed, returned to the cool old gloomy barn, dropped down wherever there was straw, and did not move again for a long while.

While Charley Rivas and the harness maker were chaining the prisoners to log uprights over in the blacksmith's shed, the old man who rode the bay horse came to lean in the doorway to watch. But his interest did not seem entirely in the prisoners. He addressed Charley, probably because he thought Rivas would be more likely to speak out than Matthews would be, at least on the topic that had brought the old man over here.

He said, "Charley, you believe in El Cajónero?"

Rivas looked up. "Do you?"

The old man settled more comfortably in the doorway before answering. "Well, I've seen them gold coins he tosses in at folks during the night."

"Isn't that good enough for you?"

"Not exactly. Lots of gold coins around. Not everyone'd give 'em away like he does. But, Charley, I've heard that story since I first come here as a child. He's got to be older'n I am, and I can tell you riding around all night, then ridin' back, then shootin' someone, then bein' somewhere else . . . Besides, the way I heard it he only goes after someone who picks on folks in Mex-town."

Rivas rose, studied the prisoners, their

chains, and was wiping his palms down his trouser legs when he said, "Far as I know, that's what he does."

"But last night —"

Rivas interrupted. "That young feller Cartwell's Texan busted up inside. He was from Mex-town."

"Yeah, I know that, but —"

Charley walked out into the yard. Behind him the harness maker stood gazing at the old man. Eventually he said, "You got to be hit over the head? You can ask questions until the cows come home and all you really got to do is look at the facts."

The old man's eyes widened. "You believe in him, Bart?"

"As sure as you're standing there. Now I got to bed down. No tellin' when Frank'll take a wild hair and start yellin' for us all to get astride again."

Chapter Sixteen

THE RIDE BACK

Just before dawn, Marshal Butler arose. He did not rouse the others, but he made enough noise rigging out the horse he'd reclaimed from the Cartwell remuda to awaken people anyway.

While the others were cursing, reaching for their boots and lustily clearing their pipes, Frank went over to the smithy.

The prisoners were awake. They looked haggard as they eyed Marshal Butler in the doorway. One captive stared hardest, and he was the man Butler spoke to. "Tell me what happened after we left."

Colonel Esparza's son shrugged. "He hit me on the head. Then he untied me. That's all I can tell you."

"What did he look like?"

The youth turned irritable. "How would I know? I was facedown in the dust, remember?

221

He came up behind me. That's all I knew until I came around with my horse tied to a bush and could move my arms."

Butler considered the youth for a while as sounds of stirring men began to fill the yard. The other prisoners watched him in silence. Eventually the youth fidgeted under Frank's stare and said, "When are you going to feed us?"

Butler said nothing. The sounds of men calling back and forth increased. Hunter Calkins and his riders were over near the barn too. Frank recognized Calkins's voice.

The marshal looked at the other prisoners, then addressed a graying older man with a badly pockmarked face. "You chased the man who shot the colonel?"

The *bandolero* bobbed his head. "Yes."

"Did you catch him?"

"No, señor. We couldn't find him. We looked very hard." The *bandolero* glanced around at his companions as though for verification, and they dutifully nodded.

"Which direction did he take?" Butler asked.

The graying man started to gesture, remembered the chains, and desisted. "East for a while, then north into some *malpais*." The man shrugged again. "It was black rock. We could not read his sign up there. But we still searched. For a long while. Then we heard shooting and rode back far enough to see all your possemen down there. So we watched. When you were ready to ride away, we followed you."

"Only five of you?"

The Mexican stared at Marshal Butler. "Because we saw you load the bullion box on a mule. There wouldn't be any other reason, señor."

"Did you see the man who shot the colonel?"

"No. Only a glimpse. From a distance."

"Was he a large man dressed in black and riding a black horse?"

"No, señor. He was not large, and he was riding a *grullo* horse."

Butler turned as Bart Matthews walked up to say the possemen were ready to load the prisoners and head for Peralta. Butler was agreeable, but as the captives were crossing the yard under the hard gaze of the watching possemen, he tapped the colonel's son and pointed to a horse whose reins were looped over one of the big rear wheels of a wagon. Butler's own animal was also tied there.

He stood with the youth until the prisoners had been put astride, hands lashed in back, lead ropes to the saddle horns of possemen. The pockmarked *bandolero* gazed at the Cartwell mule carrying the bullion box and wanly shook his head.

Hunter Calkins came up, nodded, and said, "The harness maker told me about what happened last night." Calkins looked rueful. "Couldn't prove any of it by me. By the time we got back, we'd put in a full day. I was asleep before I climbed into bed."

Butler thanked the stockman for the use of his horses, promised to take up the matter of restitution for the food and horses, shook Calkins's hand, and jerked his head for the young *bandolero* to mount up. He did not tie the *bandolero*'s arms in back, but he took both of the mount's reins.

As they were lining out of the yard, someone called to Calkins. "Keep your powder dry."

Calkins laughed.

It was chilly. Dawn was near, so visibility was fair. But Charley Rivas loped ahead anyway. When they were well under way, Marshal Butler turned toward Elias Esparza. "Where were you when the fight started?"

The youth was not in a good mood, which was understandable. He took his time answering. "I was there," he eventually said, and Butler contradicted him.

"No, you weren't. I'll ask you one more time. When we came up there was a sentry northward, near the lip of the arroyo we came up by. There was another man a long way southward. I don't know what became of him, except that he must have run for it. And there were three men sitting with their backs to us beside the colonel. One more time: Where were you?"

The youth glared straight ahead without answering until Marshal Butler leaned and spoke again. "Where did you get the *grullo* horse? When you caught us, you were riding a bay horse."

The implication did not become clear to the younger man until they had covered about a hundred feet. Then he turned and looked steadily at Marshal Butler. He said nothing for a long time, then spoke as he turned back facing the country ahead.

"I couldn't let him do it."

"Do what?"

"Take all that gold and stay up here to make a settlement."

"He told you he was going to do that?"

"Yes. Right after we recovered the bullion box and those gringos fled. He said our revolution would fail. He told me the *pronunciados* were only interested in plundering, that when the route armies caught up with them, our side would be defeated. . . . He was going to abandon the revolution."

Butler watched the younger man's profile,

then almost imperceptibly wagged his head. Youth and idealism. One went with the other. Maybe the colonel had known that too, which might be why he'd talked to his son as he had.

"You shot him?" Butler asked.

"Yes. I couldn't let him betray the revolution."

"Your own father?"

"Yes. You don't understand. I waited until they were eating. I walked out to the nearest horse —"

"A *grullo?*"

"Yes. I walked out, caught him, saddled up and mounted . . . aimed, and fired. Then I ran as hard as I could." The youth was silent for a long time before continuing. "I watched the men trying to find me and crossed a glass-rock slope. They were still up there searching when I turned back and reached camp."

"After we got control?"

"Yes."

"Why didn't you run for it?"

"Because I believe in the revolution. . . . It wasn't hard in the confusion to join the others and get captured." The youth shot Butler a look. "The revolution matters; it can't fail. My country is being ruled by an old bandit who cares for nothing but himself."

Butler rode along for a while in silence before asking another question. "Did your father know who it was that shot him?"

The youth shrugged. "I don't think so. None of them did." He turned. "How long did it take for him to die?"

"A long time. You shot him through the body. He bled to death, but it was a long while."

Silence settled between them again. Up ahead, Charley Rivas looked small in the distance. Matthews and the old man with the bay horse were leading Cartwell's mules. The old man seemed no different than he had the day they had ridden out of town, except that his face was covered with a scraggly gray beard and his clothing was filthy.

Butler rode along watching the old man. He was tough and he was old, but not a hundred years old.

The youth eventually asked how the water wagon happened to be waiting behind the land swell, and Butler told him about the note. He also told him the legend of El Cajónero, which the youth seemed to accept without question. Butler made a soundless sigh. Mexicans on both sides of the border seemed to ingest superstition with their mothers' milk.

Butler had the solution to the mystery of how El Cajónero had shot the *bandolero* officer — he *hadn't*.

That settled one point for Marshal Butler, but it left other points in limbo. He asked the youth again if he hadn't caught a glimpse of the man who had knocked him senseless from behind, and as before the answer was short.

"I told you," young Esparza said. "I don't even remember him coming out of that thicket. All I know is that someone hit me on the head and when I came around I was free, with my horse tied nearby. . . . You think it was this El Cajónero? Why would he let me go?"

Butler made a death's-head grin. "Why would he do most of the things they say he does?"

"You don't sound like you believe in him."

That was not easy to answer either. "Well . . . all I know, Elias, is that the grandfather of people in Peralta knew of him, and I've yet to meet anyone who is maybe a hundred and fifty years old."

The youth said no more.

The chill dissipated as the sun rose. Visibility was perfect. A startled coyote burst out of a thicket as the cavalcade passed and became a streak of tawny fur as it fled. Perhaps if Hunter Calkins had been present the coyote would have been shot. But the posse riders were from town; they had little reason to feel as bitterly toward coyotes as stockmen did.

The stage driver came up to say one of the captives had told him he had tried to find Jacob Cartwell and the men who had escaped with him, and that he had tracked them due south. The driver then gestured. "We're goin' due east. If Cartwell could make real good time — maybe while we was sleepin' last night — he just might be somewhere up ahead. An' if he is, sure as hell he's goin' to see us crossing in front of him."

They were passing through brushy country again. Although Marshal Butler did not believe Cartwell would run all night to get this far south, he loped ahead to tell Charley what the stage driver had said. Charley began to angle around so that the cavalcade would not approach any of the northward thickets. He also unshipped his Winchester and rode with it across his lap.

When Butler got back where the others had halted, he leaned to catch the reins he'd dropped and straighten up with them. His prisoner scoffed. "It's too far. No one on foot could get this far from where we caught the gringo horse trader."

Butler thought the youth was probably right, but he had learned long ago that caution kept a lot of people out of an early grave.

When they finally had rooftops in sight,

Butler twisted to look back. Hell, his strap-steel jail cells would be full to the seams.

He settled forward to wrestle again with some of the inexplicable things that had happened. He was engrossed in thought when Charley stopped stone-still up ahead and sat his horse like a wooden carving.

A murmur ran down the line. There was an emigrant wagon up ahead that seemed to be listing to one side, which meant a broken wheel. A rawboned large man with an unruly shock of iron-gray hair was leaning on it watching the horsemen approach. A woman wearing a shawl and bonnet peered over the listing tailgate until the man said something, then disappeared inside and eventually climbed down from in front with a long-barreled rifle, which she handed to the man.

Butler passed Elias Esparza's reins to the nearest posseman and loped ahead. Charley looked back and waited. When they met, Charley said, "Somethin' strange, Marshal. When they first seen me, there was three or four of 'em working at raising the back end of the wagon. Now there's only the man and the woman."

Butler freed the tie-down over his holster and began walking his horse. Charley rode with him, but without taking his right hand off the carbine in his lap. When they were within hailing distance, Butler called ahead. "Mister, get the rest of them out of the wagon."

For a moment the man did not move, and when he did he only twisted far enough to lift the soiled old canvas and speak to someone inside the wagon.

Farther back, the posse was watching. They saw the same thing Butler and Charley Rivas saw: rifle barrels, one over the tailgate, the others from beneath the old canvas.

The man raised the gun he was holding, balancing it across his body with both hands as he called back. "Who are you?"

Butler's reply was brusque. "Marshal Butler from Peralta, with some *bandoleros* and possemen. Who are you?"

"Emigrants trying to find the southerly route out to California. Our destination is Oregon. . . . We broke a wheel."

"You got a spare?"

"Yes. We was fixin' to put it on when we saw you coming. If you're really the law, the Lord be praised. Since we cut off from the others to come down here, we've been scouted up by just about everyone."

"Did you go through Peralta?"

"Yes sir, we did, an' we got the feelin' we wasn't welcome. . . . But we're used to that." The man grounded his rifle, but the other guns did not waver. "Come ahead," he called. "Just you two."

Butler eased up his rein hand. As he and Charley rode ahead, Rivas said, "Havin' a family like that'll pretty well keep him safe."

Butler said nothing. He had a glimmer about these people, and if he was right it would explain why they hadn't been welcomed in Peralta — and, for that matter, very few other places.

He and Charley halted about twenty feet back and saw the ratchet wheel-jack in place. It had not yet been raised. There was a spare wheel lying nearby. The wheel on the near rear side had four broken spokes. All this supported what the old man had said. But the rifles inside the old wagon were still aimed and, presumably, cocked.

Butler leaned on his saddle horn. "Goin' to Oregon?"

"Yep. We been a long time on the road, mister."

"By any chance you folks from Council Bluffs?"

The man inclined his head. "An' other places. Originally from Illinois."

Butler let go a long breath and continued to lean on the saddle horn. "You're a long way from Oregon, friend. The road you're lookin' for is a few miles south. But there's a war goin' on down in Mexico. You'd be better off to go due north to one of the freighter roads and go west up there."

The man had been studying Butler. He relaxed against the wagon. "I'm obliged," he said. "My name is Jason Lee."

The marshal nodded. "This is Charley Rivas. I'm Frank Butler."

"The law from that town back yonder?"

"Yes. Farther back is a posse and some prisoners. . . . Mister Lee, you mind a personal question?"

The man stiffened. He had reason to anticipate the question; just about everywhere they'd halted for the past months, people asked the same thing. "Depends on how personal," he replied.

"Are you Mormons?"

"We are."

Butler smiled. "Go north to the first freighter road, then go due west. And every place you find water, top up your barrels. It's dry country until you angle back southward in California, and even then water's hard to find."

"Thank you, Marshal."

"Need some help with the wheel?"

"No, but we're obliged you asked."

Butler stood in his stirrups, flagged for the riders farther back to come ahead, then took

Charley with him southward of the stranded wagons. When they could make out more details of Peralta, Charley said, "You see them women? They're all about the same age. Couldn't be his wife and daughters."

Butler's reply startled the dark man. "They're his wives."

"All three of them?"

"Yes. You've heard of Mormons, haven't you, Charley?"

"No. Not that I remember. You mean they can have more than one wife?"

"As many as they can support."

They were on the outskirts of town, with the sun sliding off center, before Charley spoke again. "Just how does a man go about becoming a Mormon?"

Up ahead, several men shouted. They had seen both parties of possemen returning. Their shouts were taken up throughout Peralta. Butler forgot to answer Rivas as people, mostly men and boys but also a few women, started to run out of town in the direction of the sunken-eyed, filthy, unshaven, and gaunt possemen.

Butler did not notice Charley stand in his stirrups looking back toward the crippled wagon, which was now standing higher as the new wheel was being bolted into place.

Chapter Seventeen

THE RETURN

Butler entered town from the west, and the excited people who had rushed to greet the returning possemen finally saw the prisoners. A lot of the relief and enthusiasm diminished as they stood and stared.

Elias Esparza, still being led by Marshal Butler, spoke dryly. "Friendly people, Marshal."

"What did you expect? Border jumpers with bullet belts crossed over their chests been raiding and killing up here for years."

By the time Butler was tying up at the rack in front of the jailhouse, his posse riders had begun to slough off, some toward Evinrude's barn, others toward their homes. The old man on the bay horse hovered in front of the jailhouse to watch the prisoners being herded inside. When that job had been done, he whooped and invited other possemen to Jess

Hobart's place for a drink, and got enough takers to leave only a middling crowd of silent onlookers out front.

Butler locked his prisoners in the two strap-steel cages of his jailhouse, smiled, and walked away. As he was barring the massive, steel-reinforced door between the cell room and his office, John Grover walked over from his general store with a flour-sack apron rolled up and tucked into the waistband of his britches. He saw the pile of belt guns atop the desk and pursed his lips in a soundless whistle. As he started to speak, the roadway door was flung open and two straining possemen walked in carrying the bullion box. Grover's eyes flew wide as they put the box down, nodded, and walked out, closing the door behind them.

The lawman sank down and leaned back as he nodded in the direction of the box. "Open it," he told the merchant.

Grover leaned to free the hasp and lift the lid. He seemed turned to stone as he stood in that uncomfortable position staring. When he finally dropped the lid and turned, Marshal Butler said, "I got no idea about whoever originally owned that stuff, and if I did, I don't know about getting it back to the owners with a war going on down there. If they shoot people for their boots, what would they do to someone with that loot?"

236

The merchant was not interested in the marshal's words. He was interested in the value of the box's contents. As he turned toward a bench to sit down, he asked, and Butler gazed at the box dispassionately and shrugged. "Damned if I know. We haven't counted the money nor looked real close at the other things."

Grover's eyes widened. He looked almost indignant. "How long have you had the box, Marshal?"

"Since yesterday."

"And you haven't tallied it? Marshal, there is a fortune in that box."

"Uh-huh, and I figure the man who traded three hundred horses for it'll be along — if he's still alive — to claim it."

"Marshal! Those things were stolen from churches! They were looted from homes and haciendas!"

Butler gazed at the merchant. "Would you try to find the owners and return it, John?"

"Of course!"

Butler's laugh was mirthless. "Sure you would." He stood up. "I'm dirty, hungry, and dog tired." He went to the roadside door and held it open. After the storekeeper had departed, Butler went back to his chair and sat awhile gazing at the box.

Stripped of all extraneous considerations,

the bullion box belonged to Jacob Cartwell. He had traded three hundred horses for it. That the loot had been stolen from a number of sources, mostly from churches in Mexico, was for someone else to sort out. Butler's job was to return the appropriated property to whoever he knew owned it.

He left the jailhouse, locked up from out front, and went to the cafe, where men were lined up along the counter like buzzards on a fence waiting for an old cow to die. He had scarcely found a seat before the questions began. The Mexican cafeman walked up, rolled his eyes, and yelled over the voices for Butler's order. After he had given it, he answered questions until a weasel-faced, skinny-eyed man built like a toothpick said, "I heard you rode right into an ambush, Mister Butler. I also heard when someone found a gun and give it to you, you didn't make no effort to get the drop on some feller named Cartwell."

The voices died away. Butler and the malicious-eyed man looked steadily at each other. Eventually Butler said, "Sort of big odds with one gun among us and maybe thirty or so guns against us. The ambush? I sure did; rode right into it — but our purpose was to find those sons of bitches, so we found 'em."

The cafeman returned with food. As he was

placing it atop the counter in front of Butler, the sharp-featured man started to speak again. The cafeman turned on him with fire in his eyes. "Where was you when the committee rode out? In fact, where was you when Jess and Pete and the others rode out later? If you come in here to make trouble — don't! Or I'll throw you out on your face!"

The cafeman's ire dampened the mood all around. Some diners paid up and departed; others went back to their meals in silence.

Butler winked at the Mexican cafeman. "I need a big bucket of stew and a bucket of coffee for my guests across the road. . . . By the way, did you ever hear of a *bandolero* called Colonel Esparza?"

The cafeman straightened up, still scowling. He got a deep crease across his forehead before he answered. "No. Not that I remember. In Mex-town we hear many names from down there." The man shrugged beefy shoulders. "Esparza's a common name, Marshal. But I can ask around."

Butler replied as he picked up the eating utensils. "Naw. It's not that important."

The cafeman went back to his cooking area, and one by one the other diners departed, no doubt confident they could get the full story up at Hobart's place, where as many of the possemen who cared to after all they'd been through would gather along the bar. Among the imbibers at the saloon was the old man who had ridden back to town on a thinned-down bay horse. He would prove to be a source of tall tales for as long as others would pay for the drinks to prime him. Inevitably, as time passed, the feats of others would diminish in importance as the feats of the old man became more heroic.

Marshal Butler took the buckets back, fed his prisoners, refused to be drawn into any conversation with them, and took the empty buckets back to sit beside the roadway door until he returned them. A number of questions required answers. One was what, exactly, he was going to do with the captured *bandoleros*. They had invaded the United States. They hadn't actually perpetrated any crimes that he knew of. In fact, they had made a point of not doing anything that would draw attention to themselves, and for a very good reason — three hundred horses desperately needed down in Mexico.

They had attacked Jacob Cartwell, had evidently shot two of his riders. But in Marshal Butler's opinion, that crime had been offset by Mexican losses when he and his possemen had sneaked up out of the arroyo and killed two *bandoleros*.

Butler finally walked up to Hobart's saloon.

He got a surprise. A youngish man who occasionally substituted for Jess was behind the bar. When Butler asked, the man said Jess had straggled in looking like the wrath of God and had gone up to his room at the hotel with strict orders he was not to be disturbed.

Butler took a bottle to a far corner and got comfortable. He was tired, wrung out, and the meal he'd recently eaten at the cafe heightened his sense of drowsiness. But the problems in his mind prevented sleep — for a while, anyway.

On the South Desert the law was most often made, or interpreted, on the spot, and Butler did not want to have to care for those damned *bandoleros* any longer than he had to. He downed a stiff jolt, blew out a flammable breath, and resolved the *bandolero* problem between the first and second drinks.

He would turn the sons of bitches loose, let them take their horses, but not their weapons, and get the hell down where they belonged — with his personal promise that if he ever saw any of them in his territory again, he'd shoot them on sight.

With that problem disposed of, he returned the bottle to the bar, paid for what he'd taken from it, and went up to the rooming house. It was still broad daylight as he kicked out of his boots, sank back on the bed without bothering to remove his shellbelt and gun, and closed his eyes.

When he awakened, the sun was climbing. Other rooming house residents had left the wash house with a slippery floor, soggy towels, and heat that fogged the piece of glass propped in front of the wash basin for the use of shavers.

He bathed, soaked like a shoat, dried off, put on clean clothing, and shaved. He felt a little better. As he returned to his room, Charley Rivas appeared in the ajar doorway looking shiny and rested, fed and capable. He waited until Butler was putting on his hat before speaking.

"The mother of the man that Texan beat to death is waiting for you down at the jailhouse. She asked me to come up and ask if you would talk to her." Rivas saw the look on Butler's face and looked out the window. "What else could I do? He was her youngest son."

Butler jerked his hat low and marched out toward the roadway. When he and Rivas were in sunshine, the lawman finally spoke. "I've had to do this before, Charley, and I'm not very good at it."

Rivas said nothing, only shrugged as they strode in the direction of the jailhouse.

The woman was elderly. She wore the fixed

expression of someone who had been accepting the adversities of life since childhood. Her eyes were swollen from weeping. Charley did not enter the jailhouse with Frank. He'd already spent an hour with the woman and was not eager to be with her now.

Butler removed his hat as he kicked the door closed after himself. He offered a kindly greeting to the elderly woman and went to his desk to sit with clasped hands. He explained as gently and as tactfully as he could what had happened.

The woman already knew. She needed details less than she needed someone to talk to, someone to offer comfort. She raised a wadded small handkerchief to her eyes as she spoke. "He was a good boy, Marshal. He never got into trouble. There was a nice girl, the daughter of a relative of Jésus Obando, the packer . . . I talked to him before he and the packer went south last month. Who would ever think it would be the last time? When he returned, I wanted him to go see the girl. He said maybe. When he returned he was too tired; Señor Obando had left him with the mules down near Angostura, and he'd had to bring them back by himself. Then someone in Mex-town said the committee was going to ride, and he left. He did not even belong to the committee; he believed in the law, Marshal. Mother of God,

I can't understand why it had to be him. He was so young, such a pride to his mother, his brothers and sisters. Marshal . . ." The woman paused to push the wadded handkerchief tightly into her face.

Butler got her a cup of coffee, which she refused. She rose to place a work-roughened hand lightly on his sleeve. "But he did the right thing, didn't he?"

"Yes, señora. I don't know what to tell you. I'll miss him too. The whole town will. Let me do something for you."

"No," she said, lowering the handkerchief and trying to smile. "No, Marshal. He respected you. He said you were fair, that you . . ." She broke down again, but this time she went to the door, pulled it open, and went out into the pleasant early-day sunshine.

Butler watched her heading toward Mex-town from his doorway, continued to stand there after she had passed from sight, and finally crossed to the cafe, which was nearly empty this late in the morning. He got more pails of stew and coffee, then returned. When he went down into the cell room, the prisoners pushed up close with their tin cups. Butler did not ladle it out, but opened the doors, told the men to help themselves, and stood back until they had finished before growling them back inside and locking all but one of them in.

He took Elias Esparza up to the office with him, told him where to sit, and went to lean on the desk. He told Elias what he was going to do with the *bandoleros:* turn them loose.

Young Esparza's eyebrows climbed. He said, "I don't understand you, Marshal. We are your enemies, and we invaded your country."

Butler laughed. "There weren't enough of you to invade a chicken house. Enemies? You're not my enemy unless you want to be. But if any of those men in the cells ever come up here again, I'll shoot them on sight. You make them believe that."

"Yes." Esparza settled against the back of his chair.

Butler stood gazing at the youth. "I guess it's all right to pronounce, because Mexico's had some pretty bad, corrupt governments. But you're young. If you get on a horse and take your guns every time some two-bit revolutionary makes a *grito,* eventually you're going to get killed."

Young Esparza smiled at Butler. "I'll tell you something. I've been on raids north of the border six times, but never have I met any of the people to talk to." The youth shrugged. "Marshal, I killed a man in your country."

Butler continued to lean on the desk, arms

crossed. "I got to tell you, Elias, I think your father was right. What's the sense of everlasting revolutions that don't succeed, or that do succeed, and put men just as bad or worse in the palace in Mexico City? Leave it, start over, raise a family, be a credit to your town."

"I still killed him, Marshal."

Butler went around and sat at his desk. "That'll be on your conscience as long as you live. If I was a vindictive son of a bitch, I'd say that's worse than gettin' hanged. Kid, go back with the others. Think. Think what your father wanted to do. Someday you might decide you owe him something. The only way I know for you to make peace with his memory is to do what he wanted to do."

Young Esparza stood up and avoided the lawman's gaze. "Do we get our horses?"

"Yes. But not your guns."

"When can we leave?"

"After dark tonight."

Esparza's eyes kindled with ironic understanding. "They might try to kill us?"

Butler rose to return the youth to his cell. At the reinforced oaken door he turned and said, "You've raided up over the border six times. Others have done it twice that many times; stolen horses, burned buildings, robbed and plundered. . . ." He opened the door, jerked his head and followed the younger man down to the cell, locked him in, and without another word or glance returned to the office. There he barred the cell-room door and stood a long time imagining the town's reaction when, tomorrow morning, it was discovered that Marshal Butler had freed the *bandoleros*.

Later, when he was stepping up onto the plankwalk in front of Grover's store, the merchant came out drying his hands on his flour-sack apron. He got very close to Marshal Butler and spoke in a conspiratorial voice.

"If you leave the box in the center of your office, sooner or later someone is going to try to steal it whether you lock the jailhouse or not."

Butler agreed. "They sure might." He left the merchant looking after him with his mouth agape.

Bart Matthews was behind the counter at his shop, concentrating so hard on where to place tin templates for a new saddle that he did not hear Butler walk in until Butler said, "Care to take a little ride?"

Matthews turned and spoke as though he had not heard. He pointed to the stretched-flat big cowhide on the worktable. "Look at that! Worse every blessed year."

Butler looked. "Something wrong with it?"

Matthews reddened. "You blind, for Chris-sake! Look here, and there, and down along both sides of the backstrap. You know what them little round marks are?"

"No."

Matthews snorted. "Course you don't. Well, I'll tell you. Them was made by bots. Botflies lay eggs where the critter can't reach. High up in the middle of the back, which happens to be the best part of a hide to use for saddles. Lays them damned eggs, the things burrow down through and stay in there until they're ready to climb out an' fly away. And look at that! Damned scars where they lived. How'd you like to ride a saddle that looked like it had the smallpox? . . . Wait a minute; what did you say?"

"I asked if you wanted to go for a ride."

The harness maker drew up to his full height. His brows dropped, and his eyes bored into the man slouching at his counter. "Last night . . . let me tell you something, Frank Butler, last night after I soaked in hot water and rubbed liniment in places I didn't even know I had, I made a solemn promise: I wouldn't never ride out with another posse as long as I live."

"Bart, the posse's not going. Just you an' me."

The older man's little pale eyes narrowed, turned crafty. "Is that a fact? We been ridin' together for days, and now you figure to go out and want me to ride along. Frank, I ain't over riding with you this last time. I may never get over it. You know how old I am? Well, it don't matter except that I'm too old for ridin' around starving, nearly dyin' of thirst, livin' off scraps and gettin' shot at by damned border jumpers. . . . Where are you going?"

"Just out an' around."

"Oh no, you're not. I've known you a long time, but it just come to me now that you're a connivin' whelp. . . . Riding around where?"

Marshal Butler straightened up off the counter as he replied. "I got all that loot in the stage-company box down at the jailhouse. I got to put it in Grover's big safe at the store. And I got to find Cartwell's carcass. If he isn't dead — and I'm bettin' he is, since no one lasts long out there without water — then I got to find him before he figures out what happened to his loot and comes into town to get it."

The harness maker's eyes widened a little. "An' if he is dead, what then?"

"I don't know. We can talk about it while we're riding. Maybe file a claim against it for that young buck from Mex-town who died at Vasquez Spring, and for the possemen who ended up with it."

"When do you want to go?"

"Before sunrise tomorrow."

Chapter Eighteen

RESOLVING PROBLEMS

Marshal Butler dragooned two townsmen into helping him carry the bullion box across the road. John Grover was waiting in the doorway drying hands that didn't need drying on his apron while looking up and down the roadway. He hadn't been enthusiastic when the marshal had braced him about putting the bullion box in his safe. Not because he believed anyone could blow the safe open — they couldn't unless they used a lot of dynamite — but from years in a more or less lawless country Grover knew that most robberies were accomplished with guns, not blasting powder.

Butler hadn't told him he would be out of town the following day. If he had, Grover would not have consented to provide a safe place for the bullion box.

After the box was safely stored, Grover

watched the pair of helpers who'd carried it, pause to buy a couple of sacks of tobacco before walking out into the roadway. Then he said, "Frank, overnight is all. You got to get it out of here tomorrow."

Butler neither agreed nor disagreed. He smiled and left the store.

Up at Hobart's saloon during his final round of the town, he told Jess Hobart what he had done and asked him to have a couple of the local vigilance committee loaf around down in the vicinity of the general store. Not that he believed an attempt would be made to get the box, but rather to make damned sure no one did. By now everyone knew about it.

Jess, fully rested and back to work, nodded solemnly as he asked a question. "You're not goin' to be around?"

"No. I'm goin' to try and find Cartwell."

"What in the hell for?" exclaimed the saloonman. "That son of a bitch is somewhere out yonder shriveled like a mummy."

"All right. I want to make sure one way or the other, because that loot belongs to him."

"What! After he kept us prisoner and let that Texan beat the lad to death?"

Marshal Butler leaned on the bar. He'd expected cooperation, and this was turning into an argument. "Jess, something's got to be done. The longer we keep that loot in Peralta, the better the chances are that it'll draw trouble."

"What'll draw trouble, Frank, is if you find Cartwell alive and bring him back to town. There's not a man who rode with you that wouldn't like to get their hands on him. By now folks in Mex-town know what he allowed that Texan to do to the lad who died. Messicans can be sons of bitches when they're fired up." Jess leaned on the bar. "You better not find Cartwell alive."

"Will you see that a couple of men watch for trouble at the store?"

Hobart continued to lean. "Yes. When'll you be back?"

Butler had no idea. "As soon as I can. It's a long ride out there."

"You goin' alone?"

"Bart's goin' with me."

The saloonman thought for a moment before pushing back off the bar. He shook his head but said nothing until the marshal was turning. "Frank, one question. If you find him dead — then what?"

"I don't exactly know. I'll have to figure that out when I get back. Just keep that loot safe."

When the lawman reached the rooming house, the man he'd left behind the bar on the opposite side of the road southward was still wearing an expression of monumental disgust.

Bart Matthews eventually strolled over to the bar for a nightcap. The saloonman nailed him with a jaundiced stare and said, "You're crazy."

Matthews's eyes popped wide. He straightened off the bar. "What did you say?"

"Goin' out with Frank to find Cartwell."

"Oh . . . fetch me a drink."

By the time Hobart returned with the bottle and glass, Matthews had had time to order his thoughts. He spoke as he watched the saloonman fill the little glass. "Maybe, but if he finds Cartwell dead, I'll be his witness."

Hobart scowled. "What difference will that make?"

Matthews raised the jolt glass very carefully so as not to spill a drop. "Because if the bastard's dead, why then Frank's got to figure out what to do with all that loot — and he said somethin' about maybe makin' some kind of distribution among the fellers who rode with him."

Matthews dropped the whiskey straight down, unaware of the stare he was getting from the opposite side of the bar until he put the glass down and blew out a fiery breath. Then he smiled. "Jess, a man ought to support his local lawman, wouldn't you say?"

Hobart gained time for thinking by making a wide sweep of the bartop with a damp rag. "He never said any such a thing. You're makin' that up."

"So help me, Jess, that's what he said word for word. An' why not? Hell, after all we went through, dang near dying out there, starvin', get shot at, threatened."

"He can't do that, Bart."

"Yes he can, by Gawd. If Cartwell's dead."

"He'll have heirs."

"Not in the Peralta country, he won't. Besides, he's no better'n a common outlaw. As for handin' back the loot, who knows where it came from?" Matthews refilled his glass and grinned over the rim of it. "Frank's the law. It's up to the likes of you an' me to back him up." Matthews downed his second jolt. His eyes brightened, his lanky body loosened all over, and his sly look appeared. "Jess, you want some Messicans to ride in here and say that loot belongs to them, an' ride away with it? They'd laugh all the way back across the border."

Hobart was not thinking of Mexicans. "Anyone know how much that loot is worth in U.S. money?"

Matthews had no idea, but he could see the crack appearing in the saloonman's lofty principles and acted to widen it. "Thousands, Jess.

Them gold coins alone make a hell of a pile. And all that gold stuff, an' them jewels . . ." The harness maker rolled his eyes, dug out four bits in silver, and dumped it atop the bar. "Keep the change," he said, and walked out of the saloon into a velvety dark night.

Jess Hobart made another big sweep of the bartop, then walked to where a pair of be-whiskered freighters were thumping the bar for service. He did not even look at them as he listened to their requirements and turned to fulfill them.

What bothered him was not that the loot might be distributed, but how such a thing could be done. As he scooped up some silver from the freighters and went along to put it in his cash drawer, he decided Matthews had been right: It *was* up to folks to support what-ever their local lawman did. After all, Frank Butler was a fair man. Over the years Jess had seen him do things that did not seem to be exactly according to book law. But this close to the Mex border on the South Desert, where every lawman was pretty much a law unto himself, Jess had never witnessed any-thing he disagreed with.

The damned army never helped; it never even arrived until ranches and towns had been plundered and burned. They watched the bor-der, made illegal sorties over the line to fetch back some renegade or fugitive, and patrolled or stayed forted up during the soggy season. The army did not interfere with local judicial processes; it knew little about them and did not want to know about them.

Jess closed his saloon after midnight, locked up after hiding the cash drawer under the floor of his storeroom, and stood awhile breathing fresh air before heading for his room at the hotel.

When he passed Marshal Butler's door he hesitated, but there was no light showing under the door. It was too late to rouse folks, so he went along to his own room, got ready for bed, and lay back, arms under his head, staring at the ceiling for a long while. Bart hadn't put an actual dollar value on the loot, but he'd said enough to keep Jess awake a long time.

It was just as well Bart Matthews hadn't knocked on the marshal's door. Frank was not inside. He was down at the public corrals at the lower end of town helping the *bandoleros* rig out. Very little was said, and even then it was in whispers, but there was no doubt about one thing: the *bandoleros* were pleased and might even have felt some gratitude. Every one of them had heard stories of gunfire executions and hangings when their kind had been caught north of the border.

Young Esparza led his saddled horse out of the corral where Marshal Butler was leaning, watching, and smiled in the darkness. "Maybe you should come with us, Marshal." He jerked his head in the direction of the darkened buildings across from the corrals. "What will you tell them? In Mexico if you did this, they would shoot you."

Butler considered the youth. "That's the point I tried to make to you. This isn't Mexico."

"Marshal —"

Someone made a night-bird whistle. Everyone stopped moving and stood perfectly still. Butler turned very slowly to watch the livery barn nighthawk walk into the middle of the alley and stand wide-legged as he mightily yawned and gazed up at the awesome vault of heaven. The sound of trickling water reached as far as the scarcely breathing men at the corrals.

The nightman shuffled a little, then trooped back up the barn runway. The men at the corrals went back to work, only more swiftly now.

When they were ready to ride and led their horses out, Butler told Esparza to make sure they did not run, but walked their animals at a slow, quiet walk until they were well south of town.

Esparza nodded as though he did not need

the instructions. He stood hip-shot with reins dangling from his hand as he looked steadily at Frank Butler. Finally, without a word he turned, swung into the saddle, and softly said, "*Adiós, jefe.* I wish —"

Someone hissed, and Elias reined away and led off out of Peralta at a slow walk.

Butler waited until he was satisfied the liveryman with the weak kidneys would not reappear. Then he went up the dark alley as far as the rooming house, climbed back into his room by the same window he'd climbed out, and sank down fully attired on his bed to wait another couple of hours before arising again.

He overslept.

When he reached the livery barn, Matthews was sitting out front on an old bench looking mad enough to chew horseshoes and spit rust. The nighthawk, having found Matthews poor company, had gone back to the harness room to finish his nap.

Matthews stood up glaring. In a barely restrained whisper he said, "What in the hell — I been waitin' for an hour. I thought you wanted to get an early start."

Butler went after his horse, led it out front, and swung up without a word. But when Matthews would have turned up the main roadway through town, Butler grunted and led him into the west-side alley he'd recently traversed on foot. They left town with every reason to believe no one had seen them.

Matthews offered a piece of jerky with lint on it as a peace offering for his earlier anger. Butler accepted it. They rode quite a while without speaking.

They had several hours of chill to ride through, and even after dawn arrived it still would not be warm for a while.

The harness maker was convinced that if they found anything, it would be the desiccated remains of dead men. Not that this bothered him. He was typical of his kind and time. An enemy was someone to be buried. Period.

They could no longer see Peralta when Marshal Butler swallowed his peppery lump of jerky and said, "I turned the *bandoleros* loose."

Matthews snapped straight up in the saddle. He was too astonished to speak for a while, and when he finally did speak all he said was: "Why?"

"They crossed the line, took delivery of some horses, and that's about it. Every day border jumpers cross the line. Most of the time they kill people and raid all over hell. This bunch just wanted horses. Bart, there wasn't any good reason to hold them."

"Well, hell, they shot up Cartwell's crew."

Butler turned his head. "We'd have done the same thing."

"But we're 'Mericans. You're the law. We'd have a right."

"Bart, folks would have lynched them if they could, and even if we held them, kept them alive until we could get an army judge over here, we couldn't get a conviction for anything but border-jumping, and that'd mean a bawling out from the army, confiscation of horses and — back to Mexico . . . Bart, they'll be back south of the border by morning. I don't think they'll come back. . . . You know where that leaves us?"

"Where?"

"With the bullion box. Let's lope a while. We got lots of ground to cover."

They loped side by side. Matthews squinted until his eyes were nearly closed and asked how in hell they'd find anyone up ahead when the consarned thickets ran east and west from hell to breakfast.

Butler's reply was reassuring without sounding very confident. "No one can move very fast or very far on foot in this country. We didn't see sign of them when we brought the prisoners in from the Calkins place."

"Yeah, but by now they've had time to get that far — if they're not dead in one of them thickets." Matthews's eyes suddenly brightened. "Track 'em," he exclaimed. "Go over toward the ranch, cut north then east, pick up their sign, an' track 'em south."

Marshal Butler gazed at his companion. "By golly, that's a real good idea."

The harness maker looked at his companion with lowering brows. "You was goin' to do that anyway."

"Well, maybe. Somethin' like that. You got any more jerky?"

The harness maker handed over a shriveled stick, and offered something else as well. "You want to keep the saliva flowing, Marshal, try this."

Butler looked at the gnawed plug of molasses-cured and shook his head. "Tried it once. No, thanks."

"You didn't like it?"

"Yeah, I liked it. It didn't like me."

They had been riding almost due west for a long time. The harness maker was scowling long before he asked when they'd turn north.

Marshal Butler's answer was curt. "As soon as we know for a fact they didn't sneak down and steal horses from the Calkins place. Bart, they got to have two things: horses and water. There are only two places they can get 'em out here: Calkins's yard or Peralta. If they get mounted at the ranch, we can track 'em come sunup. If we don't cross their tracks before we get that far east, we'll know that's about what happened. If we *do* cross their tracks goin' south, we'll know they're headin' for town."

Matthews slouched along in silence for a long time. His horse was on slack reins and seemed to reflect the looseness of its rider. Now and then Matthews would turn aside to spray amber, but he said nothing until Frank abruptly drew rein to swing to the ground.

Matthews came out of his reverie and also dismounted. At a great distance behind them, false dawn was firming up. It did not improve visibility very much, especially if a man was watching the ground from the saddle. But if a man walked along leading his horse, he could see tracks very well.

Chapter Nineteen

A LOOSE END

From the place where Butler dismounted there was a long front of underbrush leading north. It was unhealthy looking and not as tall as its equivalent farther west or south. But that would not matter much to men desperate for water and horses, especially after nightfall.

Twice the marshal paused to study the ground and twice he shook his head before continuing to walk. Behind him the harness maker climbed back atop his horse. It did not require two men to seek fresh tracks.

The chill increased. They bundled up inside their coats. Once, they disturbed a small band of wild cattle who had no doubt heard them coming from a fair distance. They leapt out of their beds and fled like the wind. Their noise was heart-stopping for a moment. As Butler resumed his hike, he looked back. Matthews rolled his eyes, eased the six-gun back into its holster, leaned, and spat.

Not a word passed between them for a long time as the sky hovered between fish-belly gray and pewter. But visibility steadily increased right up to the moment when Marshal Butler halted, grunted, and sank to one knee.

Matthews joined him, trailing a pair of rawhide reins. Eventually he said, "Ain't enough light to tell how many, but sure as hell they crossed out of the underbrush walkin' south — an' that means they decided to head for town, not the Calkins place."

Butler rose, dusting his leg as he replied. "Calkins is closer. . . . They must have had canteens along."

Matthews was indifferent as he stood looking at the boot tracks. "How long ago, I wonder. Maybe late last night?"

"Good thing it wasn't an hour ago, or they'd have heard us."

Matthews was turning to mount when he said, "We better get back to town."

Marshal Butler replied from the saddle. "No. I'll ride ahead. You sashay out a ways in case they changed course. Sunrise is close. Be careful, Bart. A man on a horse riding through this scrub sticks up like a sore thumb."

Matthews said nothing as they turned southward. Up ahead, where there were infrequent stands of scrub, he veered slightly to his left. He watched Butler from time to time, because the marshal was following the fairly fresh boot tracks. When Butler halted, Matthews did likewise. He rode over when the marshal beckoned.

They sat awhile gazing at pressed-flat ground where men had rested, then stood in their stirrups. But there was nothing to be seen southward.

Matthews rubbed a stubbly jaw. "It'd help to know how far ahead they are. This is pretty fair bushwhacking country. A man could lie on his belly down there and let you get close enough to hit you between the horns with his eyes closed."

As Butler resumed riding, he studied the eastern sky. The pewter look was becoming streaked with soft pink. It would not be long before the sun popped over the curve of the world. That would be considered a blessing by just about every other creature on the South Desert. But not by Butler and his riding partner, who would be exposed from the saddle horn up as they worked their way through underbrush following boot tracks.

Butler swung off moments before the sun jumped up to flood the world with brilliance. Matthews did the same, grumbling to himself he had a lifelong conviction that if the Good

Lord had meant for people to walk he'd have given them four legs and would have given horses two legs. Obviously, since he hadn't done that, his notion was for men to ride horses, not walk ahead leading them.

Dismounting did not entirely mitigate the peril. There were clearings of sterile ground where nothing grew. Anyone crossing them could be seen by watchers, and neither of the men from Peralta thought for a moment that Cartwell and his riders would not be keeping a watch rearward as well as forward.

There was one blessing: the cold eventually diminished enough for them to remove their coats and stop long enough to lash them behind their cantles.

They each had a canteen, but thus far had not used them. Nor did it seem likely that they would have to for another hour at least.

The tracks Frank Butler was following were alternately very clear and less clear where Cartwell and his crew had crossed caliche hardpan. In places, desert winds had scoured away all the dust. But Butler had no difficulty. When the tracks seemed very fresh he stopped, watched for movement in the near distance, then started out again, a little more slowly and a lot more warily.

Matthews had a suggestion to make at one of their halts. One of them could ride out and around and be down where the fugitives emerged into open country. The flaw to that, as Butler pointed out, was that the men they were pursuing were also watching ahead, and if a horseman appeared in the open country southward, they would see him as surely as God had made prickly pears.

Matthews went over where he'd been keeping abreast and continued walking, but with his Winchester at his side, held there by a hand around the steel and a finger inside the trigger guard.

Once, he thought he saw something to the west, some distance to Butler's right, but when he squinted all he saw was a fair-sized thicket of thornpin. Although he watched for a while, he did not see movement. A man's nerves played tricks in situations like this. He jettisoned his cud, cleared his pipes, and continued to walk, thinking back to his old grandmother — dead many years now — who had begged him to leave off driving other people's cattle, find a nice job in some town, and settle down.

She had been right; that's what he should have done. He *had* settled down in a town, but many years later than she had meant. And that hadn't really been what she'd meant anyway. She'd meant Bart should have a family of his own, and sure-Gawd it was too late for that.

He looked over where Butler was hiking along, saw the tie-down thong hanging loose, and freed up his own belt gun too.

Some fat birds about the size of quail sprang into the air a fair distance ahead and went flinging in all directions. Bart stopped in his tracks; to the west of him, Frank Butler was also dead-still. They exchanged a look, tethered their animals to the thornpin, and started stealthily ahead. It did not have to be some belly-down son of a bitch waiting in ambush. It could just as easily have been foraging coyotes that had flushed the birds. Except that coyotes, with the scent of men in the air both northward and southward, would have departed long ago.

The sun was climbing, and there was a hint of heat. The overcast had not reappeared, which probably meant that the desert springtime was passing, that shortly now summer would arrive and with it the most grueling time of the year on the desert.

A heat haze was in the offing. It was nothing either of the stalking men could see, and were not thinking about in any case. But when it arrived, the perfect visibility that usually accompanied early summer would be noticeable only when the wind blew. Otherwise, distances had a faintly smoky, blurred indistinctness.

Butler almost stepped on a huge, hairy spider. The creature waited until the very last second, when the boot was descending, then went sideways faster than the eye could follow.

Some distance to Butler's left, the harness maker was slackening until he was barely moving at all. He reminded Marshal Butler of a hunting dog: his eyes were fixed on something ahead, movement keyed to moments when whatever he was watching looked elsewhere long enough for Bart to take another forward step.

Butler could see nothing, so he halted in place to watch as Matthews repeated his start-and-stop movement several times, then sank abruptly down in the scrub brush. Butler took the cue and also sank down, but he had neither seen nor heard anything — except his heart in its dark place, and that didn't count.

Time passed. The coolness subtly changed to heat, the sky began to acquire one of those brassy-blue glazes, and the sun seemed pegged in one place.

Matthews was stalking something, inches at a time on all fours. Butler leaned to locate his partner and saw only underbrush. He watched for thornpin limbs to quiver and listened for the faint sound of a body moving through the brush.

There was not a sound for a long time.

Eventually a man's voice sounded quietly. "Put the gun down!"

Butler got lower in the underbrush. He could not see very well, so he listened.

"Move that gun, you son of a bitch, and I'll kill you!"

There was no mistaking who had spoken. Butler considered crawling ahead on all fours but did not do it. At this moment the slightest movement or noise would be the kind of distraction the harness maker did not need.

It was a long wait until Matthews spoke again. "Now the six-gun!"

The pause was not as long this time.

"Now stand up with your hands atop your head. . . . Mister, you horse me around and I'll blow your guts out. *Stand up!*"

Frank Butler saw the man rise. He was dead ahead about fifty feet. If Matthews hadn't detected him and Butler had kept to his onward course, he would have walked right down the man's gun barrel. Butler got to his feet. The filthy, bronzed man looking at Matthews turned abruptly when he detected other movement. He and Marshal Butler looked straight at each other.

Matthews did not stand up until he heard the lawman speak. "How far ahead is Cartwell?"

The ragged, sunken-eyed man looked from

one of them to the other without speaking until Matthews cocked the Winchester he was holding belly high.

"I don't know how far ahead. Maybe a mile."

"Did you see us?" Butler said, and the rangeman nodded. "As soon as the sun come up."

"And you were left behind to bushwhack us?"

The rangeman took his time replying this time. "To let you go by, then get your horses."

Butler and Matthews approached the man. They recognized him from Vasquez Spring but did not know his name and did not ask it now. The range rider waited until Matthews had kicked his weapons away, then asked if he could put his hands down. Matthews nodded. "Yeah. What'd you fellers do for water?"

"Used up what was in our canteens. Made it last until about midnight last night, then figured to reach Peralta before things got bad."

Matthews looked stonily at the prisoner. "You got any idea how far you are from Peralta?"

"Well, not exactly, but Jacob'd been there before. He said we could make it."

Matthews wagged his head. "You'd have done better to go back to the Calkins place.

They got both water an' horses. It's a long way to Peralta on foot."

"Jacob said we'd head for Peralta. There'd be horses an' water there too."

Butler eyed the man. "And something else?"

The rangeman turned his attention back to Butler. "Yes, something else . . ."

Butler relaxed, leaning on his Winchester. "Old fuzzy-face don't give up, does he? That bullion box is locked in a big steel safe, and the whole town knows about Cartwell. You'd stand about as much chance of getting that Mex loot as a chicken in a fox run."

The rangeman began to relax a little. He looked from one of them to the other. "You gents got some water?"

They had canteens on their saddles, but neither of them made any move to get them. Matthews shrugged in Butler's direction. "Shootin' would make too much noise. I'll split his skull instead."

The rangeman turned gray beneath his tan. Butler interceded by asking a question. "How many were with you?"

"Three, countin' Jacob. Those double-crossin' *bandoleros* hit us when —"

"We know about that."

Matthews stepped close, yanked off the man's trouser belt and shellbelt, and pointed to the ground, his intention clear. The rangeman's filthy, torn shirt darkened with the sweat of fear. "You can't leave a man lyin' out here tied up."

Matthews was unrelenting. "Sure we can. It won't be for long. By tomorrow you'll begin to shrivel, but by then you won't care."

The rangeman addressed the badge on Frank Butler's shirtfront. "That's murder, for Chrissake!"

Butler asked a question that surprised both the other men. "Where is Cartwell from?"

"Texas. Originally, anyway. He moves around buyin' an' sellin' horses. Some Messicans come onto him and offered to trade for three hunnert head, which was about all he had."

Butler interrupted. "We know about the horse trade. You and the others rode for him?"

"Yes. After he made the deal with the Messicans, we hired on."

"Is Cartwell married?"

The captive stared. "Jacob? Married? If he ever was, I never heard of it. He sure as hell ain't never rode off while I been riding for him. Naw, he ain't married. Once he told us around a supper fire the worse thing a man could do was get into double harness with a woman."

Matthews gazed at the marshal. Butler looked back, and the harness maker's lips lifted in a faint smile. What the bushwhacker had said did not preclude the possibility of marriage, but it almost did. As far as Matthews was concerned, it was a satisfactory reply. He said, "I'll fetch the horses if you want to watch him," and turned away.

As soon as the harness maker was no longer in sight, the rangeman made an impassioned plea not to be left to die under the sun in the middle of a waterless desert.

Butler said nothing. He watched the man and waited. When Matthews returned leading their animals, Butler took the reins of his horse, upended the carbine, and dumped into the boot. As he was facing back around, Matthews spoke to the rangeman.

"I got an idea, mister. You walk ahead of us on Cartwell's tracks. Don't look back nor make any signals with your arms. Now pick up that carbine, shuck out the loads, and start walking. When you see your friends up ahead, you stop and point 'em out to us. . . . Mister, you so much as sneeze and I'll shoot you in the back. Now, pick up the gun and empty it."

As the reprieved rangeman was levering his Winchester empty, he said, "He knows you're back here. If I shot a couple of times, he'd think —"

"Just shut up and walk," Butler exclaimed.

"Remember something: You'll be between us and them. Now start walking."

Their prisoner stood staring until Matthews swore and shoved his canteen at the man. Then, with a growl, Bart yanked it away before the prisoner had finished drinking. "You want to founder yourself? *Walk!*"

Fresh sweat burst out all over the rangeman. He looked at Matthews, poised to ask a question. Matthews leaned, pushed his Winchester into the man's soft middle, and cocked it.

The range rider turned and started walking.

The heat had settled into something that would get worse as the day advanced. The distance they had to cover to reach Peralta was not great for mounted men, but it would take all the starch out of anyone walking through it on foot.

The marshal and harness maker rode awhile, then dismounted and led their animals. It was Butler's opinion that Cartwell would halt somewhere up ahead where the underbrush provided meager shade. Even if his riders were like the prisoner — lean, sinewy individuals capable of walking a long distance — Jacob Cartwell was not. He was large and fleshy and heavy enough to have to lift each boot out of ancient dust and, eventually, gravelly earth to continue walking.

But the sun was directly overhead before

they came upon a place where men had sat in breathless shade. The prisoner needed another drink. This time he drank from the lawman's canteen, and as he handed it back he said, "We agreed to go down there an' get his loot back for him, because he promised each of us enough of it to live a long time doin' nothing. But I'm not goin' to get myself killed. . . . He's not goin' straight into that town. He's goin' to lie over until night."

That did not surprise Frank Butler. In fact, as they'd moved along he had considered Cartwell's options, and the one he was surest of was that the stockman would attempt nothing in broad daylight with the town wide awake.

He told the rangeman Cartwell could not get at the loot even if he had dynamite, because it was locked inside a big steel safe. Then Butler smiled at the man. "And it's not at the jailhouse. He's got to find it."

They were preparing to move out when their prisoner spoke again. "I never been in Peralta. Jacob has. At least he told us he had. . . . Marshal, he ain't no schoolboy."

Matthews studied the position of the sun, drank warm water from his canteen, and looped it back around the saddle horn. When they struck out again, the prisoner said, "Them Messicans was after the box when they snuck up on us and we figured they was fifty miles away headin' south. Marshal, that leader of theirs struck me as being real *coyote*. If he didn't get the box, he sure as hell ain't goin' to forget it."

Butler said, "He's dead. He got the box and we got it from him."

"Where are his riders? They —"

"They won't come back for it. Save your breath. You're going to need it before we reach Peralta."

A red-tailed hawk was making wide, circling maneuvers overhead, each circle overlapping the previous as the bird allowed roiled upper air to carry it steadily away.

The hazy heat came, and Butler left his companions to scout ahead. They were approaching open country not far from town. If Cartwell stopped there to rest and hide in underbrush before attempting to cross the open country to the outskirts of Peralta, he would not be much farther ahead.

Butler scouted east and west, then returned to the tracks and followed them almost to the final stands of thornpin. He halted. The tracks led directly into the final big thicket. From where Butler was standing, he could see beyond.

There were no tracks leading out of the thicket to the open country.

Butler was turning back, confident he was very close to the hiding place of the rangemen, confident, too, that they would lie out here until dusk before approaching the town, when three men came almost soundlessly out of the brush on both sides of him.

The largest of the men was full-bearded, big and thick, and drenched with sweat. He held a leveled six-gun, which he cocked as Butler stood stock-still. Cartwell had been sweated down by his exertion, but he was still massive. At this moment, there was not a shred of mercy in his expression.

He motioned with his cocked gun for Butler to drop his weapons. Not a word was said. Evidently Cartwell knew that the marshal had not ridden out alone, because when Marshal Butler would have spoken, the big man put a finger to his lips and scowled.

Butler wanted to swear. This was the second time he had walked into a Cartwell ambush.

If the town blacksmith or the old man who rode the bay horse had been out here, Butler never would have been able to live down this second blunder.

CHAPTER TWENTY

A LONG AFTERNOON

They dumped him on his face, tied him, gagged him with a filthy bandanna, and left him lying there. He could raise his head only enough to watch them disappear in the surrounding underbrush. He swore into the gag.

Unless they surprised the harness maker as they had the lawman, there was going to be a fight. He lay waiting with sweat running into his eyes. For Matthews, the odds were insurmountable.

There was no shooting. They came up around and down from the north behind Matthews, who was talking with the captive. Just before they got close enough, the captive started talking more rapidly and loudly, something that made Matthews eye him wonderingly. Within moments it would have occurred to the harness maker something was wrong, but he did not get enough time.

The captive, glassy-eyed and dripping sweat, abruptly stopped rambling. An unmistakable sound came into the depthless silence. Jacob Cartwell cocked his six-gun behind Matthews.

The captive slumped, raised a shaking hand to fling off perspiration, and stepped from directly in front of Matthews. If anyone had shot from behind the harness maker and the slug passed all the way through, it would also have struck the captive.

Cartwell walked closer, eyes fixed on Matthews. He gestured with his six-gun. "Shuck the weapons."

Matthews obeyed, giving the big man look for look, saying nothing and waiting. He recognized the other two from Vasquez Spring — and got the surprise of his life when Cartwell let his gun hang at his side as he addressed the man Matthews and Butler had captured.

"Worked real well," he said, and made a bleak smile in the harness maker's direction. "His belt buckle, mister. He pointed it to reflect sunlight. We saw your friend coming and was waiting."

Matthews slowly turned to look at the captive. The rangeman would not meet his glance.

Cartwell's other two mangy-looking rangemen walked closer. One of them brushed hair from his forehead as he said, "That's the mouthy old bastard, Jacob."

"I know. The harness maker from town. Well, mister harness maker, turn and walk straight ahead until you come onto your friend trussed like a turkey. And mister harness maker, be real careful."

Matthews obeyed to the letter until he saw Marshal Butler on the ground, then knelt to loosen the bindings. Jacob Cartwell came close, pushed the barrel of his six-gun into Matthews's neck, and told him to stand up and move clear.

Matthews obeyed, but he protested, "You got him disarmed. What more do you want?"

Cartwell gestured for someone to untie the lawman, then turned his back on the marshal to address Matthews again. "Where are your horses?"

"Back yonder, tied in the brush."

"Just two?"

"There's only Frank an' me. Two horses."

Cartwell sent another man to find the animals and bring them back. Butler was sitting up rubbing his wrists. The remaining pair of rangemen were back a short distance, out of reach and still holding their six-guns.

The large, bearded man moved toward shade before speaking again. "Where are the others?" he demanded of Marshal Butler, and scowled when he got an answer.

"There aren't any others."

"You're lying!"

Butler got to his feet and flexed his legs a little. "Go see for yourself," he said. "Backtrack us. Only two sets of hoofprints."

When the rangeman arrived leading the two horses, Cartwell told him and the man who had been a captive to go back and read the sign. As the two men departed on horseback, Cartwell used a limp bandanna to mop off sweat. He did this without taking his eyes off his prisoners.

Eventually he holstered the Colt and, looking straight at Marshal Butler, said, "You're crazy. No one in his right mind would come out here like you done with only one man."

Butler was almost ready to agree. "To tell you the truth, after the *bandoleros* scattered you I didn't expect to find you alive."

Cartwell considered that, found it at least likely, and stowed the soggy bandanna. "Marshal, you comin' along makes things better for us. We're goin' into your town for my bullion box."

"How do you know it's down there? How do you know the *bandoleros* didn't get it? That's what they came back for."

Cartwell answered tersely. "Because we was sneakin' back after they run us off, and saw

282

you come up out of that draw. . . . Saw somethin' else too: Saw that young buck shoot the head Messican and bust out of there in a dead run. Saw that before you come up out of that arroyo. Marshal, we was fixin' to massacre them border jumpers when you come along. They was settin' there like jackrabbits. . . . You come over that rim and hell, there was too many of you. . . . So we just watched an' shagged you part of the way back to that old ranch, but it was too far an' we was too worn down. But that Mex sentry you didn't catch, he snuck southward an' saw you headin' for Peralta with them Messicans you caught, and all them other fellers. Too damned many for us . . . Now then, Marshal, you're goin' to help us get my bullion box. Set down an' rest. We're not going to leave hiding until sundown. *Set — down!*"

Butler and Matthews sat. There was very little shade anywhere because of the position of the sun, not that it would have mattered much, because the temperature remained high.

Frank Butler eyed the sweating large man. Eventually the marshal said, "Mister Cartwell, you traded three hundred horses for that loot. Where the Mexicans got it — down there — don't figure into things very much up here."

Cartwell sank to the ground with the soggy

bandanna in one big fist. "You agree what's in the box belongs to me?"

"As far as I can see, it does."

Cartwell mopped, scowled, mopped some more, and finally spoke. "Then why you got it hid?"

"What were we supposed to do with it, leave it out in the middle of the desert? You an' the Mexicans aren't the only ones knew we had it. As I see it, they paid for your horses with that stuff in the box. My job is to mind things up here, not in Mexico and not whatever *bandoleros* bring up here. Sure, they looted churches and ranches to get that stuff, but down in Mexico. And that's up to the Mexicans, not me."

Jacob Cartwell sat in sweaty silence for a long time staring at Marshal Butler. As he sat there, his men returned to report that they'd found the trail of only two mounted men. That made Cartwell roll his eyes, but he said nothing until he mopped his face again.

"You're tellin' me," he said to Butler, "that the law down here ain't goin' to stop me from gettin' that box?"

"Its contents are payment for your horses, aren't they?"

Cartwell stared in long silence.

One of his riders eased up to say, "Jacob, that bastard's workin' some kind of scheme on you. They don't figure to let you ride in down there an' ride out with the box."

Bart Matthews glared. "You heard the lawman. What're you tryin' to do, start a fight?"

The rangeman grinned at Matthews showing brown-stained teeth. He raised his six-gun and cocked it as he aimed it. Cartwell snarled irritably. "Put that damned gun away!" He returned his slaty eyes to Marshal Butler. "There's something wrong. You wouldn't let me ride off with that box."

"Sure I would. Maybe the town wouldn't, but I would. It was a horse trade. They're made every day down here. I told you, what border jumpers do up here don't bother me unless they go to raiding."

Cartwell picked out the key words. "The town wouldn't? What's the town got to do with it?"

"For one thing," Butler replied. "Your Texan killed one of our possemen back at that sump spring."

"Damned Messican," exclaimed Cartwell in scorn, and got a fierce retort from the harness maker.

"Don't matter about that. He was one of our town possemen."

"Well, one of you shot my rider."

Matthews spoke before Butler could. "Like hell we did. How could we? You had our guns and we was all in camp."

Cartwell's brows dropped. "Someone did. An' it was done in revenge for the Messican. I sure as hell didn't do it. Neither did my riders or the *bandoleros*. They didn't even know anything was wrong until that gunshot."

Butler was watching Matthews and saw the sly smile coming before Matthews said, "El Cajónero did it."

The mean-eyed man who had interrupted before did so again. "I heard about El Cajónero. They believe some mysterious big feller ridin' a black horse comes around takin' revenge. Another damned Mex cock-and-bull story like they got in Texas among the Messicans."

Cartwell raised a big hand to silence the speaker. He was not interested in anything but the bullion box full of loot from Mexico. "What about the town?" he asked again.

Butler answered candidly. "Well, your Texan killed that posse rider. Folks didn't like that. You held us prisoner, an' they didn't like that."

Cartwell leaned. "What are you gettin' at, damnit?"

"For the dead posse rider, money to make things easier for his mother. For the men who rode with me, payment for what you put them through."

Cartwell began to redden, but his voice remained soft as he said, "How much money?"

"Five hundred in gold for the posse rider. Top wages for the others."

This time that mean-eyed man exploded. "You crazy damned idiot," he shouted, and turned to Jacob Cartwell. "You goin' to set there an' let this tinhorn town marshal tell you what you got to do, for Chrissake? Let me take care of 'em an' we can get back to our plan about goin' in there tonight and takin' the box."

Cartwell sat, expressionless and silent, until Butler addressed him again. "That box is full to the lid," the marshal said. "Better to get most of it than none of it."

That remark tipped the scales for Cartwell. He leaned, eyes deadly, and replied, "We'll get all of it. We don't need to pay off no Messicans nor a bunch of saloon bums."

The mean-eyed man gloated. "Good try, lawman, just not good enough." He turned. "Jacob, I can walk them back through the brush a ways and sock them away. They ain't no good to us anyway. All right?"

Cartwell's ire prompted his reply. "Fred, you shut up. If you shot 'em, they'd hear the noise in Peralta."

"I wasn't goin' to shoot 'em, Jacob. I was —"

"Gaddammit, *shut up!*"

The rangeman reddened and walked away, his eyes slits in a stubbly face.

Butler and Matthews watched his departure with a single thought. Fred whateverhisname-was meant serious trouble.

Cartwell lumbered up to his feet, studied the dozing pair of saddle animals, and put a slow glance on his other riders. They looked back from blank faces, and one of them said, "These horses will do, but we got to have two more, an' one of 'em's got to be pretty big."

Cartwell ignored the remark, which was intended to mean an average size horse could not carry him, then went over to drink deeply from the harness maker's canteen. He passed it around. His men nearly emptied both canteens, and none of them offered a drink to the harness maker or the marshal.

Time passed slowly. There wasn't much relief from the heat until the sun angled down the western sky. And it would have to get very low before the stunted brush could provide shade.

There was little talk. Now and then Cartwell or his men would walk down to the final fringe of protective cover and squint in the direction of Peralta. They could see riders and four-wheeled rigs passing along.

Once, a hurrying mud wagon came rocketing from up north, leaving a feathery wake of dust behind.

The man who had signaled with his belt buckle sidled up to speak briefly with Cartwell, who abruptly turned and went to stand in front of his seated prisoners.

He said, "Where is the box hid?"

Matthews looked malevolently at the man they'd captured, who turned his back.

Cartwell pulled back a thick leg for a kick. Frank spoke before he got set. "It's in a big steel safe in the middle of town."

"You know the combination?"

"No."

"Who does?"

Butler looked up at the large man without answering. The kick came with surprising speed, Butler fell over backwards and blood trickled from the corner of his mouth. Matthews moved to jump up, but one of the riders jammed him viciously in the kidneys with a gun barrel. Matthews gasped and staggered, sat down, and tried to lean far back to ease the pain.

Cartwell smiled at him.

Matthews was reaching back with both hands when he said, "You damned fool. He don't know the combination, and neither do I. But if he had, you just fixed it so's he couldn't tell you."

The mean-eyed man called Fred bent from the waist, put his face close, and spoke. "This here safe in the jailhouse?"

"No."

"Where is it?"

"Ask that mangy bastard we took prisoner. It's smack-dab in the middle of town, an' unless you got dynamite you'll never get it opened. An' I'm not sure dynamite would do it."

Fred straightened back a little, studying the harness maker. "General store," he said. "They always got steel safes. Right, harness maker?"

Matthews nodded without speaking. The pain in his back was as bad as any he'd ever experienced. He kept his eyes on the ground, because they would have shown murder if he'd looked up.

Fred turned in triumph toward Jacob Cartwell. "You ever done anythin' like this before?" Fred asked, and before Cartwell could reply the man said, "I have. Couple of times in Texas."

"Dynamited a safe?"

"Naw. You don't need dynamite. It'd bring the whole damned town down on us. . . . We find the storekeeper, take him down there, peel off his boots an' socks, and roast his feet over a little fire." Fred's grin widened. "It'll work. Fellers I used to ride with told me it works every time."

Matthews leaned to roll Marshal Butler so the sun would not be on his face, wiped blood from the lawman's mouth on his trouser leg, and straightened up very slowly, looking around for the man who had hit him in the back. The man was watching him, expressionless and still holding his six-gun. Matthews memorized every feature of the man's face, then asked for water.

When a nearly empty canteen was tossed down, Matthews leaned, propped Butler up, and trickled water into his mouth. The marshal spat, choked, coughed, then swallowed several times.

Cartwell yanked away the canteen and shoved Butler with a boot toe. "Sit up. You ain't hurt. I've been hurt worse'n that and didn't even stop talking. Now then, Marshal, it's gettin' along. Soon as it's dark you're goin' to lead us over there. Be quiet about it. Lead us where we can study the town from an alley, somewhere folks won't be able to see us. . . . An' when we've got our bearings, take us to the house of the feller who owns the general store. You understand all that?"

Butler's mouth was swelling. He dabbed it lightly with his handkerchief and nodded his head without attempting to speak. The mean-eyed man came forward, fists clenched. Cartwell turned on him in a fury. "Once more you try an' run things, Fred, an' I'll break your gaddamned neck! Now get down there where you can see the town an' keep watch. *Do it!*"

As Fred turned to obey, Cartwell glared and wagged his head. "Trouble. Nothin' but trouble since the day I first set eyes on him." He sank to one knee in front of Marshal Butler. "You know the storekeeper, do you?"

Butler nodded again. Now, along with his torn mouth and jaw, his neck was troubling him, a result of the way his head had snapped back under the impact.

"What sort of feller is he? *Marshal!*"

Butler could answer this question without evasion, because if they caught John Grover they'd find out anyway.

"He won't give you any trouble. He's a storekeeper, like most other storekeepers you've met."

"If we roast his feet . . . ?"

"You won't have to do that."

"What's his name?"

"John Grover."

Cartwell remained kneeling for a moment longer, then rose to look at the oncoming dusk. The two men closest to him also looked up.

From down at the verge of the thicket Fred called softly, "Can't hardly make things out no more."

Cartwell nodded, turned, and told the other two men to get the prisoners on their feet and walk behind them leading the horses.

Chapter Twenty-One

INTO THE NIGHT

Fred was right. When they emerged from the thicket and were on the open country northwest of Peralta, about all they could make out as the swiftly passing dusk turned to night were a distant dark blur and lights. They set their course according to the lights, moving without haste through stored-up heat from a long day that the earth, rocks, and underbrush continued to give off.

Fred, out ahead just far enough so that those following could make him out only as a shifting vague shadow, was obviously concentrating on the lights ahead. He neither paused nor spoke as he walked.

Jacob Cartwell's other two hired riders were bringing up the rear, leading the horses. Cartwell walked beside his captives, big, grim, mostly silent in anticipation.

Matthews ventured a comment. "You better

do this fast and be long gone before sunup, Mister Cartwell."

The bearded man looked around without missing a step. The statement required no reply. Cartwell faced forward.

When they were close enough to detect town sounds, Cartwell growled for everyone to be damned careful, which was another unnecessary comment.

Butler's lower face on the right side was purplish and badly swollen. His torn lip had stopped bleeding some time earlier, but it would start again if he spoke.

His neck hurt, more now than it had after he'd been kicked. He was thirsty and lethargic. He'd taken a lot of abuse this past week or so, and even the rest he'd had between interludes with Cartwell had not really rebuilt his energy or his resistance very much.

Bart Matthews walked at his side, occasionally eyeing him. Matthews knew when people were reaching the limit of their endurance. He'd lived a long time; human beings, their frailties and their strengths, were not new to him. And he had a long memory. Every step reminded him of his injured back. A couple of times he searched out the man who had slammed a gun barrel into his kidney area. If that man had been watching, if it hadn't been dark, and if the rangeman's attention hadn't been unwaveringly fixed on the lights ahead, he might have felt uneasy.

Fred stopped and waited until the others came up. They were about a half mile from the west side of Peralta, and while they could make out shapes and lights fairly well at this distance, they themselves would still be invisible to anyone looking northwesterly from town. From this point on, the danger would increase. Fred told Jacob Cartwell it might be a good idea for one of them to scout ahead. Cartwell, still resentful toward the mean-eyed man, refused the idea, which Butler thought was a mistake. Evidently so did Fred, because as he started moving he wagged his head.

A dog barked in the distance, which could have simply meant raccoons were in the trash barrels, a frequent nocturnal event, or that a civet cat was prowling. The reason Butler thought otherwise was that the dog was barking on the west side of town, the direction from which they were approaching.

Other dogs joined in, and since this barking came from different areas the original barking lost whatever significance it might have had for the townspeople.

Matthews nudged Marshal Butler in the darkness and jutted his jaw. Fred was approaching the center of town. That seemed to interest the big bearded man too. He said,

"General store in the middle of town on the east side?"

Butler answered in one word. "Yes."

"And, now then, just where does the store-keeper live?"

Butler replied again without hesitation. "He's got a room at the hotel. It's at the north end of town."

"He might be at the saloon, or —"

"He don't drink. A little around Christmas-time is about all. This time of night, my guess is that he'll be sleeping like a log."

Throughout this exchange, Matthews was regarding his companion from wide eyes. John Grover did not live at the rooming house; he lived with his family on the east side of Main Street out a short way where he and other merchants had built wooden houses with cu-polas and white paint and wooden fences.

Cartwell hissed at Fred, who stopped and turned. "Hotel's at the north end of town," he said. "Storekeeper's got rooms there."

Fred nodded, altered course, and went out ahead again. The dogs were raising hell and propping it up. Someone was playing Jess Hobart's off-key piano at the saloon, and his accompanist was making all kinds of caterwauling sounds with a harmonica. The harmonica player had no sense of cadence or timing; he was always a bar or two behind the pianist. But this late at night Jess's customers would probably be too maudlinly smoked up to notice or to give a damn.

It was still early, too early for folks to be abed, although the people of Peralta usually did not sit up very long after supper. Most of the dogs' barking had stopped.

Hobart's place was doing a fair business, considering it was a weekday night. The harmonica player finally quit, possibly hooted into silence, but the pianist continued. His repertoire was limited. He had played "Lorena," the old Confederate army song, four times, and when that irked Hobart's customers, he switched to hymns, of which he seemed to know quite a few.

He was rendering a very forceful version of "Rock of Ages" as Fred reached the back alley on the west side. Fred stirred up some dogs again, then ignored them as he leaned in shed shadows until the other men came up. Jacob Cartwell told the men leading the pair of horses to tie them.

Butler jutted his jaw in the direction of the rooming house. "Yonder," he said through his battered lips.

They hovered for a few moments. Then Cartwell said he wanted to look the general store over first.

Matthews took over the lead from Fred, led

them down the alley a few yards to a trash-littered weedy open space between two structures, and pointed. The front of the general store across Main Street was dark. Cartwell stood looking toward it before turning toward the harness maker. "Got a back door, has it?"

"Yes."

"Where is the safe?"

"If you go in from the loading dock out back, you only got to walk about fifteen feet. You can't miss it; it's painted gray and stands against the north wall." All of which was the truth.

Cartwell turned back and waved for Fred to lead northward. They had progressed about half the distance toward the north end of town when a pair of unsteady individuals appeared up ahead muttering and grumbling. Cartwell hissed and set an example by moving quickly into shadows behind the jailhouse.

The unsteady individuals snugged up close to the alley entrance of someone's cow shed and stood a long time searching the heavens. Butler recognized both of them: old gaffers from among the tarpaper shacks at the opposite end of town. Where they'd gotten money to buy whiskey he had no idea, but he did know none of the old men from down there needed little more than a sniff of a cork to get drunk.

One of the waiting men leaned and whispered to Cartwell. "Got bladders like a horse," he said about the time the men finished. Then the two old men turned southward and shuffled straight past the hidden, breathless watchers, looked neither right nor left, and continued along until their shuffling eventually died.

Fred led off again, but kept closer to the far side of the alley, where there were backs of buildings that faced Main Street.

Matthews walked beside Marshal Butler without looking at him. His guess was that Butler had lied about where the storekeeper lived on the spur of the moment. And while that was fine as long as they were not in town, now they were, and Butler had better have a workable plan in mind. Cartwell did not need either of them anymore, and he had at least one man who would be glad to crush their skulls with a gun barrel.

They arrived on the far side of the rooming house. One light glowed feebly, not from one of the rooms, but from the middle of the hallway leading from out front to the rooms.

Fred looked at Butler. "You live there?"

"Yes."

"Then won't nobody get upset if you an' me walk in, go to your room, an' open the window, will they?"

Cartwell looked daggers at the mean-eyed man but said nothing. Butler responded to the question without elaborating. "That ought to work."

Fred glanced at Cartwell, who grudgingly inclined his head and asked Butler where the window was.

"Down the west wall. Count off three. The fourth one's my room."

Cartwell gestured. "Get on with it."

Matthews watched the town marshal and Fred turn right at the front of the old barnlike structure. From this point on, he would be unable to help Marshal Butler no matter what happened. He turned toward the men around him; they too were watching. As Butler opened the rooming house door, one of them said, "Gettin' closer, Jacob."

Cartwell stood like a log, silent and grim. Nothing more was said until Matthews pretended to hear something behind them and Cartwell hissed for everyone to take cover again.

This time Cartwell and one of his riders disappeared among shadows on the west side of the alley. Matthews and the other man rushed to cover on the opposite side. The man with Matthews craned around, then said, "I don't see nothing."

Matthews moved close. "I didn't *see* anything, I heard it. Someone walking. Listen. From the south."

The man cocked his head, leaned a little, and Matthews raised an arm as he stepped even closer. "There! See him?"

He hit the rangeman as hard as he could along the slant of the jaw on the right side. The man went down, struck a discarded steel buggy tire, and turned loose all over.

Matthews tried to alleviate the pain in his right hand by flexing the fingers as he leaned and, with his left hand, disarmed the man whose neck was cocked at an awkward angle where he'd struck the edge of the buggy tire.

He knelt to pull loose the rangeman's shellbelt and fling it over his shoulder. He said, "Hit me in the back, will you, you son of a bitch," and raised the pistol high. The crumpled form in front of him did not look right in feeble starlight. Matthews slowly lowered the weapon and shook the man, who flopped a little. Then he released him and leaned down with his ear to the man's nostrils. He wasn't breathing.

Matthews rocked back in astonishment. He couldn't have hit him that hard. He had never in his life been able to hit anyone hard. He'd been fast in brawls, but never very powerful.

He reached to tentatively shake the man again. This time the body flopped less, but the head, cocked at an odd angle, fell off the edge of the tire. Matthews gazed a moment, then used both hands — the man's neck was broken!

Under his breath he muttered what had been his lifelong vocal response to things that angered him, startled him, or worried him. "Son of a bitch!"

He rose and peeked out to locate Cartwell and his companion. When he did not find them over yonder in the darkness, he paused in brief confusion. He was free, he was armed, and Butler was inside the rooming house unarmed with the mean-eyed rider.

Without another glance around, he hurried toward the main roadway and made no sound until he stepped onto the plankwalk heading north. His footfalls on the planks sounded, to him anyway, like a herd of buffalo in a headlong charge.

His luck could not last long. When Cartwell did not see his rider emerge behind the harness maker, he would cross over and find the man dead.

Matthews had no time to speculate about the big man's reaction. He was nearing the front porch of the rooming house. He had no plan, or any idea where Butler might have taken Fred. Probably to his room, because he'd told them where it was.

Matthews stopped, flattened against a rough wooden wall, and breathed deeply as he listened. All he heard was "Rock of Ages." If Cartwell and his rider found the dead man and saw his empty holster, and sure as hell they had by now, would they run for it or would they try to make it up to Marshal Butler's window?

They'd head for the window, warn Fred that the harness maker was loose and armed — and maybe Fred would kill the marshal after all. If he'd felt like doing that back yonder in the underbrush where there had been no real peril . . .

Matthews went against his better judgment. He moved to his left in the direction of the dark alley and crossed over. He had a tingling sensation between the shoulders, because if they were still in the alley they'd see him slipping down the side of the rooming house.

There was some soft earth underfoot that nearly tripped him. As he stepped wide to get past, his heel sprung a trap that had been half hidden.

Matthews nearly fell, caught desperately at the wall, and balanced there as he raised his foot. He used the pistol barrel to pry the trap loose, and swore savagely to himself as he got free of it.

There was an open window about fifteen

feet ahead. It was the only opened one for the full length of the old building. Whether Cartwell and his companion were already inside, he had no idea.

If they were inside, Marshal Butler was in trouble up to his butt. He could not produce the storekeeper, because he was not there. He gambled that they had not yet got up here.

After inching along the warped old rough siding, he flattened himself beside the window to listen. At first there was nothing, then a voice Matthews recognized snarled. "What'n hell they waitin' for? Chrissake, by now they could've crawled this far on their hands and knees!"

Butler remained silent. He never took his eyes off the man called Fred, not even when he went to the window to look out. He did not put his head out, because he knew the nervous man behind him would brain him. He stood there looking and listening. All he heard was "Rock of Ages."

When he turned, the mean-eyed rangeman was leaning with one ear pressed to the hallway door. He had a death grip on the six-gun in his hand.

Butler said, "Something went wrong."

Fred turned on him in a fury. "That took a lot of brains to figure out, didn't it? Shut your damned mouth and keep it shut!"

Butler risked trouble. "You can still get out the window and back to the horses."

This time when Fred turned, his slitted eyes were icy but moving. "I told you to shut up, you —"

"Go ahead and shoot. You wouldn't get a hundred yards."

The rangeman straightened away from the door and started for the window. As he approached the marshal, he waggled with the six-gun for Butler to precede him. "We'll both go. You in front. And stay in front!"

In this kind of a situation, things usually happened fast. This time they didn't.

Butler went to the sill, rocked forward a little looking out, and saw the harness maker against the wall outside. Turning his head in a different direction as though he had not seen the gun hand raised shoulder high or the strained face, he swung a leg out. Behind him Fred muttered a warning. "You try an' run for it, an' I'll blow you open from in back!"

Butler did not try to run. He stopped a yard or two away from the window and turned back to watch the rangeman make a swift jump and a soft landing.

Then the rangeman pointed the gun at Butler and said, "Don't use the alley. Go out around the houses and keep at a walk."

Butler did not move. The harness maker

straightened up slowly with a thumb pad on the knurled hammer of his weapon.

"Drop it, you son of a bitch! *Drop it!*"

Fred hung in place like a tightly wound spring, eyes darting. Matthews was behind him, out of his line of sight. He aimed for the rangeman's shoulder blades and cocked his six-gun.

Fred dropped like a stone, a blur of movement in the night. He rolled twice before coming up swinging his weapon. He did not know exactly where the harness maker was, so he started to swivel his six-gun.

Matthews fired. The lancing flame of a muzzle blast could be seen, and the sound of the blast was deafening to the men closest to it. Matthews lowered his muzzle and fired twice more. It wasn't necessary, but he did not know that.

Butler was bending to take the rangeman's weapon when shouts burst out from the roadway. Several doors slammed, and the sound of boots rattling over duckboards could be heard.

Across the road, the pianist was still playing. He had abandoned "Rock of Ages" and was playing "Nearer My God to Thee."

Matthews stood with the gun hanging at his side. "That damned fool. There wasn't no call for him to try that."

Butler shrugged without comment. After the harness maker had had time to think about it, he would understand that a man like Fred *did* have to try it.

Inside the rooming house, several lamps sputtered to life. Farther up the wall someone rattled a window open, stuck his head out, saw two standing men with guns in their hands and another man sprawled at their feet, jerked his head back inside, and slammed the window.

CHAPTER TWENTY-TWO

A CHANGE OF LUCK

Butler dropped Fred's six-gun into his empty holster and led off in a loose run toward the outer limit of Peralta to the west.

His destination was the horses; he was convinced that regardless of Jacob Cartwell's avarice and resolution, he would now try to flee. If he had known Cartwell had found the dead man beside the wagon tire, he would not have changed his opinion.

Matthews, whose aversion to this kind of exercise was deeply implanted, nevertheless loped in the lawman's wake.

The sleepy town awakened around them. Someone in the rooming house bawled like a bay steer that there was a dead man along the west wall, then stuffed his nightgown into his britches, grabbed his pistol, stamped into his boots, and went to join several other men gazing at the corpse. Someone said, "Where's his gun?" Someone else replied, "You blind? He ain't got one. Whoever shot him took it with 'em."

Jess Hobart arrived. He knelt, rolled the corpse onto its back, and gasped. "He's one of Cartwell's men. He was one of them as kept us prisoner out at the sump spring. I'd know him anywhere." Jess leaned to take advantage of the feeble light of a lantern being held high by the hotel's proprietor.

Other men leaned too. One of them spoke in awe. "Christ! That was real close range. Why'n hell'd he shoot him three times?"

No one replied. Jess got to his feet scowling. "If *he's* here, then Cartwell is too. An' the rest of his crew. How he done it, come this far and all, I got no idea, but I can sure guess why he come. For that damned box full of Messican loot."

Jess unconsciously wiped both hands on his barman's apron while gazing at the dead man. Eventually he addressed the quiet crowd of onlookers. "The marshal's got to be told."

A lanky man with a prominent Adam's apple said, "He ain't in town, Jess. Ain't been all day."

"You sure? He said he'd ride out, but he should be back by now."

"Well, he ain't. I looked for him. Somethin' got into my henhouse and strung dead chickens all over. I wanted him to help me find it."

Hobart looked around. "Where's Bart?"

"Harness shop door's locked," a hostler from the stage company's corral yard volunteered. Jess Hobart stared at the man, who added, "Been locked since early morning when I took some tugs down to have 'em sewed."

Jess continued to dry his hands. He looked around, saw the blank faces, the questioning eyes, and heard someone mutter to the effect that somethin' damned wrong was going on. He said, "The safe! Frank put that bullion box in Grover's safe at the store. Come along."

The small gathering trooped around front with him. There was not a sound, and the roadway was empty from one end of town to the other. The lanky townsman with the prominent Adam's apple intruded into the saloonman's moment of indecision by saying they'd better get the vigilance committee organized and put guards around the general store. He also asked how many men Cartwell might have with him.

Jess thought back to the period he'd been Cartwell's prisoner. "Maybe six or eight. But after the fight, I don't know."

That settled it for the townsmen: they agreed with the lanky man that the local vigilance committee had to be called out. They all trooped over to the saloon for some refreshment before circulating throughout Peralta to get things organized.

If they had still been in the roadway they would have heard a quick, sharp shout somewhere in the vicinity of the alley on the west side of town. A prowling townsman with a large-bore old scattergun in both hands had crossed through the littered area between two buildings and had discovered a warped old discarded buggy tire with a dead man lying beside it.

The finder stood stone-still in shock for several seconds before raising his eyes to look out into the alley. He saw a loping wraith come out of nowhere, followed by another one. Both had six-guns in their hands. The townsman turned and went lumbering back across the road in the direction of the saloon, just about the only lighted building in town.

The two wraiths had come in from the west. Frank Butler was in the lead, with no intention of going directly to the tethered horses and possibly running into Cartwell in the alley.

But there was no sign of anyone. The horses had been standing with head-hung patience, no doubt both thirsty and hungry. When they picked up faint sound from the west, both their heads came up.

Butler stopped and sank to one knee. He could see the outline of the animals but little else. He watched for movement of a human form.

Matthews dropped beside him, shaking his head. "He ain't that crazy, is he?"

"What're you talking about?"

"Frank, he's not here. Those horses was dozin' before they heard us."

Marshal Butler was silent for a long moment. Then he stood up. "*I* wouldn't be," he told the harness maker. "But that box don't mean that much to me. Let's turn the horses loose; they'll find their way down to the livery barn."

They did so after approaching the horses very cautiously. Butler in particular had become very wary of ambushes.

As soon as the bridles had been removed and draped from saddle horns, both horses turned southward down the alley in the direction of the barn at the lower end of town. The closer they got to the scent of hay and water, the faster they walked.

Butler led off in the direction of the general store, again moving with extreme caution, so much so that eventually the harness maker, whose disposition was not inclined toward caution, said, "For Chrissake, can't be but two of 'em now."

The marshal's reply was dry: "There could be a hundred; it only takes one mistake and one bullet."

Matthews hiked along in stony silence. The two men went southward almost as far as the livery barn, crossed the road at its darkest point, passed through the smithy's rear yard, which was treacherously full of cast-aside iron and steel, reached the east-side alley, and started up in the direction of the loading dock behind Grover's store.

A lean, dark dog with a long upright bony tail sprang from between the slats of a dilapidated fence and confronted them in a fighting stance. It did not bark; it growled deeply. Matthews swore at it, which only increased the dog's belligerence; it showed big white teeth.

Matthews started to bend down for a stone. Butler stopped him as the dog settled to spring. Matthews came back up very slowly, mad enough to tackle the dog barehanded. Butler said, "That's the dog John Grover turns loose inside the store at night."

"Well, we can't just stand here all —"

"Bart, they never leave that dog out."

Bart caught the implication and squinted past the dog. "They're inside?"

"Got to be," replied the marshal, and Matthews dropped his gaze to the dog again. "How did they get past that son of a bitch?"

Butler made a guess. "Opened the door, maybe stood behind it until the dog had run outside, then jumped past and closed the door."

The harness maker said, "Fine. Now what do *we* do to get past him?"

They couldn't without either shooting the watchdog or fighting it. Either would cause a noisy ruckus. Butler led the way back the way they had come but only as far as a sagging gate on the east side of the alley. They closed the gate after themselves and went northward again, this time having to pick their way carefully through litter, flower beds, and vegetable gardens. They aroused more dogs, but none as willing to fight them as the bony-tailed dog in the alley.

Matthews reached to tap the marshal's shoulder. "Grover keep dynamite in the store?"

He didn't. By town ordinance, explosives had to be stored at least half a mile from town limits. Grover kept explosives in a thick-walled little stone house about that distance from town. He did store dynamite caps in his icehouse across the alley; but caps by themselves could not do more than scratch the paint on Grover's safe.

Butler's reply to the harness maker's question was to shake his head as he leaned to peek through fence slats.

Matthews said, "You see him?"

"No. But I can't see very far southward." Butler straightened up, very gently prying the slats apart. When he had sufficient room, he looked out. The dog was still in the alley, but about a hundred feet southward. Butler eased back. "We can try," he told the harness maker. "It's fifty-fifty that he won't bother anyone so far from him."

They climbed through, stopped with their backs against the old fence, and watched the dog. Neither man moved nor spoke.

The dog faced fully around but made no motion toward them and did not growl. Matthews whispered. "Why does John keep that dog?"

"To discourage burglars."

Matthews nodded slightly. "He should do that, all right. But I didn't know he had a dog."

Butler switched his attention to the rear door of the store. It was closed, but he would have bet a year's wages it wasn't locked.

The dog went over to a trash barrel to lift its leg, but did not take its eyes off the men against the fence.

Butler's attention on the door was increased when he heard a noise beyond it, inside the store. There were tools in the store, but nothing that could be used to prise the safe open.

He jerked his head. Matthews alternately watched the dog and the closed door. When they got up close, the dog ignored them to go sniffing back and forth down the alley. Evidently the animal found its unaccustomed freedom fascinating.

Butler leaned, heard something, and straightened up looking at the harness maker. "They're not going to break into the safe. We could stay out here, out of sight, and nail them when they come out."

Matthews cast a final glance in the direction of the dog before answering. "An' suppose they go out the front door?"

Inside, something very heavy struck the floor, making a solid but not loud sound. The harness maker said, "They got the damned door off somehow."

It had certainly sounded as though they had. Butler raised the hand holding the Colt, reached with the other hand to see if the door was locked, and, when it yielded to his slight pressure, looked at his companion. Matthews nodded; he was ready to storm inside.

But Marshal Butler did not wrench the door open. He very gently eased it outward, hoping the hinges would not squeak. They did not.

The scent of the store's interior came out to the marshal and harness maker. It was an amalgam of oiled wood, pleasant mustiness, spices, and leather. The store was as dark inside as the interior of a boot, and there was not a sound until a man whispered, "The goddamned anvil fell. Now what do we do?"

The answer was slow arriving. "You sure there ain't any dynamite sticks?"

"I told you, Jacob, I looked in every drawer an' on every shelf, in the office and the storeroom. . . . If we had the storekeeper —"

"We don't have him, so shut up about that. See if you can jockey that anvil in place again so's I can get leverage across it to the door."

The next sound came from a man straining hard, words coming in gasps between panting breaths. "Jacob, the whole damned town's out there."

"I don't care. They don't know we're in here."

"They'll figure it. . . . For Chrissake, hold that block steady — this thing's heavier'n a horse!"

An abrupt explosion of pent-up breath sounded as Cartwell said, "Now, then, lend a hand on the end of this bar."

"It ain't goin' to open, Jacob. You hear 'em out there? We'll be lucky to get back to the horses."

"Lean, dammit. Shut up an' lean down on the bar."

Butler reached back, tapped Mathews, and started past the door. The same blackness that hid the straining, grunting men up ahead somewhere also hid Matthews and the marshal once they were inside.

There was another explosion of pent-up breath, this time accompanied by hair-raising profanity in a deep, growly tone of voice. "Rest a minute. Damnation, that door should have sprung open."

The second voice, not as deep and clearly anxious, responded as though the door of the safe was suddenly unimportant. "Listen to me; we got to leave off and get the hell out of here. We can come back with dynamite. Jacob, there's a whole town runnin' around out there."

"Once more," Cartwell growled, but the man behind him refused. "No more. You can stay. Me, I'm gettin' the hell out of here."

Butler heard Cartwell shifting his considerable weight and thought he knew what the large man was doing. He raised his six-gun and said, "Right where you are! Not a move by either of you."

Someone made a noise taking down a quick, deep breath. It did not sound like Jacob Cartwell. Butler told the men to move toward the center of the store where he could background them with roadway light, which came mostly from the sky.

One set of boots moved; the other set did not. Bart spoke to the motionless man. "Move! Get over there!"

The answer was a probing lash of muzzle blast and a deafening report that covered the sound of someone moving heavily to one side. All noise from the roadway stopped so abruptly that for a long moment there were only fading echoes.

Cartwell's slug had missed the lawman and his companion by two feet, sailed out the open rear door, and struck a distant stovepipe, bringing it down in a cloud of soot.

Butler barely raised his voice as he said, "One more chance. Drop them." What seemed to be an eternity of silence followed.

The reply was another blind shot and more sideward movement. Butler tried a sound shot; through the echo of this shot he heard a gun sliding along the floor. "The other one too," he called out, and again Cartwell fired at what he thought was the place an antagonist was standing.

Matthews swore, fired, moved, and fired again. A high squawk was heard, followed by the noise of a body falling. But the rangeman had not been hit; he had dropped to the floor.

He yelled. "I got rid of the gun. I quit!"

Matthews fired again. This time a genuine glass window in the front of John Grover's store shattered into hundreds of pieces. Beyond it, the sounds of running feet and yelps were audible even over the gun thunder.

Butler could dimly make out the big steel safe. In front of it someone had placed a large block of wood. Atop the block was an anvil. Nearby lay a thick pry bar, bent from pressure.

The marshal's eyes were becoming accustomed to darkness. He could discern counters, shelves, barrels, even the old iron cannon heater used in wintertime to warm the building. But he could not make out anything that resembled a big bearded man.

He half expected what would happen when he called out again, but he called anyway. "Cartwell! There's no one left but you. There's no way out. Pitch the gun away and stand up, arms high."

There was no answer and no gunshot. Matthews pitched a can of tomatoes; nothing happened. He risked moving slightly; still nothing happened. He finally pushed his Colt ahead and began shifting left and right until he nearly stumbled over the man on the floor, who looked up from a white face.

A thought had just occurred to Butler when Matthews called to him. "Where is he?"

Butler started to answer, but behind him in the alley a dog started snarling, loud and menacing. That noise was followed by fence slats breaking. Butler jumped up, spun around, and ran toward the door. A flash of scarlet, a thunderous explosion, and a shower of splinters from the upper jamb of the door distracted the marshal.

He jumped into the alley, ignored the snarling dog, and stopped when he heard someone running hard beyond the fence among the dark houses there.

When Matthews walked out, eyeing the dog askance, Butler said, "I don't know how he did it, but he got around us in there and left out the back."

Matthews reloaded from his shellbelt and spoke while eyeing the menacing big dog whose fangs shone brightly. "And Grover thinks that mutt would protect his store?" He slammed the six-gun into his holster and spat in the dog's direction. "That dog don't attack, Frank. He's got by on his mean look. Watch this."

Matthews roared a curse and sprang at the dog. It fled.

Chapter Twenty-three

SHOWDOWN!

They stood in the dark alley for a moment, listening to the turmoil around front where armed townsmen were again cautiously stalking the front of Grover's store. Glass from the big front window lay as far as the opposite side of the roadway. John Grover had had the glass freighted from Missouri wrapped and double-wrapped in straw and blanketing. It had cost him a fortune to get it here and installed, but he'd thought it worth the expense.

There were infrequent shouts in front of the store. Matthews recognized a couple of the voices and looked disgusted. "Next summer they'll tell how they done the whole thing themselves. . . . Frank?"

Marshal Butler stood a moment before saying, "If he went over where the horses were . . ."

"He won't find them."

"So he'll try the livery barn, where there are plenty of other horses."

That was likely, unless of course Cartwell came across the many animals stabled among local residences. But Marshal Butler's gamble on the livery barn was basic: when people who lived in towns or cities thought of horses, they thought of livery barns.

It was, the marshal conjectured, the best of two alternatives. The second alternative would be to try to locate Cartwell as he fled, which was also more dangerous, since searching yards at night could result in irate challenges from householders — and shooting.

What did not occur to Marshal Butler was that a desperate man fleeing in panic might not stop at the livery barn, or even approach it. Especially someone like Jacob Cartwell, who was no stranger to trouble.

Butler and the harness maker went down the alley, staying away from the center of it despite the darkness. Shouts erupted behind them from the direction of the general store, where townsmen had stormed through the wreckage to emerge in the alleyway. Matthews muttered something unkind about the noisy men and hurried along with Marshal Butler.

They came to the smithy and turned into the litter again, reached the front of the shop where they could see the livery barn, and paused to look and listen.

The place seemed deserted. Northward, in front of the general store, there was plenty of activity; to the south there was none. Matthews would have shouldered past to cross over, but Butler stopped him with an outflung arm. Without speaking, he turned back and started south again. Matthews followed without a sound. When they were beyond town and among the shacks of the old gaffers, they were invisible to anyone farther north.

They crossed the road and reached the alley. Butler paused to listen. All he could hear was the ruckus around the distant store. He passed along the west side of ramshackle buildings, keeping the barn opening in sight. If Cartwell was in there, or if he'd already rigged out and was ready to run for it, he would appear in the back alley. He would not rush out into the front roadway to flee, not where half the aroused town would see him.

Bart tapped the lawman's shoulder and leaned to whisper: "One of us could go out an' around and come down from the north."

Frank shook his head without replying; Cartwell would not try fleeing northward the full length of town.

One of the men up near the center of town fired a shotgun. It sounded like a small cannon. Bart abruptly halted, but Butler continued toward the rear barn opening. He knew Cartwell had not been the cause of the blast.

When Matthews caught up, he was muttering to himself. There had been no other gunfire after the scattergun blast; some nervous Nellie had probably fired at a shadow.

Butler stopped two feet from the doorway. Bart was behind him waiting for Butler's next move. Neither of them was prepared for the sudden scream, high and shrill, that came from Mex-town behind them. It was accompanied by a flurry of gunshots, then more screaming.

Butler spun, pushed past the harness maker, and began to run. He was a yard ahead when a large moving shape burst clear of the jacals on the west side, making a desperate run due west. A six-gun lanced flame and roared as a fleeing man on horseback swung sideways in his saddle. He had seen movement at the end of the alley down where the first jacals stood.

Matthews fired back, tracked the racing shadow, and fired twice more. The horseman twisted backwards and emptied his six-gun. Matthews did not hear the last shot. He crumpled across the facedown body of Marshal Butler with no knowledge that the fleeing man's first shot had downed the lawman.

The weight of the harness maker roused Frank Butler. He felt warm stickiness on his upper right leg as he pushed clear of Matthews, struggled upright, and crab-hopped back to the barn, entering without making sure it was safe to do so. He led forth the first horse he saw, saddled and bridled it standing mostly on one foot, ignored the horseman's rule of never mounting inside a building, and got into the saddle. With the uproar in Mex-town getting louder, he reined west and booted the horse over into a belly-down run.

The bleeding was aggravated by motion. Butler looped the reins, leathered his Colt, and sat sideways. He pulled forth his bandanna and tied it tightly above the injury. The bleeding did not stop, but it slowed to a trickle.

The marshal's earlier tiredness was just a memory. He had a pounding heart as he slackened only occasionally and long enough to pick up the sounds of a racing horse. Then he continued.

Cartwell did not deviate from his westerly course, which made it easier to hear him up ahead. But he either knew he was being pursued or thought he would be, which in either case amounted to the same fate if he were ridden down.

Fifteen minutes into the horse race, Frank Butler slackened a bit to save his animal as much as possible. While making the chase, he calculated the probable end of it. He had no idea how good a horse Cartwell had stolen in Mex-town; as a rule, they did not have very good animals down there, but some were big enough and fast enough to overtake most other horses.

What encouraged the lawman most was Jacob Cartwell's size. Regardless of the horse's size and toughness, it would be handicapped in a race by Jacob Cartwell's weight.

Without a carbine, Frank Butler was handicapped. But he was sure Cartwell was no better off. He'd carried a Winchester from the verge of underbrush where they'd spent the afternoon, but Butler did not remember him still having it after they reached town. He may have left the weapon with the tethered horses.

He heard Cartwell's horse getting farther ahead, but held his own mount to a fast lope. No horse could maintain the pace Cartwell was forcing his to keep. As the distance widened, Butler let his own animal out a notch. He was now less concerned with catching up than he was with keeping Cartwell within reach, as long as he could hear Cartwell, his confidence in ultimately overtaking him increased. One of them was going to run out of a horse if this kept up much longer. Butler did not intend to be the first man afoot out here.

They were alone in a fading darkness with no sign of Peralta or anything else man-made.

Cartwell, with not much knowledge of the area, was heading straight for an Indian reservation, but he would never arrive there on the horse he was cruelly roweling.

Butler heard Cartwell curse when the horse began to fail and stumbled. He let his own mount out another notch. Cartwell was down to a shambling trot on a horse close to being wind-broken, but still moving. Finally, Cartwell flung off the ailing horse and lumbered toward some half-hidden big gray boulders.

Butler halted well out of six-gun range, dismounted, and looked for something to tether to. He squatted at the base of a gnarled, stunted, very old and very dead tree with the horse breathing deeply behind him where it was tied.

Dawn was on the way, but darkness yielded grudgingly to the first hint of a pink blush along the farthest horizon.

Cartwell's horse wandered away on unsteady legs. The big man in the rocks could make out Butler's tethered animal without being able to distinguish its rider, who was backgrounded by the tree, the horse, and stands of northward underbrush.

Butler saw Cartwell's head slowly appear over a boulder, swiveling from side to side as though Cartwell thought whoever had chased him was now stalking him with the advantage of poor light and many shadows.

Butler settled down and examined his wound, which ran blood the moment he slackened the knotted bandanna. He cinched the cloth again and felt pain. It was a nasty gash across the top of his upper leg, the kind that bled a lot but was not serious as long as the bleeding could be held in check.

But it was painful. Regardless of which position he assumed, the pain did not abate. The chances of Butler's being able to cross the distance to the natural fortress where Jacob Cartwell was hiding were all but nonexistent. Butler worried less about this than likelihood that pursuers from Peralta would be a long time arriving, long enough for Cartwell's stolen horse to recover at least some of its wind and strength.

The distance was too great for accurate six-gun firing. In fact, almost any fair distance was too far for accuracy with a handgun.

The sun eventually arrived, and Jacob Cartwell could see in the distance, a man sitting in front of his horse. He called to him.

"That you, Marshal? Hard to tell from here."

Butler did not reply, except to glance up once. He was examining the six-gun he'd taken from Cartwell's mean-eyed rangeman. It was old but perfectly balanced, and it hadn't been used to tighten wire, crack nuts, or drive nails, which were common practices among rangemen.

"Butler?"

The marshal finished with the weapon and leathered it, tipped his hat, and gazed in the direction of the forted-up big man, still without making a sound.

"Butler! Listen to me! I got a proposition for you."

This time Butler replied. "You shot a friend of mine back yonder. Only thing I want from you is to walk out of those rocks with your hands straight out in front."

Cartwell was silent so long Butler thought he would not call again. But eventually he did, because there was one dead-sure certainty now that sunlight made their tracks readable: angry horsemen were coming from Peralta.

"You can have what's in the bullion box, Marshal. All of it. All I want is your horse."

Butler snorted. "I already got the box."

"I got a money belt under my shirt. Nine hunnert dollars' worth of greenbacks in it. That's for your horse and for not shootin' me when I ride away."

"The horse isn't worth that, Cartwell. But I'll pass my word not to shoot you. All you got to do is walk out into the open. No gun! Just walk out!"

Again silence descended. It continued until Butler turned from watching the boulders to watching the country between where he was sitting and Peralta. He thought he detected dust, but it was too distant to be sure. He turned back as Cartwell called again.

"Butler? I'll walk out with my gun. Man to man. Whoever's left standing gets the horse. You got guts enough for that?"

Butler laughed. "Guts enough, but too much brains. All I got to do is sit here. They'll be along."

This time when silence descended it was not broken, and after a while Marshal Butler, with an uneasy feeling, shaded his eyes to study the field of big boulders. He traced out the pattern of their disarray. He thought it might be possible for a man to crawl among them on a curving northward route until he got into the thicket behind Butler, which ran up as far as the dwindling rocks and well beyond it.

He moved, and the pain came instantly. He gritted his teeth and got up onto all fours. He could not stand, because the injured leg, swollen to nearly twice its size now and turning blue above and below the tightly knotted bandanna, would not lock into place.

He crawled past the horse, got into the thicket, and had to stop and lower himself to the ground for a moment.

He was not in sight of the rocks now, but if the large man was stalking him and could come in from behind him . . . the horse threw up its head, peering intently eastward in the direction of Peralta, then gradually shifted its stare almost due southward and remained like that for a long time.

Butler also looked in that direction, and thought his eyes were playing tricks on him by making a mirage of a horseman in the faint, far distance. Then he had his attention diverted when the horse suddenly swung its head and stared in a different direction, this time toward the trailing-off area of Cartwell's rocks.

This he took seriously. To test the validity of his suspicion, he called out, "Hey, Cartwell, I got a proposition for you."

This time there was no reply. No sound at all. Butler grunted to himself and inched along deeper into the thicket on all fours. He left a trail of bloody droplets in his wake, but that was not going to make a difference. Cartwell was not going to stalk him from the south; he was going to come from the northwest.

Butler pushed in as far as he could go, ignored the thorns, and squared around facing the direction from which he expected his adversary. He marveled that anyone as big, thick, and solid as Jacob Cartwell was able to creep through the underbrush without making a sound.

The sun climbed. There was no intense heat yet, but there would be. The area was dead-still and silent. Butler's leg attracted deer flies, which he waved away. He felt thirst coming. He had light-headed moments, then moments of resentful anger. He wanted to yell out asking what was taking the big man so long. He instead mopped off sweat, dried his gun palm, and waited. He was sure he knew exactly what the bearded big man was doing; he was coming, but because he could not do it swiftly without being heard, he was progressing a foot or so at a time, easing aside wiry limbs, as he passed.

Northward, some birds as small as cactus wrens sailed into the thicket and worked their way down to the ground searching for seeds. Their pleasant little chirping sounds carried. Butler shook his head. Those birds would not have landed if they'd known a man was crawling through the underbrush nearby. Butler had to credit Jacob Cartwell, who had been so silent the birds hadn't heard him.

The birds might feel safe and secure, but the marshal didn't.

Finally, there was a whisper of sound. It was dead ahead of Butler. It had been made by some kind of ground varmint scuttling for dear life from something it had encountered and mightily feared.

Butler shook off sweat, tipped his hat brim lower, and poised his six-gun with a thumb on the hammer for instant firing.

He did not see Jacob Cartwell; he saw only a large fist at ground level snaking from beneath a thornpin bush, fist and arm leaving tracks in the dusty soil.

He had to make an instantaneous upward correction of where the large body was that was connected to the hand holding the six-gun.

The guns went off simultaneously. One second later, another shot sounded. The tethered horse fought its knot but came up on it when the gunfire ceased and silence returned. Eyes bulging, nostrils distended to their limit, the animal made a rattling snort.

The other horse, picking grass around the base of rocks and bushes in the distance, raised a listless head, then dropped it to resume its search for food.

CHAPTER TWENTY-FOUR

A PATRON SAINT

Peralta wasn't quiet, but it was certainly not as noisy as it had been earlier in the day. At Hobart's saloon, which had been deserted for most of the morning and part of the afternoon, the bar was crowded by men whose conversations fed upon themselves, repeating the same questions and supplying the same answers in an atmosphere of tobacco smoke, whiskey, and profanity.

Most of the information was correct, but not that concerning the shoot-out that occurred somewhere between Mex-town and the livery barn. It had come from the lean-to shack on the rear of the harness works where Bart Matthews had been carried well before noon, washed, examined closely, and bandaged. All of this had been accomplished while the harness maker was conscious and swearing, occasionally at the top of his voice, as when Jess

Hobart had insisted upon cleansing his scalp wound with salt dissolved in hot water.

But speculation about what had happened later, before townsmen had been drawn southward and had found Matthews lying in a puddle of blood, and after Marshal Butler had ridden hell-for-leather after someone they now knew to be Jacob Cartwell, was only sketchily detailed by the riders. The riders, mostly from Mex-town, had gone in pursuit and had returned to town in midafternoon with the injured town marshal and the corpse of a large man who'd been head-shot at close range.

The remaining details could not be filled in by the big bearded man, and Butler was up on his bed at the rooming house passed out from a dose of laudanum the local midwife had provided.

Jess had done the disinfecting and bandaging under the critical gaze of the midwife. Peralta had no physician. The nearest one was many miles northward, and it was generally agreed that hauling Marshal Butler that far in a stage would probably finish what Cartwell had started.

When Pete Evinrude could make himself heard, it was to complain about the condition of the horse the lawman had taken from his barn, and to ask if the Mexicans who had returned the other horse to its owner knew enough to bring that animal back to normal very carefully in order not to induce founder. No one in the crowd answered until a resident of Mex-town, who'd had just enough popskull to resent the implication, spoke up. Mexicans, he told them in a sharp voice, had been handling livestock on the South Desert since before Pete Evinrude's forefathers had come to the New World. Other loud voices prevented this exchange from growing into anything worse.

The cafeman walked in still wearing his soiled apron. He had made a special broth and had spoon-fed the lawman before he passed out. In reply to questions shouted at him, the cafeman rolled his eyes and said, "That old *curandera* is with him. He looks dead, but she swears he will wake up feeling good. Not real good; he lost blood. Weak, she said, but on the mend." Someone handed the cafeman a shot glass, which he emptied in one gulp. Then he blinked a couple of times and looked irritably at a man who repeated the same question. He replied as another man tipped a bottle to refill his glass.

"I told you. He looks dead to me. But he's breathing. The woman says he'll sleep all night and maybe part of tomorrow morning."

"Where was he hit?"

"In the upper right leg. A bloody gouge, but it'll heal. The second time between his right arm and his ribs, gouged him in both places. Impact at close range peppered him with burnt powder an' knocked him against a gray rock. There's a little bump, but aside from knocking him senseless, it wasn't as bad as his other hurts."

The cafeman downed the second jolt, turned, and left the saloon on his way home to Mex-town. By the time he got down there, he would have had difficulty finding his butt with both hands, and in fact although people surrounded him he waved them off.

One old man, nearly toothless with parchmentlike dark skin, followed Charley Rivas to his jacal and stopped him before he could enter. His question in Spanish was simple. He asked if the lawman would live.

Charley turned with a broad hand against a ramada upright. "*Si, viejo,* he will live. But . . . he won't dance a fandango for a long time."

The old man's expression of anxiety cleared. As he turned away, he muttered something in Spanish. "Thanks be to God."

By the time morning came again, the *curandera* had fallen asleep in her chair. Butler saw her, rolled his eyes toward the front-wall window, and could see as well as hear Peralta busy around him. It was cool, so he assumed it was early.

When he moved he discovered a bandage around his upper body and one around his arm. His head did not ache but, as Rivas had said, he hadn't hit his head very hard; it didn't require much of a blow on the head to produce unconsciousness.

The midwife, who slept lightly, opened her eyes without moving, regarded Marshal Butler a moment, then groaned, stretched, and heaved up out of the chair. "I'll tell them to feed you," she said on her way to the door.

Butler spoke quickly. "Wait. How did I get here?"

"They brought you back in a blanket sling between two horses. You were out of your head most of the time. Marshal, you got a bump on the head and a bullet went between your ribs and your arm. The worse injury is that gouge across your leg. Did you get that before you chased that big man?"

"Yes. We were running toward Mex-town when —"

"I know all of that, Marshal. So does the whole town."

"How?"

"From that evil, terrible talking harness maker."

"Is he all right?"

"I doubt that he is in God's eyes, but he'll be up and around before too long. I heard from Charley Rivas that when they told him they'd fetched you back to town in a sling he swore a blue streak and promised to track the big man down if it took the rest of his life."

"Cartwell? They brought him back too?"

The woman had her hand on the door latch. "Yes, they brought him back."

"How is he?"

The woman gazed a long time at Marshal Butler before replying. "I guess a person could say he's better off than you and the harness maker. He ain't in no pain. He's dead."

The woman walked out and closed the door after herself, leaving Marshal Butler looking at the door. He tried to remember and failed. Not until after he'd slept again and awakened with the sun sinking was he able to fit bits and pieces together. But even then, although his memory was improving, he could not recall anything after he'd squeezed off the shot in the direction he'd thought Cartwell's body had to be.

There were callers. Jess Hobart, wearing his barman's apron, smuggled in a pony of brandy and shoved it under the marshal's pillow as he straightened back to solemnly regard the bed. "How do you feel, Frank?"

"As long as I lie still, not too bad. How's Bart?"

Hobart snorted. "Damned old screwt; when we was all doin' our darnedest to help him, he cussed a blue streak."

"Did he say 'son of a bitch'?"

"No, but he said everything else. Did you know he can swear for three minutes an' never repeat himself?"

Butler smiled, which was one movement that brought no pain. "How bad was he hit?"

"Alongside the head on the right side. It took a nick out of his ear. You know what he said? He said if it looks like a jingle-bob he's going to have the scar changed, otherwise folks'll think old Calkins earmarked him like he does his cows." Jess wagged his head. "What'd the midwife say? Any infection?"

"No. — She said not to tell you, but the salt you used is a good disinfectant."

"Didn't have anything else, Frank. I sent for medicine on the morning stage."

When the saloonman departed, John Grover walked in. He did not smile, but he at least asked how Butler felt before saying, "You got any idea what it cost me to have that front winder brought down here by freighter? Sixty goddamned dollars — cash. Who blew it out?"

Butler could not recall. "No idea, John. How's the rest of the store?"

"Busted up. They tried to prise open the door of my safe, the idiots. We found one on the floor, scairt pea-green, an' locked him in your cell room. Frank, I'd take it kindly if next time you got something that needs safe-keeping, you'd take it some place else."

The merchant departed. Butler sighed and rolled his eyes and brought them to the door, which opened. Maria Elizondo, the sister of Jésus Obando, walked in carrying a large flat pan covered with a cotton cloth. She smiled a little tentatively. "Marshal, we went to the old mission and prayed for you." Her lively dark eyes studied his face. "You look much better. When they brought you back, you looked dead."

He couldn't return the compliment, because her eye was still swollen and discolored. He watched her put the pan on his dresser. When she turned she said, "*Rellenos*. Jésus's wife and I made them. Can you eat?"

Butler lied bravely, but in fact the fragrance coming from the covered pan did stir some sense of hunger in him. "Every one of them," he said, and thanked her. She seemed willing to stay, so he jutted his chin in the direction of the only chair. "Is Jésus out with the mules? The last I heard, someone said he had two down with the colic."

Her dark eyes widened. "I didn't know

about that." She shrugged. "But we don't live next door. No, he isn't out with the pack train. He has been gone, though. I asked his wife; she said she had no idea but that she thought he was looking for some younger mules to replace his old ones."

She rose and smiled again. "Please get well."

He smiled back. "I'll do my best. And thank you again."

He was asleep when the midwife peeked in. She closed the door without a sound and departed.

Evening was settling when the midwife returned with hot broth. She sniffed, raised the cotton cloth, regarded the *rellenos* a moment, replaced the cloth, and pulled the chair to bedside before rousing Marshal Butler. His eyes focused slowly as the woman held a large spoon poised. "Open your mouth. There, now; that'll build up your blood." She jerked her head disdainfully in the direction of the covered pan. "Mex food don't stick to you. It smells nice and all . . . open wide."

When the broth was gone, the woman sat squarely on the chair regarding the lawman. "You'll be fine. It'll likely take a week or so. If you'd lost more blood, they'd be pattin' you in the face with a shovel. You sure looked a bloody mess when they brought you in. . . .

Mister Grover is mad as a wet hen."

She paused, which gave Marshal Butler a chance to speak. He did not tell her that she was right about the broth, although all the sleep he'd had no doubt was partly responsible. But he did feel much better. What he told her was that it seemed reasonable to him for the town to take up a collection and replace Grover's window.

That got a reaction. "Not from me he won't get a red cent. John Grover charges four times for what he sells. My husband used to freight for him. He saw the ladings. He told me it's no wonder that 'possum-bellied Scrooge has a big house and all, from what he charges." She stood up. "There'll be folks who'll donate, Marshal, but I ain't one of them. Greed! Tha's what this world is all about. Greed pure an' simple . . . How's your leg feel?"

Butler gingerly moved it. Miraculously, there was a dull ache but no sharp pain. He raised the blanket to look beneath it. The swelling had diminished a little, and the discoloration was beginning to fade.

He looked at the midwife. "Much better," he told her.

She stood up to approach the bed. As she leaned, Butler clung to the blankets. But she did not want to see the leg, only the body bandage and the wrapping around his arm.

She made no attempt to unwrap anything; she inserted two fingers, pulled, and squinted at what she could see. He asked how the wounds looked.

She was stepping back when she answered. "I never saw anythin' like that before, Marshal. Scabbed over real good, no infection, almost no swelling. You must live right. . . . are you a prayin' man? Because somebody or some*thing* sure's been lookin' after you."

She smiled. It was like crackling cardboard, but there was no mistaking her change of mood. She leaned to gently brush hair off his forehead. "Somebody's sure looking after you. Hell, Marshal, you'll be up and around in another week or two. Maybe less. You got a patron saint, have you?"

As far as Butler knew, the midwife was not a religious person. Anyone as rough and cynical, and who could swear like she could, would probably not be a keeper of the faith. He grinned up at her. "Patron saint? Yes'm — El Cajónero."

Her smile winked out and her eyes hardened. As she headed for the door, she gave a loud snort.

Butler laughed.

It was dark when Bart Matthews came in with an enormous, lopsided bandage on his head. His old hat was atop it like an afterthought. They exchanged a glance. Then Matthews lighted the lamp on the dresser and went to the same chair the midwife had used, sat down, paused as he studied the marshal, and finally spoke. "Well; Cartwell's in John Grover's icehouse along with that subbitch I took care of outside the hotel. That weaselly subbitch is in one of your cells whining to whoever brings him grub, and John Grover's mad as hell about his winder."

"How d'you feel, Bart?"

"Like I been yanked through a knothole. How about you?"

"Better by the hour."

Matthews paused to carve a sliver off a fresh plug of Kentucky twist and pouch it before he spoke again. "Hunter Calkins was in town today. He asked about a big gold cross, said it come from Cartwell's bullion box."

"It did. When I can ride, I'll take it back to him."

The harness maker nodded understanding. "We used hell out of his horses and all." He looked for a spittoon, found none and went to the window, let fly, and returned to his chair. "Couple fellers come by to see me this afternoon . . . sort of indignant you set them *bandoleros* loose. They said folks're talking about that around town. You know what I told 'em? That it was the wisest thing you ever did. Even *bandoleros* don't forget someone doin' 'em a favor. I told them I'd bet my life that bunch will never bother Peralta. Of course, there's other bands, and there'll be other revolutions." Matthews shrugged. "What the hell — what you did at least bought the town a reprieve from that particular bunch, and besides, what'n hell else could you do with 'em?"

Marshal Butler asked dryly if the harness maker thought his statement would make much difference, and Matthews's brows dropped. "If they got any sense it will. If they don't have no sense an' start bellyachin' around me, I'll overhaul their plows."

Butler nodded, satisfied the harness maker would make the attempt. But he was not a young man.

They talked for another half hour. The harness maker departed when he saw that Butler was struggling to keep his eyes open.

Chapter Twenty-five

EL CAJÓNERO

As the midwife had said, there was no explanation for the marshal's quick recovery. Maybe he hadn't lost as much blood as it seemed. Maybe some of that blood on him when they returned him to town was from Cartwell. But whatever the reason, Frank Butler was on his feet sooner than anyone would have predicted — with a cane supplied gratis by John Grover, who had not mellowed about his window, but who *had* decided providing the cane was good business in view of how everyone in the countryside thought Marshal Butler was a genuine hero.

Summer was at hand. Even the mornings were hot now, which made folks revert to their summertime custom of sleeping during the hottest time of day, having supper around ten o'clock at night, and arising ahead of the sun when their world was blessedly fragrant and cool.

Orville Shoup, the Mexican cafeman, took full advantage of predawn coolness by doing his cooking at that time. Later in the day, his kitchen became a furnace. He fed Marshal Butler an early breakfast. There were no other diners. He leaned on the counter and said, "You know a woman in Mex-town named Estella Obregon?" At the faint frown on the lawman's face, he added, "She's the mother of that young rider Cartwell's Texan beat up so that he died."

Butler nodded. "What about her?"

The cafeman leaned closer and lowered his voice. "I got an idea couple days back."

The marshal sat poised with a knife and fork in his hands. "What idea?"

"Well, it's been a while."

Butler nodded about that.

The cafeman shot a narrow-eyed look around and leaned still closer. "El Cajónero, Marshal."

Butler's eyes widened. "He flung money through her window?"

"No. Seems to me by now he should have. My idea is for you to do it for him."

At the look on the marshal's face, the Mexican reared back and wiped both hands on his apron and smiled like a conspirator.

"Maybe he'll do it, but I heard you figured to divide the loot in that bullion box among

350

the possemen. I thought maybe if you'd ride through Mex-town in the dark like The Undertaker does . . ."

Marshal Butler stared for a long time, then went to work on his meal. When the cafeman had about decided it wasn't such a good idea after all, that at least the marshal didn't seem to like it, Butler looked up. "I figured to give her the lad's share. Maybe a little more. But I figured to just walk down there and —"

"Marshal, you don't know something about that: I know her. I know all her family. They wouldn't take money from you." The cafeman rolled his eyes. "But El Cajónero is different. You see? He's been almost their patron saint for a hunnert an' fifty years. He's sort of —"

Butler was muttering. "Patron saint? El Cajónero?"

The cafeman shrugged beefy shoulders, crossed both arms across his chest, and leaned against his pie table.

Butler resumed eating. Nothing was said between them until he'd finished and the cafeman was refilling his coffee cup. Then the lawman said, "It wouldn't work."

"Why not?"

"Well, for one thing El Cajónero is a myth. For another thing, I got nothing against them having their legend, but I don't cotton to the idea of keeping it alive."

The cafeman quietly mentioned the one thing that was always used when the element of myth was brought up. "The gold coins, Marshal. Everyone's seen them. In Gringotown the merchants take them in payment. . . . Marshal, if he's a myth . . ." The cafeman shrugged again and stepped back holding the coffeepot. "I'll tell you something, Marshal: When I go into the grave you got no idea how many confidences will go with me." The cafeman put the pot aside. "I know nothing. You know nothing. An old woman with nothing to give but a son who was killed, she knows nothing — except that El Cajónero is a protector of the victims of Mex-town."

Butler paid up and limped across to the jailhouse. An hour later, with the heat bearing down and the roadway nearly empty, the cafeman came to the jailhouse door and said, "It was just an idea. Not a very good one." He shrugged. "I know the old woman. I don't often hurt for people, but I do for her. I'll forget I mentioned it and so will you."

Butler leaned on the desk. "Wait. I own two horses, Orville. Both are bays."

The cafeman stepped squarely into the doorway, nearly filling its width. "I own a black horse, Marshal. I don't ride him much anymore; I'm getting too fat. But I drive him on a buggy."

"Big horse, Orville?"

The cafeman's conspirator's smile came up, very wide. "Eleven hundred pounds. Big as the horse El Cajónero rides."

Butler continued to regard the Mexican as he slowly leaned back in his chair. "Where is your horse, Orville?"

"In a faggot corral in Mex-town behind my house. Gentle, Marshal, gentle as a baby. Even a man with a bandaged leg would have no trouble . . . Marshal?" When Butler did not respond but sat gazing into space, the cafeman repeated, "Marshal . . . ?"

"Behind your cafe tonight after you close up. El Cajónero rides a Mex saddle. You got one?"

"Yes, I got one. He wears black pants and a black coat."

Butler nodded. "The black pants and coat I wear to funerals. I'll meet you behind your cafe after midnight. All right?"

The cafeman was turning away when he said, "How much gold money?"

"Five hundred dollars. That's what I figured to give her."

The cafeman walked back across the road with the sun glowing unmercifully overhead. His face was expressionless, but his dark eyes glowed.

The thick mud walls of the Peralta jailhouse

were almost heat-proof. Butler remained in there favoring his wounded leg and idly watching the empty roadway for a long time. It occurred to him that what he was going to do would support the myth he did not believe in, giving it a substance he was not sure it deserved. But lately there had been some puzzling occurrences. Matthews believed, as did Charley Rivas and others. But Butler, whose conviction had been that the entire El Cajónero story was superstitious myth, had nevertheless been unable to resolve some of the things that had been attributed to him lately, a few of which he had personal knowledge. He threw up his hands. If it meant so much to the people of Mex-town . . .

He got a real jolt about an hour after the cafeman had departed; when John Grover walked in pink in the face and said, "Frank, you got to find some other place to put those dead men. My wife went across the alley to get a chunk of ice. . . . I heard her screamin' all the way in the front of the store. She'd fainted plumb away. I'm sorry, but you got to get Cartwell and that other one out of there."

Butler stood up, gripped the cane, and nodded. There really was no other place to keep bodies until burial could be arranged, and with summer at hand . . . He promised to see what he could do, and left the jailhouse shortly after Grover.

Before he tried to find another place to park the corpses, he limped over across the alley behind Grover's store. He heaved up the big latch on the icehouse, which had three-foot-thick walls. He had to leave the door partially open for light, because the icehouse had no windows.

It was gloomy, very cold, and unpleasant inside. The dead men were lying flat out atop some blocks of ice nested in thick layers of straw. The mean-eyed man Matthews had shot had both hands crossed atop his chest. They were frozen in that position. Cartwell's hands had been placed in the same pious position. Butler leaned on the cane, his breath making little clouds.

Jacob Cartwell had a little purple puncture squarely between his eyes!

Butler left the icehouse and slammed the massive latch closed. He did not go looking for another place to put the dead men, but returned to his office and sat down. He felt chilly sweat beneath his shirt as he leaned on the desk.

Always between the eyes. He thought back to another dead man whose death could have been attributed to El Cajónero. At first even Butler himself had wondered if Colonel

Esparza's killer had been El Cajónero, and doubted it because the bullet was in the wrong place.

After he knew who Esparza's killer was, he had felt relief. As he sat in the jailhouse reflecting, he wryly smiled to himself. Hell, he had subconsciously begun to believe in the legend of El Cajónero.

He went up to Hobart's saloon, bought a drink, and asked if Jess could find a couple of grave diggers. He told the saloonman why they had to plant the dead men very soon. Jess, whose saloon served as Peralta's clearinghouse for men seeking work, had put men to work as grave diggers many times over the years. He agreed to find a pair and send them out to Gringo-town's cemetery, which was about half a mile northwest of town.

Pete Evinrude walked in mopping his forehead. Jess set up a glass of beer and put a small stick of peppermint beside it, which made beer taste cold when it wasn't.

Pete leaned on the counter, looked from one of them to the other, and said, "Worst time of the year. Sometimes I wonder why any of us stay down here. Up in Colorado an' Wyoming, summers are cool and pleasant." Pete cheeked the peppermint and downed his beer, blew out a breath, and nodded toward the cane as he asked Butler how his wounds were. The

356

conversation was harmless and desultory for a while. Butler left to limp across to the harness works.

Matthews was still working on the saddle he'd started weeks earlier. He was still wearing the bulky bandage around his head. He turned from the worktable and gazed at the lawman. "Next time you ask me to go scout around a little with you, I'm goin' to take to my bed an' stay there." He touched the bandage. "I got the top of my ear shot off."

Butler smiled. "That's better'n having the slug go a little more inward. Then you wouldn't be here at all."

"You want some coffee?"

Butler declined. "No. Just wanted to make sure gettin' shot hadn't spoiled your disposition."

The harness maker put a narrowed gaze upon the lawman. He suspected sarcasm, but Butler was smiling so he merely grunted.

Outside, hot air danced in the roadway of Peralta. The only people abroad were those who could not avoid it. There was not a single saddle horse, rig, or wagon to be found on the roadway.

Butler went up to the rooming house, got his funeral pants and coat, rolled them, and took them down the back alley to the jailhouse. A little later he had an early supper. He exchanged glances with the cafeman, neither man showing any expression. He nodded casually as he placed silver beside his plate, then returned to the early dusk of a long, hot day.

He entered the general store and was told by an elderly clerk that Grover had gone home to supper. When Butler asked the clerk if he had the combination to the steel safe, he got a wary glance. "Why?"

"Because I want to look into the bullion box I got John to put in the safe for me."

The clerk considered and gave an almost imperceptible shrug. Then he went over, knelt, and worked the dial. As he was doing this, he said, "Next time there's a war, I hope it ain't fought in here. We was two days cleanin' up." He rose and swung the door open, then stood aside to watch as Butler opened the box.

Two women carrying net shopping baskets arrived. The clerk looked around at them twice before finally going to wait on them reluctantly.

Butler counted out five hundred dollars' worth of little gold coins, weighted his pockets with them, closed the box, and slammed the steel door. He nodded to the women and the clerk as he returned to the roadway.

Night was fully down. A scimitar moon was too slim to cast much light, but the rash of brilliant, high stars combined with the moonlight to provide fair visibility.

Butler returned to the jailhouse, lighted his lamp, and barred the door from the inside. He rummaged on a shelf in the storeroom until he found two little buckskin pouches, left there by his predecessor. He put half the coins in each sack, then tightened the drawstrings. The sacks were still heavy.

Later, at the jailhouse, he put on the dark clothing, leaving his shellbelt and holstered Colt beneath the coat. He stood a while in the dark doorway before blowing down his lamp mantle and leaving the jailhouse on a diagonal course.

Peralta was quiet, although there were lights glowing in the houses of townspeople eating late suppers.

He was early. There was no sign of the cafeman and the black horse when he arrived in the dark alley behind the cafe.

But the cafeman was early too. He materialized like a dark, beefy ghost and led Butler to the east side of the alley, through a sagging gate, and to a dilapidated cow shed.

The black horse was indeed big. It looked around at them with an expression of resigned curiosity.

The cafeman asked about the money. Butler held up the two pouches without saying a word, then untied the animal and led it outside. He found the stirrups too short. While lengthening them, the cafeman stood grinning for all he was worth. When Butler reached for the huge saddle horn and rose up to come down gingerly, the cafeman said, "You know where Obando the packer lives? Well, the woman you want lives in the jacal north of his corrals." The cafeman paused, then said, "I marked the side of the house with a white line."

Butler nodded, evened up the reins, and rode at a quiet walk down the alleyway. He was visible in the poor light only as something large and dark moving through more darkness.

He knew where the woman lived. Jésus had pointed it out to him several times. Obando was her friend, and occasionally employed her son.

Mex-town was quiet. The few lights that shone were feeble and unsteady; in Mex-town few people could afford lamps with glass mantles, and even fewer could afford the coal oil to burn in them. Also, there was tradition: Many people had grown up with candlelight and made candles by the dozens.

They also retired early. But their dogs didn't. Marshal Butler had scarcely reached the first few jacals when the dogs began barking. So many barked that the marshal doubted their racket would be taken seriously. Agitated dogs in the night were viewed in both Mextown and Gringo-town as both a blessing and a curse. When so many barked, mostly as a curse.

He passed Obando's corrals, heard the Mexican's mules and horses milling around at the sound of a horse beyond the faggots, and leaned to watch for the chalk mark. He was concentrating so hard that he almost missed hearing another horse. This one seemed to be approaching the center of Mextown from the east.

Butler reined quickly to the far side of the woman's residence. He swung off, stepped to the big horse's head, and poised his hand to clamp over the animal's nostrils if it attempted to nicker.

The walking horse came closer at a slow pace. Butler peeked around the mud wall and was able to make out the rider. Not very well, not well enough to see him clearly except to notice that he was a large, thick man . . . *dressed in black, riding a black horse!*

The dogs were beginning to pause between barks. Some of them gave it up entirely. The dark silhouette rode past several unlighted jacals. Butler finally could make out a few details. The rider was strongly built, and had a six-gun showing on the right side. When moonlight touched it, the handle showed pale silver inlay in the wooden grips. The man's hat was low in front. His clothing was dark, his saddle typically Mex, even the leather-covered steel box stirrups.

Butler felt his own animal move slightly. He had to jerk back behind the house to tighten his hold and gently squeeze the animal's nostrils. The horse stopped moving, but it clearly had heard, and probably scented, the other horse.

The marshal waited until the horse was still, then leaned to look again. The rider had turned northward and was out of sight on the far side of the woman's house. Butler limped around leading his own horse, but the other horse was nearly invisible again as it continued at a steady walk.

Butler mounted up, and rode alongside the same side of the house. He tossed both pouches through an open widow and kept on riding.

He did not find the other horseman, although he rode in several directions looking for him. Eventually he gave up and rode back up into Gringo-town. He found the cafeman sitting on the ground, smoking and waiting. The marshal swung off and, before the cafe-man could speak, said, "There was another rider down there. Rode past the old woman's house, came within an ace of catching me."

The cafeman took the reins, looking surprised. "Who? Did you see him?"

"Not well enough."

The cafeman looked at Marshal Butler with wide eyes. "El Cajónero?"

Butler scowled. "He was real. His horse was real. He made sounds when he walked." Butler tipped his hat back and leaned on the back wall of the general store. His leg ached, but not enough to hold his attention. He said, "I tossed the money through her window. Now I got to get some sleep."

He left the cafeman staring after him.

Butler was at his office the next morning when he heard the noise. It was all over Peralta that El Cajónero had thrown money through the window of the woman whose son had been killed with the town posse. Matthews came into the office looking delighted. "He done it, Marshal. He came last night when folks was abed and give the old woman some gold coins. Through her window like he does."

Butler nodded. "I'm glad to hear it. How much did he give her?"

"Seven hunnert dollars in gold!"

Butler sat staring. "You sure?"

"Hell, yes; it's all over town. Down in Mextown they're runnin' around like someone killin' snakes with a small stick. . . . I told you. I been tellin' you for a long time. You're too stubborn to . . ." The harness maker turned and abruptly rushed across the road to where some men in front of the general store were loudly talking.

Marshal Butler remained at his desk a long time — more than an hour. Then he rose, gripped the cane, and walked southward in the direction of Mex-town, where the increasing heat had stifled most of the excitement.

He went directly to the woman's jacal. She invited him inside, where it was still cool. Not waiting to be asked, she showed him a handful of gold coins from an apron pocket. He sat down to study them. All of them had been minted in Mexico. The detailing was somewhat crude, but there was no question of their weight and value.

He gave back the coins, told her how glad he was for her, and left. As he was passing the Obando residence, he saw Jésus's wife stringing peppers under the ramada. He called to ask her if her husband was at home. She said he was and invited Marshal Butler to stop, but he declined with a smile and walked all the way back to his office.

An hour later Jésus walked in, dropped onto a bench, and mopped his neck. "Summer's here," he said, and smiled. "Did you want to see me, Frank?"

Marshal Butler rose, limped to the roadside door, closed it, and returned to his desk. As he sat down he said, "That young feller who got killed at Vasquez Spring — he swamped with your pack train now an' then?"

Obando nodded gravely. "Yes. What about him?"

"How did you know he was killed out there?"

Obando shrugged. "I heard about it when I got back to town."

Butler softly shook his head and looked unwaveringly at the big Mexican. "Got back from where?"

"Down at Angostura and Rincón."

Butler rocked back off the desk. "Jésus, you left the lad to bring back the train by himself. You came back to Peralta long before he got back. Someone told you what some damned *arriero* out of Mexico did to your sister."

Obando was expressionless as he listened.

"You went after that *arriero* and killed him."

Obando remained like a stone carving, dark eyes fixed on Frank Butler.

"The lad's mother told me he had told her you left him to return alone with the pack string."

Obando remained still and silent.

"What I want to know, Jésus, is why you

left the lad down there and returned to town."

"At Rincón we heard about those *arrieros*. They dragged some women into their camp down there. The men were afraid and did nothing. When the women came back, they said the *arrieros* were heading for Peralta."

Butler got a drink from the hanging olla and returned to his desk. "Jésus, when the posse rode out you couldn't ride with us because you had some sick mules."

Again the big Mexican sat in stony silence.

Butler got his sore leg comfortable before speaking again. "You didn't have any sick mules. You followed us from hiding. You were the one who shot that Texan who'd beaten the lad. You followed us when we went looking for Cartwell's camp, and you followed us when we rode back to the Calkins place with the prisoners. And when Bart and I got caught by the young *bandolero*, it was you came up behind him and knocked him senseless. There were other things, a lot of them, but the last one was when Cartwell stole a horse in Mextown an' I went after him."

Obando's dark eyes showed a trace of hard humor, but he still said nothing.

"I shot at Cartwell."

Obando said, "Too high, Frank. You missed him by a foot."

Butler leaned with his elbows atop the desk.

"Anything else you want to tell me, Jésus?"

Obando slightly smiled. "You can guess the rest."

". . . You are El Cajónero?"

"Sort of," the big Mexican said, and leaned forward, moving on the bench for the first time. "Frank, a long time ago, when my grandfather was a young man, the Mexican government would not send soldiers to protect people from Indians, and it refused to allow anyone out here to own guns. So they made bows and arrows. But they were no match for the Indians, and got slaughtered. My grandfather bought guns from the Comancheros, the traders who cared nothing for anyone, only money and sometimes horses and cattle in trade. My grandfather was ready when the Comanches came. They killed many and drove the others off. When the Apaches came, they did it again. When the Mexicans came to arrest everyone for having guns, my grandfather had to hide for a long time.

"That was when he decided he would personally take revenge for everyone killed or injured in Mex-town. Only in those days that's all there was. All Peralta was Mexican.

"He trained my father when he got very old. My father trained me. They did not call either my grandfather or my father The Undertaker; they were called Vengador. Only in my time has The Avenger been called The Undertaker."

Obando continued to sit forward, large hands clasped between his knees as he looked steadily at Marshal Butler.

Butler went after another drink of water and returned to ease down with his injured leg pushed out. They sat like that for a long time. Then Butler laughed.

Jésus Obando leaned back, smiling a little. He dryly said, "It was hard on my horse," and the lawman nodded. Obando did not own a black horse, but seal-brown horses looked black in darkness.

"Go home," the lawman said. "Hey, *compañero,* I dressed in black last night and threw five hundred gold dollars through the old woman's window."

Jésus rose. "When I heard this morning, I couldn't figure it out."

"You threw two hundred through her window?"

"Yes. Well, now she's rich. Frank . . . ?"

Marshal Butler rose, limped around the desk, and pushed out his hand. "Good thing you hit Cartwell between the horns. Thanks."

"And — if El Cajónero continues to ride, Frank?"

"What are you having for supper tonight,

Jésus? We can talk away half the night about El Cajónero."

"My wife said she was told you like *rellenos*. Come anytime. We can sit outside a little before supper."

Butler favored his sore leg by leaning in the jailhouse doorway. He watched Jésus Obando walking southward toward Mex-town, heated air rising around him like transparent jelly.

Butler went back to sit down. He smiled to himself.

The employees of THORNDIKE PRESS hope you have enjoyed this Large Print book. All our Large Print titles are designed for easy reading, and all our books are made to last. Other Thorndike Large Print books are available at your library, through selected bookstores, or directly from us. For more information about current and upcoming titles, please call or mail your name and address to:

THORNDIKE PRESS
PO Box 159
Thorndike, Maine 04986
800/223-6121
207/948-2962